Sign up to my newsletter, and you will be notified when I release my next book!

ISBN-13:   9798365996755

D1528198

JACK BRYCE

To redheads with the courage to wear pigtails worldwide.

Chapter 1

The lawyer's office was as cold and lacking in personality as the lawyer himself. For the past few hours, the man had gone through the details of James's father's last will and testament, listing off what went to whom.

And nothing went to James.

The company went to James's brother — but James wouldn't have wanted to manage that anyway. The bulk of the remainder of James's father's inheritance would be used to set up a trust for two cousins that James did not get along with at all.

What the whole affair really came down to was this: he'd inherited nothing from his father.

So far.

He let out a long sigh as the lawyer closed his briefcase, pushing back his chair. "There is one last thing," the man said, fixing his cold eyes on James.

James perked up, as did his brother and sister-in-law — the only two who had actually bothered to come.

"A cabin in the woods," the lawyer muttered as his gaze shifted to his papers. "He left a cabin to you, James. 'for your happiness', he wrote."

"For my... *happiness*?" James shifted his gaze to his brother. "I didn't even know dad had a cabin?"

His brother just shrugged. They weren't really close, and it was obvious his brother just wanted to wrap this up.

James felt numb.

Numb, confused, and shocked. He didn't need money or anything — he had fostered no expectations about the inheritance, but he *had* hoped for some kind of reconciliation. A gesture of love from the father he'd been at odds with nearly all his life.

Something with meaning.

And he got a *cabin*.

He nodded dumbly, feeling as though he should say something profound and meaningful about how important this gift was to him, but all that sounded in his head was, "Why a cabin?!"

He shook his head at himself, trying to clear away the cobwebs. His hands trembled so much he barely held his grip on his glass of water as he took a sip.

The attorney gave a soft smile and continued talking as if James hadn't spoken at all. "Your father specified the cabin is free of any mortgage or debt."

A *cabin*...

"Well, young man?" the attorney said. "Are you not pleased with your gift from your late father? Will you accept the inheritance?"

James swallowed. "I just..."

A tiny thought fluttered into his mind, like a stray butterfly. What if this was some sort of cruel joke? Some sick prank pulled by his family?

James's cousins, the ones his father was close with, were real dirt bags. They never liked James — the black sheep — and it wouldn't surprise him if they'd had the cruelty to play a joke on him. Send him out in the sticks chasing a cabin that didn't exist and laugh their asses off when he returned all dejected.

"What does the cabin look like?" James blurted out. "How do I get there? Is it... When was dad last there? Is there anything... special about the place? I mean, why did he even own that cabin?"

The lawyer stared at him blankly before turning to James's brother for help.

"No idea," James's brother replied coolly.

"Let me see if there's something in the papers," the lawyer said, heaving a tired sigh as he began looking.

"Ah!" he said. "It says here the address is..." He quirked an eyebrow. "1 Forrester Trail... *Tour County*?" He cleared his throat and said, almost to himself, "Never heard of *that* place."

But James had.

Tour County.

And despite the hardships of the past few weeks, those two words conjured a smile on his face.

A happy memory.

It looked like there was some meaning to his father's inheritance after all.

"Tour County," James's brother murmured. "Isn't that where dad went hunting a couple of times?"

James smiled and nodded. "Yeah. I went with him once."

"Oh," his brother said, studying his nails.

"It was a nice trip," James said. He knew neither his brother nor the lawyer cared, but he felt like saying it anyway, as if the words could help the memories manifest.

"We spent four nights in a bed-and-breakfast in town," he said, and considered his memories of the trip for a moment. "There was something really special about it…"

He remembered driving up to Tour County with his father. It had felt as if at some indeterminable point in their journey, they crossed through a portal into another world. Colors were more vibrant, the scents of the forest fresher, and his blood seemed to flow faster and thicker.

Tour had utterly charmed him, and it had the same effect on his father.

But after the trip, James forgot all about it — as if it

had never been. In fact, he didn't recall reminiscing about the trip even once.

Not until now.

He chuckled. "I can't believe dad actually bought a cabin up there!"

"Yeah," his brother said, impatience edging his voice. "Well, I guess it's yours now."

"Will you accept it?" the lawyer asked.

That was a very practical question, and it brought to mind a number of objections. A cabin had to cost money, even if it had been paid off. Maintenance, taxes, other things — James had never owned real estate before. He'd have to get into all of that.

Maybe he could sell it?

But he had no idea what the market was like. He remembered Tour was undiscovered; there had been no other hunters there for the season.

And then there was his job.

His apartment.

He had bills to pay, obligations in the city.

"I don't know," James muttered. "I have no idea what to do with a cabin... especially not way up there."

"Well, if you don't accept it, we'll have to think of a way to get rid of it," the lawyer said, returning to his papers. "We'll sell it, and the money will then go to the heirs who *did* accept." He nodded at James's brother, his sister-in-law, and then James before rising from his chair. "Thank you all for coming."

"Hold on," James's sister-in-law said.

She gave James an empathetic look. "Are you sure, James?" She placed her hand on his shoulder. "I'm certain your father meant well, James. He just wanted you to find happiness... whatever you choose to do. Is it worth thinking about this before you say no?"

She had a point.

Maybe this was a chance for him. A way to change a life he wasn't really enjoying so far. And even though he had been at odds with his father, James still wondered what the intention behind this 'gift' had been.

Maybe it was acceptance of who James was?

A gift 'for your happiness'?

And besides, James would like to go up there once more. It'd be good to remember that trip.

Maybe he would stay overnight and return in the morning?

Surely it wouldn't be too much trouble if James needed some time to consider. Especially since they'd already made such a big fuss over everything else, including all the gifts and letters that had poured in from their many distant relatives. The whole affair surrounding his father's death and inheritance had taken weeks already.

James looked at the lawyer. "Can I have a look at the place before I decide?"

"If you insist," the lawyer said with a tired sigh. "But the sooner you can settle this, the better for all concerned."

James nodded. "Yes. It won't take long. A few days."

Chapter 2

James drove north in his banged-up old sedan. He was alone, and that gave him some time to think. Or at least to pretend he was thinking, so that he could ignore the churning in his mind and concentrate instead on what he should do once he saw his father's cabin.

Should he accept it? The truth was, he'd been in a bit of a rut ever since he dropped out of college.

His parents had groomed James for a life as a highly educated, upper-class businessman. That was what they had been, of course, but nothing about that life interested James.

James loved the outdoors, he loved honest work, and he loved a good book by the fireplace. And even though he'd ended up in the city for a job, he didn't care for it much.

Was that why his father gave him the cabin... for his happiness?

He took a left at the first sign saying, 'Welcome to Tour County'.

As soon as he crossed the county line, he sped up — a little faster than usual, actually. There weren't many cars out on these back roads.

His thoughts kept turning over the same questions over and over again.

How far away from civilization would this cabin be? What kind of condition would it be in after all these years without maintenance? Would it have electricity or running water? If not, how did he plan on making it comfortable enough to live in?

James had been to the town of Tour once before, years ago, on the hunting trip with his father. That was one of the few pleasant memories he had about the man, and he remembered the town well.

James pulled off onto the shoulder just before he entered the town limits to give the place a good look before he ventured in. It wasn't very often that people drove this way. Tour was just a hamlet.

Most houses were small and basic. During their trip, his father had told him Tour was an old town that had grown to accommodate a farm or two and a very modest logging industry. After new laws pertaining to the logging industry, the work had died down and hardly anyone lived there anymore. Most tourists wouldn't come out this far, even if they wanted to visit the woods.

And even if someone found their way out here and decided to stay awhile, they'd probably turn around and head right back to the bigger logging towns when they realized they had nothing else here except nature and trees.

But here, just outside Tour, was the perfect spot to park his car and reflect on the trip he had taken here with his father. There was a pleasant stream nearby, too. Perfect. There was something about the babbling of water that calmed his mind.

He remembered they had laughed, and his father had taught him many things about hunting and outdoorsmanship. In fact, the man had seemed changed out here. Relaxed, in touch with nature.

Prior to the trip, James and his father had not been on good terms; the man wanted James to be something he was not: a ruthless, callous businessman, a shark with a singular focus on money.

Just like his father had been.

James was not like that — he never would be.

But out here, his father had been different. His expectations for James changed, and his own stress receded.

This place had called out to James back then — and it still did so now. He smiled slightly to himself as he turned over the sensations in his mind — the fresh air, the beauty of nature, the peacefulness of it all.

They had spent the four nights at a small bed-and-breakfast in Tour, and James remembered sitting by the fire, reading in content silence.

A pleasant memory.

After that, things got back to normal, and James took his rightful position as black sheep of the family again. His father's disappointment returned, and they never caught the feeling of wonder and freedom that they had shared in Tour again.

James took a deep breath of fresh air, scented by the

surrounding pines. Already, some of the magic he had felt back then returned. Everything was more vibrant out here — more *alive*.

With a smile, he stepped back into his car. He took one last look in the mirror at himself.

The face that stared back at him seemed older somehow. More tired and worn out, although he didn't feel like he looked that bad. A little worried, yes. But well... more adult.

So he stopped worrying about what others might think and focused on what he needed to do.

James turned over the engine and pulled out. He let his fingers gently glide across the steering wheel as the scenery flowed past.

He drove through the small town; it was exactly as he remembered it, with a single street down the center and some smaller roads branching off. He paid little attention to it, focused now on following his navigation's instructions to reach the cabin.

Soon, a clearing appeared ahead, with an old barn nestled among some tall pine trees. He slowed down a little as he approached a large gate made of heavy timbers held together with big metal clamps. On the other side stood a rickety old fence with holes in it where branches were growing through the gaps.

His navigation told him this was the place.

"That can't be," he told himself. "This is a barn, not a cabin."

He looked around to see if there was a farmhouse nearby. Just when he was about to give up and head back to Tour and ask for directions there, the door to the barn swung open and a woman came out.

And what a woman!

To say this woman was the hottest farmer's daughter James had ever seen was an understatement.

She wore overalls and a work shirt that hung loosely over her firm breasts, nipples poking at the coarse fabric. Her ginger hair was tied back in a loose ponytail that reached halfway down her slim and toned back.

And even her overalls couldn't conceal a thick ass that would put most Instagram models to shame. And when she slammed the door shut and turned so James could see her face, his heart just melted at the sight of those big green eyes and plump lips.

"Hot damn," he muttered to himself, feeling his need rise.

She stopped short as soon as she saw him staring, then walked toward the car.

She halted in front of the window, James still gaping at her, and stood with her hands on her hips and stared straight into his eyes before breaking out into a grin.

She made the universal sign of rolling down the window, and James pushed the button, his sedan's window barely complying.

"Hello there," he said.

The girl stuck her hand through the open window. "Howdy yourself. You must be new to town." The smile widened on her pretty face.

"Yes," James said, shaking her hand.

"I'm Corinne," she told him, leaning against the side of his car. "And who might you be?"

He leaned closer to hear her over the idling engine. "James." He grinned again. "James Beckett."

"Beckett, huh?" she said. "Where ya from?"

"North Dakota." He pointed vaguely in the general direction. He didn't want to seem too eager, and he figured a little mystery would help set the mood. It wasn't hard for a gorgeous girl like Corinne to draw men in, and he doubted coming on strong would help him.

Besides, it was always better to be subtle until he

knew the lay of the land.

She gave a soft laugh. "We don't get a lotta folks from North Dakota here."

"Well, we're a rare breed."

She laughed, and her heaving chest made her tits bounce a little. He tried not to stare at them; they were so large and bountiful that even her shapeless and stained work shirt couldn't conceal them.

As if reading his thoughts, she looked down at her chest with an expression that almost seemed apologetic. But only almost.

"Sorry about my outfit," she said as she took one hand off the car door and ran it along her collar before pinching the loose fabric between two fingers. "It's just the old clothes I wear when working."

"I'm sure no one's complaining," James assured her, hoping he didn't sound sarcastic or come across as a creep. Instead of dwelling on how beautiful this woman was, he needed to find out where exactly his cabin was. "I take it you're familiar with this area?" he asked.

She smiled. "Yep. What can I help you with, James Beckett?"

"I need directions to a cabin," he said. "It's here in Tour County. It used to belong to my dad."

Her eyes lit up. "Your father has a cabin here?"

James nodded. "Had," he corrected her. "I, uh, inherited it."

Her pretty green eyes widened. "Oh, I'm sorry."

"Thanks," he said. But he didn't want the silence to linger, so he smiled at her. "Any idea where that cabin might be? The address is supposed to be 1 Forrester Trail, but that just took me here. Looks wrong to me, unless I'm moving in with you."

She shrugged as if she didn't mind that notion, and her smile was still in place. "Yeah, there's a cabin near here. I never saw anyone there, though. Anyway, the road leading to it is unmarked. Go down this here dirt road until you reach a fork at the creek, then go right." She gestured to a spot on the other side of a small clearing, away from the trees. "You can't miss it."

"Thanks," James said. "So, uh, you live around here?"

"Yep," Corinne replied as she pushed herself off from his car. "My farm is a little down the road. Well, good luck, stranger." With that, she started walking back toward her barn.

"Hey," James called after her, trying not to sound desperate. He watched as her firm ass swayed as she walked, and his cock gave a painful throb in his pants. "I'm still on the fence about accepting the cabin. What would you do? I mean, is Tour a fun place?"

She glanced over her shoulder, giving him a teasing look from under long lashes. "Oh, it *can* be."

Chapter 3

The cabin stood at the end of a dirt road deep within the forest.

It was nothing more than a single-story wooden building with shutters and wide eaves — and no running water or electricity. The only thing the cabin had going was seclusion; it stood far away from everything.

The area surrounding the cabin was beautiful, but it would need work, being covered in tall weeds, stumps, and bushes.

But James didn't shy away from a little physical labor.

As he pulled into the drive, he considered that he might find solace here. There were no neighbors close enough to hear, and nature sprawled all around.

And most importantly... he felt safe here.

This place was like stepping back in time. A perfect escape from the rat race of the city.

He might spend hours just sitting on the porch staring out at those trees, listening to the birds chirping while enjoying a cool drink from a bottle of cold beer.

If I accept my father's inheritance, he thought as he got out of his car. *This could be my home. I could own this land if I wanted to! I might stay here for months if I wanted to. No one would bother me.*

He grinned as his eyes roved over the surroundings and imagined himself living here full time.

He wouldn't need anything else in this world. Well, maybe a hot girlfriend to share it with now and then.

Corinne would certainly do...

James staved off the naughty thoughts of the dirty things he would want to do with that hot little farmer's daughter.

Freeing his mind, he gave the surrounding area another look and walked up to the cabin.

When he reached the front door, he hesitated for only a moment before turning the knob. But instead of opening right away, the heavy door creaked open only a few inches. James pushed on it harder until finally the whole thing swung inward with a loud bang.

Not even locked… he thought.

That said something about the small-town trust in Tour — something he didn't see much of in the city. It was also unlike his father, who wasn't a very trusting man, to leave his property unlocked.

He was really different here…

Luckily, the lawyer had given James a key, so he could lock the place up if he wanted.

James blinked at the dark interior as if something had hit him in the face.

It was so quiet inside; not even a hint of wind or sound could be heard through the old log walls. The place was dead silent. It smelled musty. Not surprising, considering how long it had been abandoned.

James stepped inside, shutting the door behind him. "Hello?" he called out, feeling silly at once. Of course, there was no one here.

He paused, giving his eyes some time to adjust to the dimness after all the light from outside faded completely.

As expected, there were two rooms — a living room with a small kitchen connected by a narrow hallway to a single bedroom. A large stone fireplace dominated the living room. He had seen the outhouse outside and a small well to draw water from. Besides an awning under which to store firewood, this was all the space the cabin offered.

Modest... but clean and sufficient.

He sighed. There were advantages to accepting the inheritance. He'd finally end the lease on his overpriced apartment in the city he hated, and he'd have a place of his own. But he couldn't commute to work from here every day; it was just too far away.

He'd have to get a job in Tour.

For a moment, he almost let the whole thing go, but then his eyes fell on a picture of his family on the mantlepiece. He was there, his brother, and his mother. All in better days, back when his father still looked happy.

Before he moved to the city and became rich.

And why would I surrender myself to the same damn rat race that killed my father? James thought.

No... maybe this place earned a chance.

James was just going to drive into Tour. If there was work in town, he'd take it as a sign that he was supposed to accept his father's inheritance and move into the cabin.

It didn't matter where or what it was. Maybe he could find some odd jobs for a while until he found something more permanent. Or maybe the local rancher needed help with his animals or something like that. That might be a way to make some extra money until he could start looking for a full-time gig.

To get to Tour, he drove back down the dirt road to Forrester Trail, where Corinne's barn stood.

The redhead was nowhere in sight, unfortunately. James wouldn't have objected to another look at the fit beauty.

After he passed by the barn, he hung right and headed for the small town of Tour.

When he finally made it to the outskirts of the hamlet, he slowed down. There weren't any cars on the street itself, and only a couple parked on the curb.

He rolled his window down, glancing up and down Tour's main street, aptly named Main Street, that seemed to make up the bulk of the town of Tour.

As expected, several shops lined both sides of Main Street — a diner, a bank, a post office, a gas station, and other businesses that ran the gamut from a general store to an auto shop.

A few old houses lined streets that branched off from Main Street, as did many of the business owners' homes. An older church stood off by itself about half a mile from the center of the town.

But James didn't see anyone offering jobs right away. This was going to take some effort, but he was determined to give it a serious try.

He pulled over into one of the empty parking spaces next to the post office. It was early yet, so no one was around.

He figured he'd go check out the restaurants first since he had experience waiting.

There was a diner that doubled as Tour's watering hole, but they hadn't opened yet. From there, he headed over to the gas station. He didn't enjoy being a gas station attendant, but it was honest work; he'd do it in a pinch if he had to.

"Hey there," a familiar female voice called out from

the general store, stopping him in his tracks. "What are you doing here?"

James turned to see Corinne walking toward him. She had her hands tucked under her armpits, as if fending off the cold.

She stopped right in front of him and eyed him up and down with a look of amusement.

She gave a smile. "Ya look like you're lost."

"Not really," James replied with a shake of his head. Then he cleared his throat and smiled at the attractive redhead. "Just taking a look at the town."

Her green eyes were smiling at him too now, and it almost felt like she knew exactly what he was thinking when he looked at her.

"Not lost, then?" she prompted him with a grin.

He shrugged. "Well... I'm actually looking for work."

Corinne's eyebrows rose. "Looking for anything specific? Or will any old kind of job do?"

"I don't mind hard labor or farm work if needed," James said, still standing there feeling slightly awkward while they talked about this stuff. "But it needs to pay for now if I want to make things work out at the cabin."

He didn't want to sound desperate to get a job. But he also wanted to start earning money to move out here into the cabin — and not have to worry about being broke.

She nodded. "There aren't many in town who need help right now... or who can afford it. But maybe I can point you in the right direction."

With that, she gestured toward the general store. "Come with me!"

Chapter 4

James followed Corinne into the general store, trying his best to keep his eyes from drifting to her perfect ass.

The general store was pretty busy, even though it was only midmorning. There were shelves upon shelves full of food items and household supplies, and more than a few locals shopping around.

Corinne walked right up to the counter.

James had to do a double take when he saw the mature beauty standing behind it, pouting as she seemed to fidget with something.

She was dressed in an outfit that looked like it struggled to keep her luscious figure within its bounds. The tight tank top hugged her large breasts perfectly, and the matching shorts barely contained her hips. Both were bright red, and the tank top had "Lucy's Deals" written on it in fading print.

She'd added a pair of knee-high cowboy boots to her outfit, making her the ultimate cowgirl MILF. She wore her blonde hair down, and her blue eyes were bright and big as she studied whatever it was she fidgeted with.

"Hey Lucy," Corinne said. "This here is James, my new neighbor, who wants to know if there is work available."

The blonde looked up at him, her blue eyes alive with a profound interest. "Well, howdy, James," she purred. "Work, huh? What can you do?"

"I'm... um... versatile," he replied without thinking. His face got hot at once while Lucy stared him in the eye.

"Hmm... I bet." Her eyebrows lifted before she burst out laughing.

He couldn't help himself; he started chuckling too.

"Well, then..." Corinne began, but was cut off by Lucy.

"I might have just what your young friend needs!" Lucy said brightly, glancing back and forth between them with a mischievous twinkle in her eyes. "If James here is 'versatile', he can help out and cut the saplings in Rovery's old lot out in the woods."

"Great idea!" Corinne said.

Lucy glanced at James. "Can you lumberjack, James? Little pine trees at first, but we might get to the bigger logs later." The bold smile on her plump lips said more than enough.

James grinned. "Yeah, sure."

"Excellent! You can start today if you want to. The day's still young!" The MILF pushed away from the counter. "Just deliver them to me right here. You got a truck?"

"If by truck, you mean a rusty sedan," James said.

She chuckled. "All right, give me a call, and I'll come pick them up instead when I get time. That'll be in the evening after closing hours."

"Ooh, a date," Corinne teased.

"Jealous?" Lucy teased. "You can come if you like."

James swallowed. He could feel his cheeks burn at

once.

"Let me give you my number," Lucy said to James, studying him from under long lashes before she pulled a piece of paper and a pen from under the counter.

"Oh, this *really* feels like guys are going on a date!" Corinne exclaimed.

Lucy grinned at Corinne, her eyes twinkling with mischief. "Not a date. He's just gonna put some wood in my truck."

Corinne doubled over laughing. "Lucy! I'm seeing a whole new side to you."

James couldn't believe this. He would've wanted to say something witty, but this MILF beauty came on so damn hard and fast. He could barely form a coherent thought.

With a smile, Lucy leaned forward, offering James a look down her shirt.

That didn't help for James's internal temperature.

Lucy wrote down her number, then pushed the piece of paper over to him. "Here we go!"

He smiled and took it. "Thanks," he said.

"You're welcome," Lucy said, holding him with her stare for a moment.

For a moment there, she actually looked a little vulnerable. The teasing smile from before turned a little shy, and a blush appeared on her cheeks.

She looked down, and James was enamored by those long lashes and the way her hands fidgeted with each other on the countertop.

"So, uh, where is this Rovery place?" James asked, trying to regain his composure while he figured out how he felt about these women.

"Along the highway, just south of Main Street," Lucy said. "A rutty road to the left. Can't miss it: it has a sign that says 'Keep Out: Private Property'."

"And that's okay for me to enter?" James asked.

"Hm-hm," Lucy purred. "It's mine. Head up the road, and you'll find a shed with some tools you can use. Call me when you finish up, and I'll pick the wood up from there. No need to remove the branches; the client will do that. And focus on the small trees; four to six feet is perfect."

"Thanks," James said with a smile. "I guess I'll hop to it." He glanced at Corinne. "Uh, I guess I'll see you later, then."

"Oh, yeah, I'm sure ya will, stranger." She winked at him.

He felt the eyes of both women on his back as he made his way outside.

Chapter 5

It took James three tries to get his old sedan to start, but once it did, he had a few moments to himself as he drove down Main Street until the road transitioned into the highway.

Damn, he thought. *That Corinne is something else!*

Who would have known he'd find such an attractive woman within an hour of arriving here?

And Lucy... what a bombshell! A true MILF! Her body was just... well, she looked like she was barely in her twenties yet had that sweet, mature thing about her that just gave away she'd be a great lay. Up for anything.

An hour in Tour, and he'd already met more desirable women than in the city.

And the best part was, they were flirting with him.

Flirting *hard*!

Well, hell. What the heck? He wasn't getting any younger; he might as well live it up now. Why not enjoy some of this free time?

He smiled to himself at his own thoughts before returning to his driving.

The rutty road Lucy told him to look out for soon came into view. It appeared to run parallel to the highway for quite a distance until finally reaching an empty field at a bend. There was a lone wooden shack sitting there on the right side.

He slowed down and turned onto a narrow dirt lane that led to the ramshackle house, wondering why someone would choose to build a shack in the middle of nowhere.

There were several trees planted in neat formations near the building, their bare branches swaying in the breeze, but there were many, many more younger pine trees among them, springy and young. Clearing them out would take more than a day's work.

James headed toward the shack.

It was unlocked. The door creaked when he opened it, and he winced.

Must be pretty old if the place is in a state like this, he thought as he entered.

Inside, he saw that the room was unfurnished except for a single chair and workbench placed against one wall. On top of that, a couple of rusty tools sat on the table at the center.

There was a single felling axe with a worn handle. James lifted the tool from the table. He noted how heavy it felt. Its blade showed signs of wear, and it must have been sharpened countless times by someone who knew what they were doing.

James shouldered the axe and headed back outside.

He had chopped firewood before, and that was about all the experience he had with it.

However, how hard could cutting short trees be?

The first sapling looked easy enough. It stood only eight feet tall.

Just to be sure he had the space for a clean cut, he walked around the tree. His eyes fell on another small pine, this one much smaller than the first, maybe six feet high or so. This seemed like something even a novice lumberjack could manage.

His fingers found the wood rough as they touched the bark, but once the tree started bending under his weight as he pushed harder, he realized it was more flexible and stronger than he'd expected.

It wasn't going down without a fight. So he applied the hatchet with strength.

He cut into the base easily at first, then stopped in surprise when the stubborn little bastard wouldn't let go. He kept chopping at the tree until it finally snapped and tumbled down.

Despite it being a short tree, James still had to watch himself when it fell.

But the second tree proved easier. After that, he was sweating from exertion, which made him feel good for the time being.

He gave a satisfied nod.

This is pretty nice, he thought. *Different from all the bullshit I used to do in the city.*

Feeling good, he continued on to the next tree.

Although the sun beat down on his head from the blue sky overhead, James enjoyed its warmth on his face. The cool wind carried the scent of wildflowers and pine needles, making the forest smell like summer.

With every little tree he felled, he got the hang of it more and more.

The axe became an extension of his arm, and before long, each swing sent the blade flying out with a satisfying *crack*!

Sometimes the axe landed deep in the trunk and stuck there, requiring a tug to pull it free; other times, the blade barely penetrated before bouncing off the trees with a dull thud.

But after several swings, all trees eventually fell. He piled the felled trees up near the toolshed.

The work didn't take that long since most were only four to six feet tall, but soon enough, he was panting. His muscles ached by noon.

Not wanting to quit too early — and wanting to impress Lucy — he took a quick break and filled his canteen up from a nearby creek he found.

He could have just driven into town to ask Lucy for water, but it felt better to be able to say he went out and found it himself.

Besides, he wanted to get back at it as soon as possible.

He drank the cold stream water down as fast as he possibly could so he could keep going without wasting any precious time.

The heat must've been getting to him because he lost track of time again, this time taking longer than usual between breaks.

As he scoured the forest looking for trees to fell, he saw something shimmer in the distance, near the creek he had discovered earlier. A large clearing opened up there, and something looked strange about the place; he couldn't quite put his finger on what exactly was bothering him until he came closer.

But then he saw: some of the shapes he had taken for trunks were standing stones.

A circle of them formed a perimeter around a much larger one lying in the center of a massive flat area. The smaller stones seemed to stand guard over the central stone like a border or fence surrounding it.

James walked toward the giant boulder. There weren't many trees around it, but some did grow from its edges and several more sat inside its wide ring, all dead and dried-out, like they'd died centuries ago and not just months.

He stared at the large rock, trying to figure out how such ancient standing stones would come to rest here where no one lived — or if someone had moved them there deliberately.

He felt like he should look into that once he finished cutting up the trees.

Or maybe now?

The ground felt different under his feet when he got closer. Not that there was a difference he noticed at first sight; the dirt was dry and cracked, the grass brown.

But somehow, there was an air of antiquity to this place; a feeling of age that set him on edge as well as intrigued him.

James stopped next to the largest of the stones in the middle, studying it intently as if looking for clues of its origins before realizing what else made him uneasy: three deep gouges in its surface ran vertically through its width and length, almost resembling claw marks in size and shape.

He doubted they had been gouged into the rock with any man-made tool.

As he studied the stone, a tiredness settled on him.

He squinted up at the sun. He leaned against the stone, allowing himself a moment's breather. His mind wandered, and the fatigue that tugged at him haunted him with strange half-images and sounds he struggled to place.

After a few minutes, he glanced down at his watch. His hands stilled at the sight of the time.

Two o'clock!

The afternoon sun was high overhead already, and he hadn't even realized it.

Shaking himself from his brief daze, James made to walk away from the stones and head toward the woods. He had more work to do.

Just as he turned, a voice drifted to him. Out of place, out of time, and it called to him.

"James," it spoke. "Come to me now, James."

And James turned to face the stones, unable to resist that siren call. Slowly, he raised his hand. Then, he placed it on the stone and he, too, became out of place and out of time.

Chapter 6

James was the beast they hunted. He heard the shouting behind them, the rage, the fury. Barking dogs, whinnying horses.

They wanted to kill him.

He realized they would soon catch up, but then a few of them would die for their efforts. That thought gave him strength. A little longer to fight, just a bit longer...

A raven-haired woman ran alongside him, her bare feet slapping the ground. "Run," she muttered, her breath already halting. "Run on ahead. I'll hold them off. Go!" She threw something at him.

It landed in front of him with a thud, and when he picked it up, he found it familiar: her pendant. A simple talisman of an unknown, green material.

On it were the emblems that he recognized as the Eleven Elements of Magic…

Time, Space, Fire, Lightning, Force, Water, Air, Life, Death, Blood, and Earth.

In between each symbol was what looked like some kind of magical runes or symbols. He clutched the necklace to his chest as he ran faster than before.

She turned, and fire raged among the trees. Men screamed as they died. The tall woman had bought him time, and James escaped.

Down the years, down the generations.

And in the darkness that crossed the ages, the woman spoke to him. "So," she said. "You return to us now, after all these years."

"Yes," he simply replied, willing the words into existence with a willpower he did not know he had.

"Good," she crooned, her voice edged with hidden promise. "Find me then. In the forest we once called home, in the house you already call home in your mind. Find me there."

Those last words were taken by the wind, carried away from him, but laden with promise.

"Find me there."

Chapter 7

James bolted upright. He blinked a few times before he recognized he lay on the slab in the middle of the stone circle.

I fell asleep? he thought.

He checked his watch. It was almost 4 pm.

The dream.

The woman — her face and features were familiar,

like a promise made to him long ago.

But for some reason, he couldn't remember who she was. Just her name: Sara.

Her call still echoed through the empty clearing.

He got to his feet slowly. His muscles protested at first, reminding him he hadn't rested well the previous night.

There was no way he was going to cut more trees today.

Reluctantly, he pulled out his cellphone to dial Lucy's number. As it rang, James glanced around again before looking up into the sky. The sun hung low over the tree-tops.

If only I had a few more days... he thought wistfully. *Then I could finish my work here.*

Maybe Lucy would let him continue tomorrow.

"Hey," Lucy answered after a couple of rings. "This is James, right?"

"Yep," he replied.

"How are things going?"

"I think I did all I could for today," James replied as he looked back down at the ground. "And..."

"Yeah?" she asked, her voice metallic through the speaker.

"I ran into a circle of standing stones out here." He

tried not to sound too excited about what he found. He wasn't sure how much he should tell her yet.

"Oh?" she said. "I don't remember ever seeing something like that at Rovary's old lot."

He shook his head. "No? Well… there was something strange about them. They were just sitting there in the grass. But when I touched them…"

He paused before finishing his sentence.

"Then what?"

"Never mind," James said. "It's silly. Uh, did you want me to leave those trees I felled right here? Or…"

"Sure, but I won't be able to come over for another hour or two. I have to keep the shop open."

"Okay," James said. He had been looking forward to see her again.

"But will you be available to work again tomorrow?"

He perked up. "Sure!"

"Great!" she said. "Drop by the store around eight. I'll fix you up some lunch, and then I'll make you dinner as a 'thank you' tomorrow."

"That's… really nice of you."

"Hmm," she hummed. "Or a sneaky tactic to make sure you'll work all day."

He laughed. "Well, that's an approach I can live with."

"Good," she said. "I'll see you tomorrow, then!"

"See you tomorrow."

Feeling a lot better, James made his way to his old sedan.

The dream returned to his mind when he drove back to the cabin. The woman — Sara — and her promise.

Find me then. In the forest we once called home, in the house you already call home in your mind.

It had to be the cabin.

He sped up, suddenly eager to search the cabin. And she was right, too: in his mind, he already called the place home.

He careened down the road, headed up Main Street in Tour, and finally came to the barn at 1 Forrester Trail where he turned onto the dirt road, taking a right at the fork in the road until the cabin came up.

It stood there like an old friend.

By then, it was getting darker out.

He parked and killed the engine, then took the flashlight from his car. With slow, deliberate steps, he approached the cabin.

James's heart beat hard in his chest as he stepped through the front door. There wasn't any electricity here. Only the last of the day's light bleeding in through the windows illuminated the place.

But it was enough for James to make out the rooms.

As if by some magic, the hatch in the floor drew in his eye. He knew where it was, even if a rug still covered it. When he pulled it away and found the hatch, he wasn't the least bit surprised.

Once more, James thought of Sara and her words that still echoed faintly within him.

Find me then. In the forest we once called home, in the house you already call home in your mind. Find me there.

He placed both hands on the handle. For a breath, he hesitated, but only a moment before he opened the hatch and went down the rickety stairs, plunging downward into darkness.

Chapter 8

The world under his feet was one of cold stone.

The cellar under the cabin did not smell musty or earthy as he had expected, and it felt a little bigger than it had any right to be.

"Hello?" James called out. "Sara?"

He ran one hand along the wall. His fingers brushed smooth stone and cool mortar.

This was a place she called home?

It was strange how everything just… clicked. He looked into the darkness, no doubt in his mind now that she was calling to him with purpose.

He trusted her summons; there was no other way to explain why he obeyed them so easily and without question.

And what he'd seen in the circle of stones hadn't been a hallucination, either. Something very real had happened there, something magical and mystical. He could feel it still echoing within his body.

"Sara?" he whispered, feeling like he might wake himself from a bizarre dream if he spoke too loudly.

But this was no dream.

"James?" the voice came from the darkness. Her words were honey-sweet whispers in his ears.

"Come." She sounded gleeful, too. As if she long awaited the chance to have him join her here in this space.

As he walked, he encountered an old workbench set in the far corner of the cellar.

On the surface lay a single book, ancient and yet wholly intact and undamaged. On its leather cover were the signs of the Eleven Elements of Magic.

No way, James thought.

"Meow."

James almost bumped his head as he jumped. He had not seen the black cat under the workbench, trailing her tail around the leg of the workbench as she studied him.

Her left ear twitched once.

"Oh, hi," he said to the cat.

She just studied him with signature feline curiosity.

The book drew in his eyes, and he picked it up.

The tome weighed heavily in his hands. The cover seemed to call to his mind, and he opened it. The pages were empty, all but the first few.

'High Magicke', it read in an imposing heading in Old English script.

But even as his eyes drifted over it, it changed into a much more legible font, and 'thees' and 'thous' turned into 'yous'.

High Magic, it read. *Also known as the magic of the High Mage.*

The High Mage.

He'd never heard of that term before, and he had to admit he liked the sound of it. There was a profound, mysterious ring here that intrigued him.

What exactly did the title mean?

Was there some kind of magical group that called themselves by that name? The High Mages? Was this a spellbook?

He scanned the rest of the text by the light of his flashlight, quickly discovering that a High Mage could cast magic by virtue of hereditary quality. However, High Magic required a specific combination of words in an ancient, forgotten language to function. It was based on the premise that by the power of the correct intent and promise — willpower, in effect — a High Mage could manifest anything.

Anything.

"Meow," the cat purred. She remained there, at the foot of the table, as if she wanted to say something. Then, in one slender motion, she hopped up, curled her tail around James's wrist, and purred.

"Uh, hi," James said. "Affectionate girl, aren't you?"

Then, her tail flicked at the pages, seemingly at random, but the movement caused a page to turn.

To a spell, it seemed.

Word of Familiar Binding.

James eyed the cat with a raised eyebrow.

This had to be a joke. No way this cat would ever...

But she looked so pleased about it all.

He took a seat beside the workbench where she sat on her haunches watching him, waiting for whatever next move he might make.

He swallowed and began studying the Grimoire.

Magic is like water from an open faucet. You only need to grab hold and drink deep.

There are only two rules when you learn how to use High Magic: One, you must bond with another who has already mastered some elements of High Magic, or else you cannot learn.

Two, the more powerful your intention and promise, the more powerful the effect of the spell, but it also makes it more likely that a person may resist or even break your spell.

These were the first things James learned on his path to becoming a High Mage.

James studied the spell to bind a familiar to him.

It was not a difficult spell, and the language wasn't too hard; some weird breed of Old Germanic.

More important was the intent and the purpose with which he spoke the words. Those amounted to a promise to bind himself to his familiar, to promise to protect and to cherish it. And finally, the spell needed a target.

A target, James mused.

Beside him, the cat mewled and looked up at James with yellow eyes. She leaned against James's leg.

He couldn't help but smile at the sight of her. His familiar; it all made sense now. She had brought him here.

He would cast the spell with the cat as his target. If he succeeded in casting the binding spell on this black cat before him — and he planned on doing exactly that — the two would become bound to each other by magic until one died or released the other.

That could take months, years, decades, centuries... who knew?

"So what do you say?" James asked the cat.

The creature tilted its head and gave a soft purr. "Meow," she replied.

I'll take that as a yes, James thought.

Then James spoke the spell, speaking slowly and clearly, trying not to stumble or rush through any part of it because that might break it.

"Vandeer tod meerdandeer.

"Furbaintenis, bainding. Lefen.

"Van deer tod meerdandeer."

The next moment, his hands began to tingle as his fingers curled around the book in his lap. He sensed that he tapped into some inner reserve of power.

It was like putting your hand on a stove with a fire under it, only your skin felt hot from the inside out. The sensation was painful — a profound burning that tore at his flesh.

And yet it seemed natural, and the power of this ritual rushed into him, filling him with strength. The pain lasted only a moment, leaving power in its wake.

His breath quickened as he waited for the spell to take effect. The room became brighter, warmer; his vision sharpened; and there came an undeniable humming in his ears.

This was real magic; ancient magic; magic that had been used since before the beginning of time itself. It felt intoxicating.

Then came the flash. It blinded him, and he covered his face with a curse.

But then he heard her voice, calling to him over and over again.

"Meow!" she said at first.

But soon enough, the sounds she made became words.

It took James a moment to realize she wasn't purring or meowing anymore. And still blinded by the flash of magic, his hearing was all he could go by for the moment.

But the cat's words coming back to him over and over through the bond forged between them by High Magic.

At length, he understood her.

"You found me." Her voice sounded cheerful, even giddy.

As his vision came back, James looked up at the cat sitting on the workbench beside him.

But she was no longer a cat...

Well, not completely.

On the tabletop sat a beautiful figure, curvy and sensual, with hair black as midnight, just as the cat's fur had been. A pair of cute, fuzzy cat ears protruded from her long hair, and there was no denying the cat's tail that still brushed the Grimoire from which James had read his first spell only a moment ago.

But apart from that, she was human...

And hotter than hell with her big breasts, luscious hips, and her perfect hourglass figure.

And it got worse. Because this woman — or better, cat girl — wore only a short, skin-tight dress and heels.

As he stared at her, he couldn't help but wonder how

it would feel to be bound to such perfection, to be trapped in the cage of those legs as they wrapped around him while he took his pleasure from her.

"You're beautiful," James said softly, astounded. He almost choked on the words — he was rarely this forward, but he simply couldn't control himself.

"So are you," the woman replied in the same sultry voice of his dream. She giggled. "And you found me. Found me... and bound me."

A dirty promise lay in those last two words. James didn't need to hear them twice; the thought alone made his heart pound faster and his blood boil.

For all her beauty, there was an inner fire that burned bright within the cat girl — one that she kept tightly under control for now, but also one she never fully stifled.

"My name is Sara," she said, and gave him a little smile. "But you already knew that."

She sat up on the workbench, a gentle swaying motion that left her dress hiked up dangerously high on her thick thighs.

It seemed like a deliberate move designed to draw his eyes down to the part of her body James wanted most desperately.

"I'm James," he replied, voice hoarse. "But you

already know that."

She laughed at having her own words reflected back at her, then hopped down from the workbench with the agility of a cat.

Her tail swished as she studied him, and her left ear gave the cutest little twitch.

"Come," she finally said. "Let's get out of this drafty place so we can talk in comfort." She nodded at the Grimoire. "And I would hang on to that if I were you."

She gave him a yellow-eyed look, then grinned and sashayed toward the ladder. James stood mesmerized by the way her luscious ass made her tight dress ripple, then grabbed the book and followed her.

Chapter 9

"So, you're going to teach me High Magic?" James asked Sara.

They sat together in the armchair in the living room. Sara had just hopped onto his lap without even asking.

James's cheeks had flushed at first, but he couldn't object.

After all, he didn't mind.

She purred softly as the fire crackled beside them, her tail absently flicking against James's legs.

"High Magic?" Sara asked, leaning forward to poke the wood in the fire, casting an amber glow across her face, accentuating the blush in her cheeks.

Her move also gave him a breathtaking view of how the tight fabric of her dress revealed the curvature of her ass, nice and squashed from sitting on his lap.

"Yes, indeed," she replied. "And I'll make sure your first lesson is a good one."

She raised an eyebrow and sat back. As she settled on his lap, she brushed her nose along the side of James's neck. The soft fur of her ears tickled and James felt himself tense up.

She glanced up at him and winked before she spoke.

"The High Mages have always been special people with very special powers — since long before there were any schools or colleges for the art of magic," she said. "High Mages are one of the few magicians who can learn magic by their Bloodline, although they require a bond with one or more familiars to learn spells."

"Bloodline?" James said, shifting his weight as he felt her constant movement on his lap cause his cock to rise.

Sara chuckled as she leaned back into him, bringing

her lips close to his ear. "Well, yes, all High Mages have magical Bloodlines, but you must understand that every single High Mage has its own unique lineage with its own benefits... and drawbacks."

"Do you know mine?" James asked.

She giggled and wriggled in his lap as he shifted his weight some more, making his cock even harder.

"I do," she purred. "Your Bloodline is called the House of Harkness, a cadet branch of an ancient European house of magic. The House of Harkness was founded in the United States. Its founder was a powerful man. But well... he made mistakes. One being when he became involved with the wrong woman."

"What does my Bloodline mean for me now? How can I use this power?" James looked up at Sara again.

"So many questions already!" she purred, a teasing note in her voice.

Her eyes shone a bright yellow in the firelight. She reached up to brush her fingers across her cheek, her black hair spilling across her shoulder blades and down her bare arms.

A shiver ran through James, and she smiled wickedly — as if she realized her effect on him all to well. She poked him in the chest with one finger and gave him another wink.

With the frenetic energy of a feline, she hopped down from his lap and stood facing him within an arm's length.

"Your Bloodline means everything," she whispered huskily, then lowered her voice an octave or two before adding, "It will help you achieve your goals."

"What goals?" James said, eyebrow cocked.

She put her hand on James's chin and tilted his head until their gazes met, hers full of meaning. Her eyes stared into James's soul; he sensed them look deep within him to see what he was made of.

And then, those bright yellow eyes lit up with excitement, a sudden flash that illuminated her whole face as if someone had hit a switch that turned a light on in a dark room.

She licked her lips. "You must answer that question for yourself, James," she said.

Then she kissed him — a long, warm kiss that left his mouth burning with need. His cock strained against his boxers as if it hungered to be closer to her.

He growled, needy for more, but she took it the wrong way and pulled back, her yellow eyes wide.

"Oh!" she cried out, pressing both hands to her chest and laughing as she backed away. "What am I thinking? I'm sorry... It's... I..." She shook her head and sighed. "I'm so excited... I should've asked... It's normal for familiars and their master to..." She fidgeted with her hands, and it was an immensely cute sight to see a woman so hot fidget nervously. "Well, I should have asked. I'm sorry."

James didn't know what else to say other than what came first to mind. "It's okay," he said gently. "I liked it." He reached up and touched his lips where Sara had kissed him.

She licked her lips. "You did?"

"Yeah." He grinned.

She blushed. "Good. I guess that means we can try again later."

But to James, there could be no later.

A need rumbled in him now, awakened by the sweetness of her lips, and he rose to his feet, no longer trying to hide the erection tenting his jeans.

"Why later?" he grunted. "We can do it now."

Chapter 10

Sara gave a lascivious smile at his words. "Now?" she purred, big yellow eyes dipping to the outline of his rock-hard cock in his jeans.

"Now," James confirmed.

She came to him almost on her tippy toes and with feline grace until she could wrap her arms around him, hugging him tightly.

His hands found their way to her back as she pressed herself against him. Her soft pelvis pushed against his hardening bulge behind the fabric of his pants as they kissed and explored one another's mouths.

Their tongues danced together while their bodies ground against each other, rubbing up against the fabric, eager to break away from those cloth confines.

Sara broke the kiss and ran her tongue along the edge of James's lip. She flicked it over his teeth before running it across the tip of his nose, making it twitch from the ticklish sensation, before she nibbled on him, just hard enough to make him wince.

Then she stepped back, still smiling, her tail twirled around James's leg. Her dainty hands moved down to grab her dress by its hem, and she pulled the garment over her head in one fell swoop, leaving her in nothing but her heels.

She wasn't wearing any panties underneath.

James gulped at the sight of Sara standing naked in front of him in nothing but heels.

Her long black hair spilled down her shoulders and back, and her nipples stood up hard as pebbles. The firelight danced between her thick thighs, revealing a thigh gap to bury a face in and — higher — a smooth and pink pussy with a perfect triangle of black pubic hair.

He licked his lips as his eyes drank in her naked beauty. Then he let out a low growl that sent chills up his spine as he felt his cock jump in his jeans like a startled bull being goaded by a red flag.

"Let's get *you* out," she purred, eyes dipping to his tent, and her left ear gave that little twitch again. "And see what my High Mage works with."

Sara helped James pull off his shirt before stepping away to lead him by the hand into the bedroom.

There, she lit an oil lamp and put it on the bedside table, then sat on the bed with her legs crossed under her. She looked like a naughty schoolgirl caught with her hand in the cookie jar, eyes fixed on him.

James's eyes lingered on her bare legs and the tight pink lips of her pussy glistening in the firelight. Her aroma called to him. His cock throbbed in his pants as she waited patiently for him to undo them.

With a grunt of need, James undid his belt and let his jeans slip to the floor, together with his boxer shorts.

His cock sprang free, firm and throbbing with need.

"By the Elements," Sara purred, her yellow eyes wide. "Your cock... I really love it!"

She giggled before she crawled forward on all fours, her delicious ass swaying as her tail trailed behind her.

She ran a finger along the length of his shaft, causing him to suck in air at the ticklish sensation.

"It's something to worship!" she purred.

A moment later, she leaned forward and kissed the tip with a reverence that matched her words.

"Fuck," James hissed. He couldn't believe how beautiful she was. How much she was everything he'd been dreaming of. How she made him feel.

A few hours ago, he wouldn't have believed what was happening to him now.

Sara giggled and pulled back, then grabbed him by his waist and tugged. She looked up at him with those yellow eyes, the firelight dancing in them. "Let me suck your cock," she crooned. "Let me taste you."

James gave a nod, allowing Sara to climb on the bed with him.

His body already ached for release as she knelt on the bed and took his cock in her hand, her lips only barely brushing his skin.

"So, so big," she murmured before finally taking his cock in her mouth.

She sucked him off with fervor, her lips swirling around the head of his cock, making it slick and shiny with her saliva. Her tongue slid out, tickling the underside of his cock. Then she slipped him into her throat, making him groan as she took him deeper, her eyes closed and a blissful smile on her lips.

As she sucked him off, she stroked his cock with her hand, making it jump and throb in her grip. She looked up at him as she bobbed her head back and forth, working him in her mouth like a seasoned pro.

"I want to drink your cum," she whispered, her breath hot against his cock.

She kept up her pace, slurping and sucking, taking his entire length into her mouth. She even let her hand drift down and spread her fingers on his balls, massaging them softly.

James's hips began to buck, thrusting his cock in her mouth as he pushed her head down on it with his hand. He moaned, sensing his orgasm rising.

She looked up at him, her eyes wide with excitement. Her hand slid up his cock to tease his sack with her fingers, then her hand crawled up to join the other around his cock, jerking him off with both hands.

James groaned, and she smiled, keeping up her pace.

"Ah," he gasped. "You're gonna make me cum."

She pulled out his cock and kissed it, then used her lips to tease the head of his cock, flicking her tongue against it. "Cum for me, James," she moaned.

He groaned and slammed his cock in, driving it into her mouth, letting her take him deep.

Sara held him, her tongue swirling around his tip, then slowly sank down on his cock, making him groan in pleasure.

She took him all the way, her lips wrapped tightly around him as she slipped him deeply into her throat, her eyes squeezing shut. Her tail gently caressed his thigh, twirled around his leg, as she worked on his cock like a needy little slut.

"Oh, fuck!" James cried out. "Yes... Oh, yes..."

He panted hard and his cock bucked in her mouth, the head throbbing.

She swallowed the wash of precum he gave her, and his cock jumped again, sending spasms of pleasure through him, ready to cum down her throat. He buried his hand deep in her full head of hair, his need rising even higher when he felt those cute little cat ears.

"Oh, God... I'm... oh, shit! I'm gonna come!"

With a deep grunt, he spurted a rope of sticky cum down her throat.

Her yellow eyes widened at the massive flood of seed

being pushed into her mouth, but she drank it all, gulping and swallowing and gagging, until James's fifth rope made her release him, coughing, and the rest of his sticky load splattered over her big tits, jiggling as she coughed.

"Fuck," James muttered as he took in that delicious sight.

Eyes wide, her left ear giving a cute little twitch, Sara recovered and pushed her ample tits up, jacking the last rope of cum from his cock to make it land on her bouncy chest. She proceeded to lick his cock clean, her eyes slightly crossed as she focused on her work.

When she was done, she licked her lips. "Wow," she said. "That was a big load."

James chuckled. "Well, you awaken a lot in me," he muttered.

She looked up at him with a sly grin, and his cock twitched as the tip of her fluffy tail ran under his balls.

She bit her lip for a moment and gave a bashful smile. "I have a question, James," she hummed, her voice husky.

James rolled his shoulders, eyes still fixed on his new conquest. "And that is?"

"Will you please eat my pussy for me?"

Hot damn…

James's heart bucked with delight at Sara's dirty request.

He nodded, smiling. "There is nothing I'd like to do more..."

She laughed, sitting up. Then she shimmied back on the bed. "How...?"

"Lie down," James commanded.

She purred, anticipating the pleasure, as she lay back, his cum still glazing her magnificent chest.

With a needy grunt, he moved onto the mattress and grabbed those long legs — one in each hand — as he surveyed his prize: her wet, pink pussy.

He kissed her belly first, enjoying how she purred and drew her tummy in as a reflexive response to his tickling kisses.

He ran his tongue down her midriff to her belly button. He circled his tongue around it before slipping it between her legs and lapping at her pussy.

Sara moaned and spread her legs for him, allowing him to continue. Her thighs were damp with her own juices. He could smell her scent, musky and sweet.

It drove him wild.

He continued to lick and lap, pushing her legs further apart. When she reached down to grab his hair and pull him closer, he did not resist. He let his tongue dance on her soft pussy lips, his tongue licking at the hood of her clit before he pushed it inside her.

Sara's eyes went wide as his tongue pushed into her. She arched her back, her hands grabbing the sheets as she purred louder. Her tail whipped back and forth under him, tickling his stomach and thighs.

"Oh, yes!" she gasped. "Oh, James, that's it. That feels so good!"

He gave her a moment to recover, then pushed his tongue deeper inside her. Her pussy was tight and hot. Her lips wrapped around his tongue, and he found himself pushing his face deeper into her, drinking her nectar.

"Oh, James!" she moaned, arching her back and pulling his head tighter into her. "Yes... oh, yes... Oh, god, yes! Fuck me, James! I want you to fuck me!"

James groaned, loving the feeling of her pussy around his tongue. Her voice made his cock twitch. He couldn't wait to feel her tight cunt wrapped around him.

But he was going to make her come first. He wanted

to hear her scream under the lashings of his tongue.

Sara moaned as his tongue flicked her clit, and she gave a desperate gasp.

"Oh, yes... I'm so close, James! I'm so close!"

He lapped at her clit, faster and faster now, and her legs tightened around him. He heard a muffled cry as she came, her pussy twitching against his tongue as she shuddered with pleasure.

Sara's eyes opened, and she looked at him with a sly grin. "You're a natural," she cooed.

James smiled, pleased that he'd satisfied her. Then he moved up and kissed her, her tongue tangling with his, as he slipped between her legs, which she immediately clamped around him.

"Fuck me, James?" she purred. "Please?"

"I will," he growled, moving into position. He laid his body over hers, his cock pressed against her soaked pussy. She raised her hips, opening her legs for him.

With a moan, he let his cock slip into her slick channel, the head hitting her cervix.

"Ah, yes!" she cried, her tail wrapping around his leg once again.

He pulled out a little and pushed in again, then again, slowly taking his time as he enjoyed the feeling of her tight pussy enveloping him.

He had never known he was so virile that he could go so shortly after getting his cock sucked, but it seemed Sara was right; he was a natural.

"Fuck, you feel good!" she moaned. "Oh, James, don't stop! I need you in me."

He didn't need to be told twice. He grabbed her hips and pulled her to him, thrusting his cock in and out of her. She cried out in pleasure as his cock hit her spot. She was tight and hot and perfect, and he lost himself in her.

He grabbed her waist and pulled her down into him, burying his cock deep inside her with every thrust.

Sara threw her arms up and bit the back of her hand, baring her cute little fangs, and her cat ears twitched as he pillaged her tight little pussy, slamming into her again and again, giving her what she needed.

Sara moaned and thrashed beneath him, her hands moving to pull up her own legs as her tail twitched and curled. "James," she gasped, "I'm... oh, I'm... coming! Oh, yes!"

Her body shook with pleasure, and he knew he would soon join her, but he wasn't ready to let up yet. She was just too beautiful to stop.

"Oh, yes," she whimpered, "Make me yours, James!"

"Argh," James grunted, pounding her harder, his

hips slapping against her jiggling ass. "I'm gonna fill you up!"

"Oh, yes, James!" she cried. "Yes... Yes... Yes!"

They both screamed out as their bodies tensed and their orgasms washed over them, making them shiver and shake.

With a roar, he spurted a juicy rope of cum into her slick pussy, filling the cat girl up with his seed. She purred with delight, pressing him deeper into her with her heels, urging him to give her every drop from his balls. He complied happily, spurting two more loads of jizz into her, before his strength waned with a dizzying suddenness.

"Fuck," he groaned, and collapsed on top of her, breathing hard.

"Oh my.... That was amazing," she purred.

"I'll say," he panted. "I've never felt better."

"Me neither," she grinned, kissing him on the cheek.

They lay there, panting.

Sara's tail was flicking back and forth on the bed. After a moment, James rolled off her, and she immediately snuggled up against him, her cat ears upright as she purred happily in his embrace.

Then she suddenly looked up at him with feline curiosity. "I have another question," she whispered.

"Oh?"

She turned to look at him. "How long are you staying?"

"I haven't decided yet," he answered. "But I... I want to know more of this High Magic... And of you. I think I'll stay at the cabin for a while."

She nodded with a broad grin that bared her pointy canines. "That's good. I like it here, and I like you, James. I'm happy you made me your familiar."

He blushed. "Well... thank you, Sara. And I like you, too."

She giggled, reaching out to stroke his face. "It's nothing. I'm glad to have you around. I've been lonely."

"How... how long have you been here?" he asked.

Her expression turned a little sad before she gave him another of her feline grins and snuggled up against him.

"Let's talk about that some other time," she purred, her left ear trembling for a second. "For now, let's just relax."

Chapter 11

James woke up with a sudden jerk, sitting upright in the small bedroom in his cabin.

Sara was gone.

What the hell, he thought. *Was it just a dream?*

But he saw his clothes discarded by the bedside, and he felt the soreness from fucking her. Her dress still lay there as well.

So, definitely not a dream.

With a grunt, he hopped out of bed, grabbed his jeans, and pulled out his cellphone.

It was already seven in the morning. He had promised to be at Lucy's store in an hour.

He dressed himself quickly, splashing some water on his face from a small bowl that someone — Sara, maybe? — had left on the nightstand.

Where was she? he wondered.

He saw no sign of Sara as he made his way to the living area with its small kitchen. He realized he hadn't had a chance to even buy something to eat or drink.

He sighed and reached into his pocket for his keys. As he ignored his rumbling stomach and walked to his busted-up sedan, his mind wandered to Sara.

He'd spent the night with her. It had been the most amazing sex he'd ever experienced, and she had been a fantastic lover. She was an exquisitely beautiful woman. He was a lucky man to have met her.

But now, she had vanished.

He was a little concerned, but he tried to put his thoughts on hold. He didn't want to worry too much. And besides, she might just be out doing... whatever it was she did.

James drove down to the Tour General Store on Main

Street, enjoying the way the early sunlight broke through the canopy of the forest. It wasn't a long drive, and he saw no sign of Corinne at the barn.

As such, he arrived a little early, so he strolled around town a little, watching the locals opening their shops or hopping into their cars. A few of them left Tour, driving back in the direction James had initially come from.

Back to civilization.

After a few minutes, the sign hanging behind the window of the general store was turned around, changing from 'closed' to 'open'.

As James opened the door, a bell tinkled overhead.

Lucy stood behind the counter. She wore a tight plaid skirt with a white blouse that made her seem like a naughty Catholic schoolgirl, and James's need rose at the sight of the perky blonde MILF.

"Morning, James!" she hummed, flinging her high ponytail back as she sent him a wave.

"Morning, Lucy," James replied with a nod. "How are you?"

"Good," she said. "Did you spend the night at the cabin?"

"I... I did," he said.

She laughed. "Sorry," she said. "I shouldn't be so

nosy. But Corinne told me you were still on the fence about moving in." She gave him a warm smile. "So, are you? Moving in, I mean?"

James smiled back. "Yeah," he said. "I think so. At least for now."

Lucy clapped her hands. "Great! I was hoping you would. The town could use a fresh face! Plus, it will be great having a strong man around. We don't get many of those around here."

"That so?" he asked. Come to think of it, he hadn't seen a single male in Tour yet... only women.

"Yup! I bet you'll fit right in, though!"

"I hope so. After all, I need a place to live. I'm not sure what the future holds, but I intend to make the most of it."

Lucy gave him another smile. "Well, you can't do that without food, and I'd like to help you with that."

She bustled around the shop, grabbing two bags and handing them to James.

"Here you go," she said. "Lunch for today. And as I promised, I'll cook you dinner tonight."

"You don't have to do that," James protested.

"Oh, I insist," Lucy purred. "I enjoy cooking and I'd love to treat you. I'll come pick you up at Rovary's at around five, okay?"

"Okay," he nodded, accepting the bags.

She bit her lip and gave him another generous smile. "Have a good day!"

"You too," he smiled.

He watched her turn to walk over to the storeroom, then carried the bags outside to his car. He placed them on the passenger seat, then got in, started the car, and drove to Rovary's old lot.

Chapter 12

The rest of the day was filled with work. James was on his own for the day, and that suited him fine.

After parking his old sedan at Rovary's, he headed into the toolshed to retrieve the hatchet and get to work chopping down the trees.

The sun stood higher in the sky by the time he finished the first short trees, and he was already sweating. His muscles ached from the hard work, and he felt like he needed a nap, but he was happy to just spend some time working with his hands.

As a side benefit, it also gave him plenty of time to consider the unreal things that had happened last night.

He had had sex with Sara. *Crazy, wild sex.* And even though she wasn't in his bed this morning, he was sure it hadn't been a dream.

And then there was the stuff about High Magic.

He had cast his first spell.

Wild...

A smile surfaced on his lips as he went to work on the third tree, having cut the second while just thinking over last night's events.

He felt satisfaction as the axe bit into the slender trunk, then continued. Chopping down trees was harder than it seemed, even if they were just short ones. Applying the blade of the axe required concentration and a solid aim. After a few swings, the axe became heavier and heavier with each time he wielded it. But his thoughts could still roam free.

He knew that he had a lot to learn about High Magic, but he didn't want to let that bother him. He would find out more when he spoke with Sara.

In fact, he was going to find her as soon as he could.

He set to work, cutting down another tree. He was exhausted, but he kept going. He wanted to finish a few more before he took a break.

Then he heard a voice.

"James?"

He turned around to see Corinne approaching. She wore cowboy boots and a skin-tight pair of jeans that showed off her wide hips and her round ass, enough to make James blink and do a double take.

She wore a plaid blouse over her jeans, tied at the bottom to reveal her alabaster and narrow midriff. The scuffed cowboy hat and the messy mop of long ginger hair under it finished the job; she looked every bit the hot farmer's daughter.

She seemed surprised to see him here. "What are you doing here?" she asked.

He shrugged with a grin. "Chopping down some trees. What does it look like?"

She raised an eyebrow, then laughed. "Oh, that's right. Lucy gave ya the job! You're a lumberjack now."

He chuckled along. "I guess so."

She laughed and studied him for a moment with her big green eyes, shielding them from the sun with one hand.

He had taken off his shirt in the late morning heat,

and Corinne took a moment to appreciate his physique, glistening with sweat.

"It suits ya," she finally said.

"Thanks. I think," he said.

She smiled. "So, made up your mind yet? Are ya staying here for a while, or are you only passing through?"

"I'm staying," he said. "I have some business with Lucy, and I just moved into the cabin. It's... really nice."

Corinne nodded. "Yeah? I've come across it a couple times and it sure looks nice and cozy. I'm glad ya found a home, James."

He smiled at her. "Thanks, Corinne. People around here are nice. Lucy, you..."

He wanted to mention Sara but realized that Corinne probably wouldn't know her.

After all, Sara was a magical creature, and James doubted she revealed herself to the other inhabitants of Tour.

"Just Lucy and me, huh?" Corinne said and laughed. "Well, there ain't too many people in Tour."

"Yeah," he said. "I noticed. Is that normal?"

"It's not that unusual," she said. "Lotsa towns 'round here are small. And Tour is one of the smallest. But we're all friendly folks. It's real nice-like."

"It is," he agreed. "I'll be glad to be living here."

Corinne gave him a warm smile. "I hope you'll be here for a long time, then. It's always good to have a strong man in a small town."

James smiled back, and she gave him another appreciative look. A few moments passed in silence before she bit her plump lip. "Well, I'd best be on my way," she said.

"Hold up," James said. "One more thing."

"Yes?"

"If you ever need any help, like at the farm or something, let me know?"

"Oh, for sure," she said, and something slightly sad seemed to pass over her face. "I'll let ya know when I need some help, all right?"

James wiped his forehead clear of sweat, then studied her as he leaned on his felling axe, wondering where her sadness came from.

But he figured it wouldn't be polite to ask her directly. Instead, he changed the subject.

"Say... what are you doing here at Rovary's, anyway?"

"There's some waste I came to pick up," she said, jerking a thumb in the direction behind her. "Good for making fertilizer."

James laughed. "You mean, like, shit?"

She grinned. "No, silly! Plant waste has its uses too."

"Oh," he said. "That's right. That's a great idea, actually."

"Thanks. I thought so," she said, beaming at him. "I bet you'll learn a lot of things here, James. And I'll be around to teach ya if you wanna know more 'bout the farming business." She winked.

"I can't wait," he said, giving her a nod.

"Me neither." She walked away from him with a little wave. "Catch ya around, stranger!"

"See you, Corinne," he said with a smile.

The lunch Lucy had packed for James was great. It consisted of a large sandwich with cold meat and cheese, along with hard-boiled eggs and crackers. There was also an apple and a bottle of clear water.

It was all delicious.

He sat by himself in the shade under one of the trees in front of the toolshed eating his lunch while staring at the blue sky, thinking over the day's events and looking forward to dinner at Lucy's.

As he finished eating his meal, he felt a gentle breeze coming from nowhere, cooling the sweat on his chest and face.

He looked up to see Sara standing beside him.

She wore another flimsy dress, white and lacy, that covered her curvy body. It was sheer, offering a view of her enticing skin, and it even had a hole for her tail.

Her raven hair was down, swaying gently in the wind. In fact, everything about her seemed soft and gentle: her clothes, her movements, even her voice.

She was almost like a waking dream. She had appeared out of nothing.

"Hi, sweetie," she said, smiling.

He stood up; his eyes locked with hers. "Sara," he whispered. "Now where did you come from?"

"Hello, sweetie," she said, walking closer. "Are you having fun chopping down those trees?"

His mouth opened, but nothing came out as he stared at her in disbelief. This couldn't be real... She just appeared out of nothing.

She came to stand next to him and gave him a hug. Then she pushed herself back so that they could look at each other eye to eye.

His hands instinctively reached around to embrace her slim waist and press her against his chest. He ran his fingers over the curves that he had been dreaming of since this morning.

She laughed, biting her lip, and purred her pleasure. "I came to see how you were doing."

"But how did you get here so fast? And without me seeing you?"

"Cats are quick," she purred. "And we move unnoticed." Her ears twitched. "Who was that pretty redhead?"

James swallowed hard before saying, "That was Corinne... She, uh, she runs the farm, I guess."

"Ah!" Sara said with a nod. "A friendly girl. She seems nice enough."

He nodded. "She's good people."

"I'm sure," Sara said, and grinned slyly. "Is she flirting with you?"

He looked down shyly at her. "Uh, yeah. I think maybe a little? But we're friends."

"Then why haven't you kissed her yet? A handsome man like you should have lots of girls swooning over him."

"You think so?" he asked, looking into those eyes again. "I mean, wouldn't you mind? If I had more... you know?"

"If you took more women besides me? No, I wouldn't

mind at all. I'm yours, my sweet, and I could never want another man." She raised a finger. "But I am no jealous lover, and I understand the appetites of a male High Mage. There is no limit to how many lovers you can take."

His jaw worked as he processed this. It sounded like a dream come true.

She giggled softly as if guessing his thoughts and slid closer to him, pressing her body against his and kissing his cheek.

With a mischievous grin, she slipped her hand down to the front of his jeans and wrapped her fingers around his rock-hard erection, stroking it gently as they stared at each other for long moments.

He gulped hard but managed not to speak as she continued.

Suddenly, a guilty expression came over her, and she looked over her shoulder. "We shouldn't do this here..."

"Why?" James grunted, his mind swimming in lust.

"I shouldn't be seen in this form outside... People are superstitious."

"What people?" he breathed. "Don't tell me you care what people say about you?"

"Of course I don't. But... we should do this later. In some other place."

Her hand slipped out, deft and quick, leaving his rod throbbing. She gave a guilty smile.

"Sorry... It's hard to control myself. With you like this..." She bit her lip as she studied his bare chest for a moment. "Will I see you tonight? At the cabin?"

"Sure," he said and grinned. "I'll be home after supper."

She smiled back, then turned away from him before saying, "I will be waiting. And remember, make sure you tell nobody about me."

With those words, she stepped back. Then, in an instant, a wisp of shadows suffused her, robbed her wholly from sight. And when it disappeared, as if swept away on the wind, the place where she had just stood was empty.

Among the trees, James saw a tiny black shape hop away.

He shook his head; he would have never believed it if he hadn't seen it with his own eyes.

James felled log after log, although Sara's teasing left his mind swimming in dirty thoughts.

After working for hours under the sun without taking a break, James paused for a bit and rested against one of the large oak trunks while eating what remained of the lunch and drank some water.

His mind drifted to the stone circle nearby, and he decided to go look for it once he ate the last bits of food.

But it was nowhere to be found. The grassy field looked exactly the same as it always did, but he could find no trace of the old stones among them.

He felt disappointment but shrugged it off.

There had been something magical about them. Perhaps he would ask Sara when he saw her again after dinner tonight.

He returned to work, once again gripping his axe with two hands before bringing it down onto a stubborn piece of wood. Chips of wood flew around his arms as the axe struck true and bit into the trunk with a loud crack.

He pulled back and began hacking at it as hard as he could. Again and again, he struck the wood with his axe, sweat pouring down his face as he panted with exertion.

Finally, he was able to bring the tree down and drag it on top of his growing pile.

He kept at it, feeling the burn of his exertion until the

sun was already halfway down again. Just as he realized the day was drawing to an end, and he'd need to contact Lucy soon, he heard footsteps behind him.

"Hey!" a familiar voice called out. "James! Over here!"

He looked up and saw Lucy walking toward him from behind the pile of timber he was currently working on.

She walked gracefully over to him and gave him a generous smile.

"My, my!" she said, shooting him a wink. "Some prime wood over here!"

He laughed and shook his head as he watched her walk over.

In her tight plaid skirt and loose white blouse, she looked like a naughty schoolgirl cosplayer lost in the woods, and the sight sent a jolt of need down to his dick, all the more thirsty after Sara kind of blue-balled him. Lucy's teasing would do little to remedy that...

He wiped his forehead clean of sweat and leaned on the handle of the axe. "Evening already?" he said, smiling at Lucy. "How was your day?"

"It was good! I did all sorts of things," she said and gave him a grin. "And you?" she asked with a coy smile. "Did you have fun chopping down all those trees?"

"It's hard work," he replied with a shrug and a grin.

He didn't really mind the work itself; it was all about the end result and not so much about how it got there. He liked doing it well, though, and he was proud of himself for the progress he had made today.

She cocked her head and smiled knowingly at him. "I see you're getting better with your axe. How many more trees do you think you could chop down before dinner?"

"I'm not sure..." he admitted and grinned.

"How about none?" she said, poking him in his ribs.

He wasn't wearing a shirt, and her touch tickled.

But it also awakened something; as if the barrier between two people who only just met began to break down.

"We'll load up my truck and you can follow me to my house," she said. "I live right above the general store. I'll make you dinner like I promised. And then... we can maybe get to know each other a little better."

He glanced down at her breasts straining against her shirt as she spoke to him, and there was a stirring in his pants as her eyes gazed up at him with that knowing look that she had given him before.

The thought of being with another woman — besides

Sara — made him feel uncomfortable at first; but with Lucy's teasing, he sensed himself slipping away. He was keen to explore that delicious MILF body, but also to know a bit more about her. She was pleasant to be around, sweet and considerate.

And he was pretty sure Sara didn't mind...

"All right," James said, shouldering the axe. "Let's load up and go!"

Chapter 13

Once the trees were loaded onto the flatbed of Lucy's truck, James followed her taillights into Tour. By then, darkness had fallen.

As they drove down Main Street, they passed by a few people heading to their homes for the evening. It was a very small town, and most people knew everyone else well enough to recognize their faces and even know what they were up to. And so they nodded in greeting or waved from their houses. Lucy waved back at them with a smile as they drove by.

James smiled to himself, thinking that some townspeople were probably none too pleased that their cute MILF shopkeeper had a dinner guest.

Then again, he hadn't seen any men in town yet.

He pulled up beside Lucy in the general store's lot. Once again, his cock poked his jeans as he saw the voluptuous MILF step out of the car. It had been a long day; his shoulders and back ached from all the work he had done and all the physical effort. But he still felt like bending Lucy over and filling her up.

And by her flirting, that might be just what the sultry blonde MILF was looking for tonight.

James opened the creaky door of his sedan and stepped out into the cooling night air. "Want me to unload those logs?" he asked.

Lucy placed one hand on a hip and smiled at him. "No, that's fine! I have a customer who'll pick them up tomorrow. They'll load it themselves." She then turned, showing him once again that way-too-hot plaid skirt. "Come on!" she said. "I'll show you my place. We can talk while I cook."

"Sounds good!" James said with a grin as he followed

her back to her house.

He had seen the general store before, of course, and it was a duplex. The top floor was where Lucy lived, and a metal stairway on the outside of the building led up to it.

Walking up that stairway gave James an upskirt glance at Lucy's tight ass, those plump butt cheeks parted by a slutty little pink thong. He got the urge to rip those off her body so he could see that luscious ass of hers better; he wondered how she would like it if he slipped a hand up now, fingers prodding her delicious ass...

He shook his head to clear his mind; the night was young. And there would be plenty of time for dirty thoughts later.

Lucy's place was cozy and tastefully decorated with many knick-knacks. It looked like she lived there alone, since there were no signs of another presence anywhere in the house.

"Wow," James said as he stepped inside, admiring the place.

The living room was full of bookshelves filled with books; but everything was neatly organized and arranged. On a wooden table in front of the couch was a little glass lamp, which gave off a warm orange light. It illuminated the room with more atmosphere than any electric bulb would have done. A worn skin rug covered most of the floor, giving the room a homely feel; there was also a glass table between two sofas with a bottle of wine and several glasses on the surface.

Lucy grinned, grabbed a remote control from a shelf in the living room, and pushed a button. The soft sounds of jazz music could be heard from a speaker near the window, which overlooked Main Street below.

"It's not much, I know," Lucy said. "But it's my place and I like it that way. Kitchen's this way!"

Lucy beckoned him to follow her past a narrow hallway leading into the rest of the house. She led him to the kitchen, where the aroma of fresh coffee already drifted to meet him.

James glanced down the hallway before following Lucy into the kitchen.

She stood before him now, holding two steaming mugs of hot coffee and handed one to him. He took it gratefully and sipped at it before asking, "Nice place. Where did you live before?"

"I moved here a year ago," she replied. "It was Rovary's old place. I inherited it when he died. He was my uncle, but since my parents died when I was young, he took care of me."

James looked at her in shock and said, "I'm sorry! That must have been really hard for you."

She smiled and said, "I won't lie; it was. But he was a good man." She then took a sip of coffee and added, "Besides, he left me something nice." She pointed up at her house as she said it.

"You're lucky to have had someone who cared about you," James said softly as he stared into her eyes.

"I guess I am," she said with a smile and reached out her hand to touch his arm gently. "What about your parents?"

"My mother died a few years ago," he replied. "And my father a few weeks ago. That's why I'm in Tour, you see. He owned a cabin here and... well, that's what I inherited."

"I see," Lucy said softly before taking another sip of coffee and setting down the mug on the countertop next to her. "What did he die from?"

"A heart attack," James replied. "He worked too hard."

James thought back on his father's death and how

hard he had worked for the last few years before he died.

"My dad ran his own company for many years," James continued. "And he was doing very well. But I guess it was too much for one man to do on his own all alone. He was always working; he never had time for his family or himself."

"I'm so sorry to hear that," Lucy said.

James gave a little smile. "My brother took over the company. No doubt, he is headed in the same direction as dad. I hope he'll come around and understand that family is more important before it's too late."

Lucy nodded. She seemed a little sad for a moment, but then she perked up and gestured at the kitchen behind her. It adjoined the living room, separated from it by a bar with three stools. "So, what do you say I start cooking and you start relaxing?"

"Uh, can I... shower first... Kind of a weird question, but I'm a bit smelly." James gestured down at his sweat-stained clothes.

"Oh, you can shower after dinner!" she said, a mischievous light twinkling in her blue eyes. Her smile brought out the sexy little crow's feet that only made her more of a MILF delight. "I don't mind a little sweat."

James laughed. "Fine," he said. "I'll shower after dinner."

She winked at him. "Now, come sit. You've worked hard! You earned some rest!"

Chapter 14

James sat down at the bar while Lucy poured him a glass of red wine.

It was a fruity bouquet, and it went down well after a hard day's work. He would've thought a beer would suit him better, but he was satisfied with the offering.

As he savored the taste, Lucy went to work.

"I'm making risotto," she said, throwing him a glance

over her shoulder. "I hope you like Italian?"

"Love it," James said, studying the way her toned back tapered down to her wide hips and thick thighs.

The ivory skin she teased him with was a delight, and whenever James let his mind roam, it was at once flooded with the dirtiest fantasies.

"That's good," she replied with a smile as she placed a pan with water on top of a stove to boil.

She leaned back against the bar and crossed her arms in front of her chest again. "So... where do we go from here?" she asked with a coy smile.

James laughed and shrugged before replying, "I don't know... I haven't thought about it." He stretched his legs out in front of him, crossing his ankles, as he grinned at her.

"How about you tell me a little something about you?" Lucy asked with a grin. "And I'll tell you a little something about me?"

"You mean like reveal all our dirty secrets?" James asked with a smile as he eyed her.

Lucy laughed and replied, "Yeah! I have some! But it's a little early for those. Tell me about you. What do you hope for in life?"

James shrugged and smiled. "Well, I care little for wealth or fame. I just want to be happy," James said with a grin before taking a sip of wine. "Not sure how to get there yet... but I will."

"Well, it's nice to find someone who doesn't have dollar signs in their eyes!" Lucy replied. She straightened and faced him. "So, tell me: what does happiness mean to you?"

"Well... You know... I'd like to fall in love and have someone love me back. Then share a life together and enjoy each other. Simple." James grinned at her with a look of innocence and sincerity.

"Sounds like you already have the beginnings." Lucy leaned forward and stared at him with her piercing blue eyes.

"How do you mean?"

"A nice cabin in Tour." She shot him a wink. "Now all you need is a woman to move in with you."

He laughed. "The cabin is very small!"

She picked up a spatula and casually weighed it. "Does it need to be big? Were you planning on getting a big family?" The look she followed up with was one of sincere curiosity... and more than a little naughty interest. "Or more than one woman?"

He laughed along with her. "Maybe..."

He stared down at his wineglass as his thoughts wandered into forbidden territory. He could see Lucy in his mind; her beautiful face looking at him with those soft blue eyes; her pouting lips that begged him to kiss them; her full breasts begging to be sucked on...

"Hey!" Lucy called out, waving the spatula at him. Her voice broke through James' fantasy like an alarm clock. "Are you listening?"

James shook himself back to reality and downed the rest of the wine. "Yes," he said, wiping a hand across his mouth. "I'm sorry." He set down the empty glass. "I was just thinking about something."

Lucy grinned and then waggled the spatula again. She laughed a bit and said, "So, what were you thinking about? I'm intrigued." She leaned over.

James swallowed and gave her a broad smile. For a moment, he considered a bullshit story.

But why not tell her how he felt?

Why not tell her that he liked her?

How much time were they going to waste with games? He liked her, and he believed she liked him, too.

Why not talk about it?

Filled with resolve, James sat up straight.

Lucy's eyes glinted with mischief.

His pulse raced faster and harder than ever before when he gazed into her eyes. It felt so right to be here with her now. Like this.

"Well?" she asked, smiling seductively at him.

"I think you're very beautiful," he said, keeping her gaze captured with his for a moment before giving her another appreciating look. He couldn't help but stare at the way her thick thighs stretched tight against her short skirt.

"Oh my gosh," she purred. "Thank you!" Her cheeks reddened a little.

Then she turned to pick up the spatula again — it seemed more like a slightly nervous fidget this time. But still, she was intrigued. In a softer voice, she asked, "So? What else did you think of me?"

James laughed softly. This was going well. He wasn't sure if Lucy had intended for him to spill his guts to her or not, but he didn't want it any other way now.

"You're nice and sweet," he said. "And you have this liveliness about you — an energy that I admire. I think I could spend a lot of time with you."

She offered a soft smile, her cheeks crimson. But a naughty light simmered in her blue eyes as she looked at him over her shoulder. "That's so sweet! I don't think anyone has ever said anything so sweet to me."

He swallowed. "Yeah... Well, there's more I might say. But some stuff should probably stay in my mind!" he said with a laugh as he finished his drink.

She laughed along, but her naughty gaze promised more than a little curiosity before she turned back to her pan.

"Good!" she called out, still stirring her pot of risotto. "Keep some secrets, mister. But tell me: that cabin, it's close to Corinne's farm, right? I think I saw it once. Isn't it little more than just a stack of logs with a hearth and bed?"

James laughed. "Basically, yeah."

"So, are you going to fix it up?" she asked. "If you get married and start a family with one — or more — women, you'll need space for everyone."

"I guess so." He shrugged, staring at her backside as it slightly jiggled while she stirred the rice. "I don't even know if I'm ready for marriage yet... And I never even considered children!"

She turned toward him again as his mind wandered into new territory once more. Her smile lit the room like the sun; it seemed brighter now than before he'd stared into her eyes.

Children... With the right woman.

"Anyway," he continued. "I'm not much of a DIYer. I always hired contractors to do work on my old place. Or... well... *the landlord* hired contractors."

Lucy shook her head and continued to stir her pot of risotto. "Not many of those around here. In fact, we're pretty short on handymen." She laughed and looked at him. "We need some good ones in Tour!" She poured another glass of wine.

"Let me know when you find one," he joked.

She fluttered her lips and waved the spatula at him. "You're terrible!" she said and laughed. "I'm sure you're a handy guy!"

"What about you?" he asked. "Are you happy with this place and your store?"

She nodded. "I love living here!" she replied. "This is a beautiful town with lots of great people! But I want to grow my business! I've got a lot of ideas but haven't had time to execute them yet." Lucy frowned. "I guess that's why I'm so stressed out all the time."

James raised an eyebrow. "Stressed out? You don't strike me as stressed out?"

"Well, there's more beneath the surface," she said, throwing him a glance over her shoulder. "We're only just getting to know each other."

He chuckled softly. That was true, though they were already friends in James's mind. Maybe more than friends. "So what do you have planned for dessert tonight?" he asked. "Is it going to be a surprise?"

She shot him a wink and leaned against the counter behind her.

Then she twirled the spatula around and studied it like it might hold some kind of secret. She licked her lips and then pursed them before saying, "It sure will be..."

Chapter 15

Lucy's risotto was perfect — savory, creamy, and delicious.

She sat across from him with an expression of delight on her face, while James dug into his food with gusto. He wanted seconds... And thirds. He'd been hungry all day.

They talked while they ate; even made plans to get

together again soon. But James could not stop thinking about one thing. Ultimately, he had to ask her.

"So... is there a man in your life?"

She grinned and shook her head, throwing him a seductive look from under long lashes as she leaned on the table, pushing her magnificent tits together with her toned arms.

The button-down shirt with the top buttons undone offered quite the sight.

"The position is open," she purred, but she couldn't contain herself and laughed at her own silliness.

James laughed along. "I'm teasing!" He laughed harder when Lucy frowned at him. "I just mean that I'm curious how you can still be single. You're a great woman."

Lucy licked her lips and continued to lean on the table, showing him those big melons that made it hard to focus. "Well... There aren't any men in Tour."

"None?"

"*None.*"

"But even if there were..." She shrugged, making her breasts bounce. "I'm picky. I have specific tastes... and preferences. I just never feel free to open up. Most people give me the idea they'll judge me."

"Really?" James asked with a raised eyebrow. "I

would've expected the opposite was true. That people are more likely to be attracted to a confident person who knows what they want."

"Not in my experience," she said.

He leaned back in his chair. "What makes it different now? Why are you opening up to me?"

Lucy sat upright and studied him. Her eyes narrowed, and she asked, "Why do you think?"

James smiled softly but said nothing, leaving the ball in her court.

He'd hit a nerve. He'd opened a door, and now it was up to Lucy to decide what she wanted to do with it.

Lucy shifted her weight uncomfortably as she looked at the ceiling before finally looking him in the eye again.

"I don't know," she said, with a bit of frustration in her voice. "I guess... It's just been such an emotional week. I have had little time to think things through."

"That sounds tough." James stared into her beautiful blue eyes.

This MILF beauty made him feel alive and energized. She lit something inside him that no other woman ever had — barring Sara. Something good and pure and powerful and all-encompassing; like a pure fire from within his soul.

"I think it's because you... you're different from the

men I've met," she said. "You're kind of intense, hm? You're a little mysterious, too. You came out of nothing with your handsome dark hair. Like a dark stranger out of some kind of romance novel. And you're not such a hick as most men I've met. You're sophisticated, patient, kind... and yet..."

She licked her lips and considered her next words for a moment. "I bet you have a rough edge, too. But it just feels like you're trustworthy. Everyone else seems so gabby, so small-minded, so petty. But not you. You're like a knight out of a story... or maybe the handsome outlaw who came riding into town at sunset." She shifted her weight and studied him more intensely now.

James smiled at that and replied, "Maybe..." Then he added playfully, "But what does that say about me?"

"That says there's more to you than what meets the eye!" Lucy laughed and held out her glass toward him. "More wine? I could use another glass!"

He laughed and nodded, pushing his glass forward. "Please!"

As Lucy poured James another drink, he lost himself for

a moment in her beautiful blue eyes, fully focused on the job.

When she was done, James took another drink before asking, "Do you believe in fate?"

She furrowed her brow in thought for a moment and shrugged with a grin. "I'm a believer in love. If that makes sense."

She tilted her head in contemplation for a moment longer. "So I guess that could include fate. Lovers can be fated." She leaned back in her chair and sipped her wine while she watched James. "Why do you ask?"

"I don't know," he said. "There's something about this place — about Tour — but I'm not sure if it's all our own doing. It feels as if there is a touch of destiny to it — like I was meant to come here."

He looked around the room with an expression of awe on his face. He didn't notice how his words affected Lucy as he continued, "It just doesn't seem like any ordinary town."

Lucy smiled gently and nodded. "Well... That makes sense, too. I would've left Tour a long time ago if I didn't feel so... bound to it. Like something needed to happen here. All my life, I felt like I've been waiting for something... or someone..."

Her eyes dropped to her lap where they lingered

before finally rising to meet his once more. "And I'm not the only one... Ask the others in Tour — well, the ones that say more than one or two sentences — and they'll agree. Something just... hangs over this place. People either leave right away or stay all their lives."

She chuckled and shook her head. "Weird, huh?"

James nodded and sat silently for a few seconds while he considered everything she'd said. His heart fluttered in his chest. She had given him a glimpse into her soul, and it made him want to keep coming back for more.

He reached out with a finger and traced a path across the smooth skin of her forearm. She shivered under his touch, which brought another smile to her lips.

"I think that sounds lovely," he said. "Not weird at all."

They sat like that for a while, silent, each cherishing the moment.

What Lucy had said resonated with James's feelings. And the discovery of magic in the cabin fitted perfectly into all of this.

There was something mystical about Tour County, and James was intrigued. He was drawn to it in ways he couldn't explain. He had sensed the same thing on the hunting trip with his father so many years ago.

Perhaps his father had sensed it too?

Maybe that was why he had purchased the cabin. Even though life caught up to him and he ended up never coming here.

And it might well be the reason he left the cabin to James. Perhaps it wasn't meant as a consolation prize for the son who didn't become a successful businessman, but as a celebration of the connection they had experienced here — to each other and to the area. It had been brief, but James had been truly happy on that trip. Maybe his dad had been truly happy, too.

And with that, James resolved to stay here. At least for now.

Something clattered on the floor, and James perked up.

"Oops," Lucy chirped.

Then, to James's utter surprise and arousal, she hopped down from her chair and got down on all fours to pick up the fork she had accidentally knocked from the table.

Her skirt hitched up, and James had a moment to appreciate that perfect ass in its skimpy little thong.

The strap was so narrow he saw part of her little rose, and the way the front of that skimpy underwear hugged her pussy lips into a tight camel toe made his cock buck in his pants.

Son of a...

Did she do it on purpose? Was it really an accident?

"Got it!" she called out triumphantly, holding up the fork. She then rose, straightened her skirt, and looked at him, blushing. "So, dessert!"

He swallowed and nodded.

"Here's the surprise!" She jerked a thumb in the direction of the hallway that opened into the living room — James guessed it led to the sleeping room and bathroom.

"I actually have a Jacuzzi. I'm something of a..." She touched her lip with her forefinger as she looked for the right word. "Bath aficionada. So... in addition to the four hundred dollars I owe you for the two days of work you did, I'll also let you use my Jacuzzi! And what's better, I'll serve you some strawberries with whipped cream."

James blinked. "Are... you... Are you serious?"

"Yes!" Lucy grinned as she leaned forward, resting her hands on his shoulders. "I'm very serious. You're new in town, and I like you, so I wanted to do something nice for you."

"That sounds amazing..." he said.

She laughed. "Well, go on! It's through that door,

then the first on the left. The bath is ready."

He chuckled and shook his head. "You prepared it for me? That's amazing!"

"You bet. Go hop in, and I'll bring you your strawberries in five minutes. Don't let me see anything!" she added with a wink.

James laughed and rose. His muscles ached after sitting down for so long, and a hot tub might just be the thing to help loosen them up. He rolled his shoulders and headed toward the bathroom.

He was looking forward to this.

Chapter 16

Lucy's bathroom confirmed what she had told him: she was a bath aficionada.

It was large, meticulously clean, and tastefully decorated. But the centerpiece had to be the Jacuzzi that sat under an archway in one corner of the room, surrounded by candles.

Lilac-scented steam rose from its bubbly surface,

suffusing the room with a calming aroma.

A couple of towels were stacked neatly on the edge of the pool, waiting for him. The light in the bathroom was soft — the glow of candles — and James felt at ease almost instantly.

He shut the door behind him and began undressing, leaving his clothes — dirty from a long day of working — in a neat pile in the corner.

The moment he stepped into the water, he sighed. It was warm, almost hot. He slid down into the soapy water and exhaled in contentment.

He leaned back against the tiled wall, letting himself relax as he looked around.

Lucy's home wasn't nearly as rustic as the cabin but there were still touches of nature everywhere he looked: dried herbs lay in baskets and jars along one side of the room, spreading a delicious wild aroma; bunches of wildflowers filled vases here and there; even Lucy's perfume had smelled sweetly floral, with a hint of lavender.

His mind wandered while he soaked in the hot water... wondering if he could convince Lucy to take him to bed tonight instead of just serving him strawberries and whipped cream in her hot tub.

He only recently met her, but she left him feeling like

that was certainly an option. Not to mention that she was gorgeous, funny, intelligent, and sexy, and she knew how to get him worked up.

"Comfy?" she called out from the kitchen.

"Very!" he said. "This is perfect!"

"Good! I'll be there in a minute." Her voice echoed from inside the house as James dunked his head underwater, then let the rest of his body slip beneath the surface before resurfacing again.

His muscles ached. It seemed so long since his last bath.

He closed his eyes, savoring the warm water, until he heard footsteps in the hallway.

Lucy came through the door with a platter laden with strawberries and a bowl filled with whipped cream. She placed it on a small table next to him, offering him another view of her delicious cleavage.

"Sorry for the wait," she chirped. Then she set down two glasses and poured them both a drink.

When he lifted his glass to toast with her, he caught a mischievous light in her eyes.

She sat down on the edge of the Jacuzzi, and the move hitched up her skirt to reveal the ample flesh of her thighs.

Smiling, she took a strawberry, dipped the bottom in

whipped cream, and held it up. "Open up," she purred.

He grinned and lay back in the tub, opening his mouth, and she first dabbed his lips with the sweet delicacy. He made to grab it with his mouth, but she pulled it back.

"Nuh-uh-uh," she muttered. "Savor the taste."

He laughed and leaned back again. "All right."

"Now close your eyes. Here it comes again."

He did as she asked. The scent of lavender made its way into his nostrils, and he felt her close in.

What touched his lips next was no strawberry.

It was Lucy's plump lips, sweet with the taste of whipped cream.

For a moment, the unexpected kiss took James aback.

But this was exactly what he had wanted.

James kissed her back, feeling his cock rise to firm attention in the tub. Lucy moaned softly against him and parted her lips to kiss his cheek.

Her tongue tickled his skin playfully while her hand brought the strawberry to his lips again. This time, she let him eat it as she leaned in to kiss his cheeks and nibble on his ears.

"Hmm," she purred in his ear. "You bring out the naughty girl in me." She chuckled, running her hand along his soapy chest.

She pulled away from his body reluctantly — not letting go of their embrace completely — and reached for another strawberry, dipped it in whipped cream, and put it between his lips before withdrawing from the bathwater once more.

She didn't say another word, but walked across the bathroom floor like a goddess, pausing at the door to give him a seductive smile before slipping out. "Be right back," she purred.

"You'd better be," he said, his voice heavy with need.

He sat up, reaching for his drink. It was cool, refreshing. He drank the whole thing, enjoying the smooth, sweet taste of the strawberry and the creamy sweetness that lingered in his throat.

Then he relaxed back in the tub again, only this time he kept his eyes open.

When Lucy returned, she had loosened her hair.

She looked at him seductively and smiled. "I should keep you here," she said. "You look like a Roman god in that bath."

He chuckled. "Well, there are ways to make me stay."

She giggled as she sat down on a stool placed against the wall. She lifted a leg, placing the ankle on her other knee, and began untying the straps of her high heels.

In doing so, she gave him a generous upskirt glance at the slutty underwear hugging her plump pussy lips.

"And what ways are those?" she purred.

James was speechless. All his dirty thoughts about having sex with her came rushing back with renewed vigor.

But instead of taking control and kissing her, all James could do was sit in the tub and watch in awe as her beautiful legs opened wide before his eyes. He liked her teasing; he liked that she postponed the moment so they could savor it more.

His cock swelled in the hot water, rising hard.

He cleared his throat and regained some of his composure. "Well, you can start by telling me those specific tastes and preferences. I still wonder why you'd be afraid that anyone would judge a woman like you."

"Ooh!" Lucy exclaimed. She removed one foot from the shoe, then switched legs as she unclasped the other one. "That's a good question."

She tossed both shoes aside, then rested her feet on the floor. Her fingers brushed through her hair to fluff it, making sure it was in place.

"I suppose the best way to describe it is that people think..." She sighed. "Well, they'd think I'm a freak." She studied him with her big blue eyes, waiting for some kind of prompt.

"A deviant, huh?" James said. "Well, I don't see people that way. I find women who enjoy their bodies very attractive. And a woman who knows what she wants even more."

Lucy nodded and looked at her hands, running them over her forearms slowly, seductively. She then giggled. "It's a bit weird..."

He laughed and leaned back. "Tell me only if you want to."

She bit her lower lip and stared at him for a moment. "I have a fetish... well, let's say I like to feel... you know... *man stuff*? On my skin. I... think that's a nice feeling."

James had to restrain himself from shooting up.

"See," she muttered, her face turning crimson. "You think it's weird."

"Weird?" He chuckled. "No, Lucy. I think it's fucking hot."

He sat up slowly and gently, so as not to startle her.

She still sat on her stool, but her posture was a bit more demure — she had crossed her legs and arms.

Her chest was heaving slightly as well; it seemed that this confession was difficult for her to say.

"So... tell me what it means, this fetish."

She looked at him, very vulnerable now. "Are you serious?"

"Of course," he said, taking another strawberry and dipping it in the whipped cream. "I'm fascinated."

She laughed a little at seeing him grab a strawberry so casually. "Well," she began nervously. "Okay, I guess... Here goes..."

"I always fantasized about doing... dirty things with, well... cum. I mean... not like a *bukkake* or something like that — I wouldn't want to be anywhere near something like that. But the idea of having my lover shoot his load on my butt..." She bit her lip, uncrossed her legs and arms, and stirred on the stool. "Or on my tummy... Or on my face... Or to... you know, lick it from another woman... That idea excites me. Very much."

The tip of James's cock was out of the water now; he couldn't help it. What sane man could have kept a lid on it in these circumstances?

Listening to this sensual MILF confess her dirty fantasies turned him on immensely.

Her eyes shot down for a moment, and she licked her lips before her gaze flitted back up to his.

And even though relating the tale seemed to turn her on a little, there was still an edge of vulnerability to her voice.

James cleared his throat. "I don't think that's a strange fetish at all," he said. "In fact, I'm sure many people like that."

She looked up at him, her cheeks a delicious red, both hands resting on her thighs. He could see a strip of her slutty pink thong.

"You think so?"

"I, for one, love it," he said.

She gasped softly.

He chuckled. "What? You didn't expect me to?"

"I... I wasn't expecting anyone else to think this was hot," she admitted with a smile.

She stared down at herself again. Her chest was heaving in her shirt, buttons struggling with her ample bosom.

She was practically radiating heat; her eyes glistened as she watched him stare.

"It is kind of weird."

James shrugged. He popped another strawberry into his mouth. "I don't think so."

His gaze lowered slowly to the outline of her panties and the visible swell of flesh between them. "Maybe in a small town like Tour it can feel weird. But I assure you, there are plenty of people who get turned on by this kind of thing." He shrugged. "Just own it."

She laughed and rose from the stool. "You know what? You're right."

With that, she raised a hand to the straining buttons of her shirt and gave him a sultry, challenging look. "Wouldn't mind taking this off, either..."

The shirt's top buttons came undone, falling away, exposing a lacy bra covered in pearl-like decorations. Then she untucked her shirt completely and dropped it onto the floor, letting it pool at her feet.

He admired the view of her body underneath for a moment before her hands fell on her waist, cupping her breasts through her tight bra. She looked down at herself, as if appreciating her own body.

James felt his heart beat a little faster when he saw how much her hands seemed to enjoy themselves.

"So, you thinking of joining me?" he asked. "The bath is very nice."

Lucy smirked but said nothing.

She reached around to unclasp her bra, revealing two beautiful breasts topped with large pink areolas.

When she finished removing the top, she leaned back against the wall. Her arms crossed over her chest, pushing up her breasts; it made them appear even bigger.

"Hmm, yes," she purred. "If there's room?"

Chapter 17

With Lucy topless before James, ready to climb into the Jacuzzi with him, he couldn't help but grin broadly.

He slid to the side, watching her as she came to him. Her every step caused her wide hips to sway and gave her full chest a perky bounce. He was hypnotized, mesmerized, and as she came to a stop next to him, a grunt of delight escaped him.

She peered down into the bath, saw the tip of his cock break the surface, and giggled. "Oh my, he looks *very* enthusiastic."

"Well, you've been teasing him all night."

She hooked her thumbs behind her skirt, then let it slip to the floor. Her slutty little pink thong rode high on her hips, and the straps squeezed into her luscious flesh.

"Fuck," James muttered, his eyes on the MILF's delicious camel toe. "You are a delight."

She grinned, then placed one shapely foot into the tub with him. "One last dirty secret," she purred as he gazed up at her thick thighs. "I also like it when I get fucked with my panties on..."

James's heart pounded in his chest as Lucy slipped into the Jacuzzi. The slightly awkward step made her jiggle in a delicious way, and he loved that slutty little thong on her.

He couldn't believe it; another day, another beauty to bang...

Luckiest guy in the world, he thought.

Lucy bit her lip as she sat down beside him, on her knees so that her belly button was still above the surface of the water. She had such a curvy, sexy body, and she knew how to show it off. "You like what you see?" she asked.

"I love it," he replied.

She laughed, her eyes fixed on his cock. "Well, so do I. And I have plenty to work with."

He glanced down at himself. His cock was rock hard already, poking out of the bath with fiery need.

"Such a beautiful dick," she purred. She moved closer, her hand going to her knee and stroking up her thigh. She looked up at him, her eyes half-lidded, as if she was just taking in the sight. "I could look at it here all night." She licked her lips. "And I bet you wouldn't mind."

He chuckled. "I'd have you do more than look," he grunted, his voice hoarse with desire. "I'd have you take it in your mouth."

Her eyes widened. "Really?"

"Yeah," he said. "I'd have you suck it, Lucy. You like to play with cum? I'll give you plenty."

She blushed, her eyes drifting down to his cock, mouth slightly open.

"I'd like to see you with my cum on your face," he

said. "And on those big tits."

"You'd like to see that, huh?" she purred, her hand slipping into the water near his cock. Her touch on his thigh was velvety soft.

He nodded. "Show me."

Her throat moved as she swallowed. She took his cock in her hand, then wrapped her fingers around it, squeezing it gently. She drew her hand along the length of his shaft, her eyes glued to the head of his cock. "It's so big."

James sat back with a groan. "Take it in your mouth."

Lucy giggled and looked up at him before lowering her head to his lap. She opened her lips, and he groaned as she engulfed the head of his cock in her mouth. She closed her lips around him and sucked, her tongue swirling. James's cock jerked in her mouth as she moaned softly.

"That's it," he said. "Just like that. Suck it."

She moaned again and bobbed her head, sucking more of him in. Her hand stroked the inside of his thigh, occasionally playing with his full nut-sack, and images of him fucking her right here surfaced in James's mind. "Mmm, that's good," he grunted.

She kept sucking, her lips pressing around him, and her free hand kept working wonders on his swollen balls. His load was coming; he could feel it.

"Lucy," he said as she pulled his cock from her mouth and planted a kiss on the tip. "I'm about to cum."

She grinned and started stroking him again. "That's okay, baby. I want you to cum."

He groaned. "It's going to be a big fucking load!"

She giggled and bobbed her head, taking him back into her mouth before pulling him out. "Cum on my face, baby," she purred. "Make me your little cum-slut." As she spoke her slutty words, she kept tugging, and James's toes curled in the bath as he lay there, all warm and comfy, ready to cum all over this sultry MILF's pretty face.

His cock pulsed, and he cried out as a thick rope of cum spurted from the tip. She opened her lips and stuck out her tongue, letting the first spurt splatter messily onto her lips.

"Ugh," James groaned, and another spasm passed through him.

This time, a king-size load of sticky cum shot from his cock, and Lucy yelped as it coated her pretty face, across her nose and cheeks. A big gob dripped down to her big, jiggling tits.

"That's it," James groaned. "Take that fucking load."

Lucy took a deep breath and smiled. "Sooo hot… Cum on me, baby," she purred, and she kept milking him, milking him until the last drop of his cum was gone.

By then, James's warm cum covered her big breasts, thick strands of the stuff connecting those luscious melons. She wiped her lips with the back of her hand, looking up at him with her cum-glazed face. "Fuck... That is so hot."

James chuckled. "Damn… You're good at it, too."

"Why, thank you," she purred as she gave him a smoldering look. "So, Mr. Beckett? Are you enjoying your naughty new cumslut?"

He grinned. "I am. I can't wait to see what other dirty things you've got planned for us."

She giggled and ran her hands over her body, squirming with delight as she eyed James's powerful cock. "It's still up," she purred.

He had marveled at that himself the other night with Sara. He was young and good to go, but he managed to cum twice in rapid succession with the cat girl.

And it looked like he might be able to pull that again with Lucy.

Eyes blazing, his gaze fell on the sultry, cum-covered blonde MILF, eyeing his cock with a profound hunger.

She giggled and gave him a naughty glance. "Such vigor... Think you can go again?"

James smirked and rose to his knees.

He lifted Lucy's ass onto the edge of the tub with her back against the wall and let his eyes feast on that delicious camel toe.

Now that her skimpy thong was wet, he could see the cute mound of pubic hair above her plump pussy lips, and he couldn't wait to pillage her.

Her legs quivered, and she let out a little gasp of pleasure.

"I can go again," he said. "I promised you lots of cum, and that's what I'm delivering."

She grinned. "You are such a dirty boy."

He leaned forward and grabbed his cock with one hand. "Spread your legs," he commanded.

With a yelp of delight, she complied, her delicious thighs jiggling as she parted her long legs for him. She leaned back against the wall, her breasts pushing up, the nipples stiff with excitement.

He moved between her thighs and pressed the head

of his cock against her pussy, rubbing it through the fabric of her thong. "So soft," he murmured.

He reached down and pushed the thong to the side. He spread her even wider, winning a yelp from her, and the sight of her glistening pussy made his mouth water.

"Hmm, yes," Lucy said, her fingers curling in his mop of hair. "Fuck me good, baby."

He smiled and leaned in, kissing her knees as he looked up at her. "You like to talk dirty, don't you?" he whispered.

"I talk dirty, and I fuck dirty, baby," she purred. Her tongue darted out of her mouth as she licked her lips. "You can fuck me any way you want. I'm your little slut."

He leaned in, letting his tongue run along the inside of her thigh, up to her puffy labia.

She was sopping wet already, and her taste was sweet and creamy. He licked up her juices, and she let out a soft whimper, her fingers tightening in his hair.

"You're a dirty, dirty girl," he said. "You like it when I eat you out?"

She nodded, her eyes half-lidded and filled with lust. "Hmm..."

"I'm going to make you come like you never came

before," he grunted, his tongue dipping into her snatch.

He lapped at her plump pussy lips, and she moaned. She tasted so good, and her tight little hole was so inviting. "You're so wet," he said. "And you're so fucking tight."

She giggled. "It's all for you, baby."

He flicked his tongue against her clit, and she shuddered. "You like it when I play with your pretty little clit?"

She nodded. "Yes, please! Play with it for me."

"You want to feel it, don't you?" he asked.

"Yes," she moaned. She bit her lip and closed her eyes. "I want you to tease me and please me."

He pushed her knees wide, and she arched her back, thrusting her pussy toward him. He dipped his head and ran his tongue through her slit, teasing her.

"You feel so good, Lucy," he murmured. He slid a finger inside her and rubbed her sensitive spot. "So soft."

She whimpered and spread her legs further, her body leaning against the wall, her arms spread out. She gripped his hair and tugged him closer.

He kept licking her, lapping at her, then sliding his tongue into her. He kept working his fingers in and out of her, finding her sweet spot, her G-spot, and she gasped and whimpered.

"That's it," he said, drowning between her thick thighs.

"Oh, God," she groaned. "I can't take much more."

"You will," he grunted. "I'll have you squirming."

She was writhing now, her hands gripping his hair, her body shaking as he continued to work her pussy with his tongue and fingers.

"That's it," he said. "Come for me, Lucy. Let me feel your hot juices on my tongue."

She let out a long, drawn-out moan and came hard, her hips bucking as her pussy clenched around his fingers.

He worked her harder, sucking her, licking her until her body went slack in his arms, and she sagged against the wall.

He crawled up, holding her, his cock resting between her thighs, and rubbed the tip against her sensitive pussy. She bucked and gasped, squirmed.

"Oh, James... Fuck... It's too... too much. Ahn... But... Don't stop..."

He gave a grunt of delight as their eyes met.

"Fuck me, James!" she called out. "Talk dirty to me and fuck the shit out of me! Fuck my brains out!"

James's ears rung with Lucy's dirty request.

Biting his lip, he slapped her sensitive pussy with his rock-hard cock, then pushed the tip against her wet folds, the strap of her slutty thong still pulled to the side.

She moaned. "Oh, god... Yes... So good. Do it, James! Fuck me!"

And he complied, pushing his cock into her with all the force he had.

She was so fucking tight, and she was tighter still from coming on his tongue, but she welcomed his cock with a deep moan of delight.

"Hmm," she purred. "Talk dirty to me, baby!"

He started to move, slowly at first, but he was so fucking horny, and his cock was so damn hard, he couldn't hold back. "I'm going to bang your brains out, you little slut," he groaned. "I'm going to fuck you until you see cross-eyed."

She groaned and met his thrusts with hers, her body rocking back and forth, her tits jiggling.

"Yes... Yes... Faster, baby. Fuck me faster. Make me

your little whore."

He slammed into her with a fury, his balls slapping against her ass. "You like being called a whore, don't you?"

She gasped for air as he pushed into her hard. "I'm a whore for you, baby," she moaned.

"For me alone," he grunted.

"You alone, baby," she purred, then yelped as he plowed into her again. "Ahnnn... Just for you!"

He rammed into her again, and she cried out, her voice echoing in the room. "You're so fucking tight, Lucy," he growled. "So fucking tight. So fucking hot."

"Yes," she moaned. "Give it to me. Give it to me hard. Fuck me. Fuck me good. Fill me up with your cum, baby. I need it. I need it so bad. I want you to fill me up with your cum."

James groaned, and he lost himself in the moment, his mind gone, his entire world consumed by the beauty of Lucy's big, round tits, covered with his cum as they bounced, and the way her plump pussy lips clung to his cock.

He fucked her with wild abandon, slamming his cock deep, making her squeal with delight, her cum-soaked tits jiggling, her fingers clutching his hair.

He kept pumping into her, his cock plunging in and

out of her tight, hot pussy. His hands were on her legs, squeezing her, spreading her, and he could feel the way she was quivering.

Her pussy was so hot and slick, and he couldn't stop himself. He needed to feel her come, and he would not let her off until she did.

"Come for me, Lucy," he growled. "Come for me again."

She moaned and looked down at him, her blue eyes sparkling. "I can't stop. Oh, James... I can't stop. Don't stop. Don't stop. Don't... Stop..."

She was crying out, her head hanging as she held his shoulders. He drove into her, hard and fast, and she screamed. "Yes, yes! Oh, James, yes!"

James pushed her legs up, her feet in the air, her pussy wet with their combined juices, and he pounded into her, his cock plunging in and out of her.

He wanted to hear her scream.

He wanted to see her face as she came, her lips parted, her eyes glazed, her body trembling.

"Come for me, Lucy," he grunted, pounding her. "Come for me!"

She screamed, her body convulsing as her pussy clenched around his cock. Her cum-glazed tits were bouncing, her nipples stiff, her pussy gushing with her juices.

He fucked her harder and faster, feeling his own orgasm building, and he pulled his cock back as far as he could without it popping out, then jammed it back inside her, thrusting hard, and she came again, screaming his name.

"Oh, god," she moaned, her voice hoarse. "Oh, James. I can't... Please cum in me... Cum in my pussy!"

As her tight little snatch clenched on him and her dirty words urged him on, he let out a roar of delight and blasted his cum into her. He slammed his cock deep, spurting his seed deep inside her. He pulled back, growling, and pushed again, filling her tight little pussy up.

"That's it, baby," she crooned. "Cum in me. I need it inside me... All of it... Ahh, fuck, it's so good."

He was panting, gasping for breath, and he was still inside her, his cock throbbing as it released his final load.

"Oh, fuck," he panted. "That was good."

"Good?" She looked at him, her blue eyes wide, her lips parted. "Oh, James. That was *perfect*."

He smiled. "You're right about that." With a satisfied grunt, he felt the utter relaxation of two orgasms in a row roll over him.

She chuckled, running a finger down to her full tits and scooping up a gob of cum. She licked it from her finger and shot him a naughty look.

"Let me go clean up real quick," she said. "You lie back and relax. Have some more strawberries, and I'll come join you when I'm clean. Okay?"

He nodded. "That sounds nice."

She giggled and crawled up from the ledge, heading toward the towel rack. She took a single towel and began cleaning herself in front of the mirror.

James watched her with a smile.

She was beautiful. Not just in the obvious ways, like her tight, toned body, or the way she was always smiling, but she was beautiful in a different way. She was a woman who had confidence and poise — a woman who knew what she wanted and what she liked, too.

He admired her. He liked the way she talked to him, and the way she treated him with such a tender edge.

He wondered what it would be like to have a wife like Lucy. A hot MILF that was a submissive little slut in the bedroom, but a strong, independent woman the rest of the time.

She turned to him with a big grin, then sashayed over, hips swaying, and slipped into the water to sit between his legs, her back to him. Her sweet scent, with a hint of lavender, filled his nostrils.

She rested the back of her head against James's chest, and his curious hands went roving, kneading her full tits and stroking her soft stomach.

"Hmm," she purred. "That's nice... I'm so glad we did this."

"So am I," James agreed, happy to be in the hot water with a beautiful woman in his arms. "This has to be one of the best days of my life."

"Me too," she purred. "Hmm. I hope it's not the last day you spend with me."

"I promise it won't be."

She sighed. "That's good. I think I really like you, James."

He kissed her hair. "I like you too, Lucy."

She turned and smiled at him. "Will you stay the night?"

James really wanted to, but he had made a promise to Sara. He had to meet her tonight at the cabin. He kissed Lucy on the cheek and shook his head. "I have some things to do at the cabin."

She grinned. "You can do *things* at the cabin, or you can do *me* right here."

He laughed. "I'm sorry. It's important. If you're still

willing, I will come back tomorrow."

She smiled. "Of course I'm willing. And there's more work to do at Rovary's if you want to." She giggled. "We could basically repeat the day tomorrow."

"I could have this be my Groundhog Day without a problem," he joked.

She laughed and wriggled her ass against him.

"So you don't mind if I leave?"

"Well, I'm a bit sad about it," she said. "But something tells me you'll be back. Besides," she added, shooting him a naughty look over her shoulder. "It's not like you have to go right now, right?"

He grinned. "No... I think I have a bit more time."

She licked her lips and slowly turned around in his arms, her mouth seeking his.

Chapter 18

By the time James left Lucy's house, it was already late.

He didn't mind, though. He was looking forward to his evening with Sara, and he had certainly had his fun with Lucy tonight.

He knew Sara would be waiting for him.

He stepped out into the darkness and ambled over to his busted-up car, rolling his shoulders and popping his neck muscles.

The sky was clear, and the stars were bright overhead.

James climbed into the driver's seat, starting the engine. He was in luck; his old, busted-up car started on the first try, and he pulled out of the driveway.

He headed down to the main road, and the trip to the cabin took only a few minutes.

Once there, James parked on the side of the road and got out of the car. There was no light in the cabin. He walked up to the door and knocked.

It felt strange, considering it was his place, but he didn't want to intrude and at least announce his coming to Sara.

A moment later, he heard footsteps on the other side of the door. The lock clicked, and he pushed it open.

Sara looked up at him, her eyes widening.

He grinned. "Hey."

She gave him a coy smile as she ran her yellow eyes over him. Her tail swished, and her left ear gave a cute little twitch at the sight of him. "Hello, James. I'm happy to see you!"

He smiled. "You're as beautiful as ever."

She looked at him with a flirty expression. "Aw, thank you! I must admit, I was a little worried you wouldn't show up."

"I told you I would," he said, moving past her into the cabin. It was his cabin, after all.

He surveyed the tiny living room, the fireplace, and the bedroom. He nodded and smiled at her.

She licked her lips and narrowed her eyes as she picked up one of the oil lamps from the small table in the living room.

She then leaned in, her face close to his.

And she took a little whiff.

"Hmm," she purred, tail swishing. "You smell like... Hmm. Have you been doing naughty things?"

He smirked. "Maybe."

She pursed her lips as she lit the lantern. To James's surprise, she didn't light it with a lighter or a match; she just muttered something and snapped her fingers before looking back at him. A small flame sprang to life.

"I thought so," she said and grinned. "Well, come with me. We have much to do."

She opened the hatch in the floor and descended. James followed, and they were in the cellar. It was dark and dank, and James could hear water dripping.

"So, what are we doing?" he asked as he followed the cat girl's swooping tail.

She wore a yellow dress that matched the color of her

eyes, and it clung to her curves like a drowning man to a buoy.

Like with the dress she wore yesterday, there was a hole for her tail, and that was just the cutest detail.

She glanced at him over her shoulder. "Tonight, you will learn your first proper spell."

"*Proper* spell?" James muttered. "What? 'Word of Familiar Binding' wasn't a real spell?"

She smirked. "Oh, it was a real spell. But it was an inferior one, at least for you. Besides, I didn't teach you that one, did I? You just read it out loud. Got it right on your first try, too; you're really talented! As is to be expected from a scion of the House of Harkness. Anyway, you will learn a better one tonight."

"What kind of better?" he asked, frowning. He couldn't imagine what else she meant by a 'proper spell'.

She turned to him and grinned. "The kind of spell that'll be helpful for your work here."

"What is it?" he asked, suddenly excited.

"You'll see," she purred, leading him down a dusty, narrow tunnel.

The cellar confused James; its layout seemed different from what he had seen yesterday.

It was hard to be sure, though, because it was dark. He could barely make out the walls.

The tunnel opened up into a larger chamber, and a warm glow of light shone down from the ceiling. The light was dim, but it sufficed to illuminate the room.

As he followed Sara's swaying tail, his eyes widened in surprise. He was in a large cavern.

All of this under my cabin? he thought.

There had to be some kind of magic in play.

A stone altar stood in the center, and several candles burned on it. The walls and the floor were made of stone, and carved wooden beams supported the ceiling.

He saw a table nearby. There was a leather book on it, and he recognized it as the Grimoire. A candle flickered beside to it. A second table stood near the wall, and this one held a basin and a pitcher of water.

Sara noticed where his eyes were going. "We will start with the basics," she purred.

"Okay," he said.

She grabbed the Grimoire and flipped through the pages, her yellow eyes gleaming in the dim light. She found a page and turned it toward James.

"You have a lot to learn," she said, "but I'll help you get started." She handed him the book. "Here."

"Okay," he said. "What am I looking at?"

"That's a blank page," she purred.

He chuckled. "Yes, I saw that. Why am I looking at a blank page?"

"We will write something on it soon! Now, you know about the Eleven Elements of Magic: Time, Space, Fire, Lightning, Force, Water, Air, Life, Death, Blood, and Earth. Yes?"

James nodded.

"Now, you've learned 'Word of Familiar Binding'. That spell is simple and contains only one Element: Life. The more Elements a spell contains, the more complex its casting and the more important your intent." She gave him a mischievous, yellow-eyed look. "Do you understand?"

"Makes sense," he said.

"Good," she purred. "Now, I will teach you how to use another Element to cast a simple spell. Elements are a very important part of High Magic. The Elements are the building blocks of everything, and if you can master them, you can do almost anything."

She placed the book on the table with the basin and grinned at him. "This is a very important spell," she said. "Go on. Focus on the water."

"A Water Element spell?" James asked.

She shook her head and chuckled. "Fire, actually... I want you to will that water into boiling."

"Uhm, okay..." James looked at the bowl. "Boiling water? Sounds kinda basic."

"Yes," she purred, smiling at him. "Willing heat, the power of Fire, upon it! It's basic, but basics are important."

"Fair enough," he agreed.

"Now, focus on the water. Just *will* it into a boiling state."

He nodded and turned toward the basin. "All right," he said. "Here goes."

James followed Sara's instructions and focused on the basin with water.

He tried many different approaches: visualizing the water in a boiling state, imagining a fire underneath it, or simply saying 'boil' in his head over and over.

Nothing worked.

"I can't seem to do it," he said.

Sara nodded. "It's not about doing it right now; it's about intent. Just keep doing what you're doing now. Focus all of your willpower on the desired effect."

James frowned and tried again.

This time, he thought about a pot on an open fire. The pot boiled over and spilled. He imagined the water splashing over the floor, and the flames jumping up and hissing as the boiling water splashed on them.

He experienced a sharp pain in his forehead, and a moment later, the image faded.

Sara was smiling.

"What was that?" he asked, rubbing his head.

"You're a natural. You've already mastered the first lesson of High Magic. Did you feel the pain?"

James touched his forehead. It felt like he had been stung by a bee. "Yeah..."

Sara laughed. "That's the power of your intent, left unchanneled by the right words. Most people with the aptitude for magic never figure out how to control their intent, and they never learn magic as a result. I suppose it's for the best. If everyone were able to cast spells, the world would be a dangerous place."

James nodded, rubbing the painful spot on his forehead with his index finger. "So, what? This is like the magical equivalent of blue balls? I got all loaded up, but I didn't manage to shoot it out?"

She laughed and came up to him, planting a kiss on his cheeks.

"Kind of..." she purred. "Don't be mad. You need to feel the power of your intent before you can wield it. Magic is impossible without the right will powering it."

He nodded. "So, what do I do now?"

"You need to learn the words..." she muttered, and her voice obtained an air of mysticism. "This is where your Bloodline comes into play, James. If you focus your intent, then turn your mind inward, you will see. Many of the House of Harkness have gone before you, and many of those have learned this spell. Call upon the memory of generations, and you will learn."

"So... I can only learn spells through some kind of ancestral memory?"

"Not *only*," she said, shaking her head. "There are other ways. You can learn them from other High Mages or even research them on your own. But for now, you need to reach back in time." She took a step back and crossed her arms. "Try it."

James licked his lips and nodded. He closed his eyes

and focused his will.

"Good," Sara purred. "First, focus on the water. Will it into a boiling state."

He used the same mental picture as before, the pot boiling over on an open fire. Flames hissing as water splashed onto them. Once again, the nagging sensation in his forehead rose.

"Turn it inward," Sara said, her voice seemingly coming from far. "Focus on your Bloodline, on your ancestors, on the memories of your family, your clan, your house. Your Bloodline is strong. It has shaped your destiny, your purpose. They have made you who you are. You are their blood, their heir. Let yourself remember."

James closed his eyes. He reached for his memories, and the nagging sensation became a throbbing pain.

He could sense it burning under his skin, and it made him clench his fists. He was desperate to pull the pain out of his body, to rip it away and be rid of it.

And just as he was about to drop it and let his focus drift, his mind moved across the ages, and he was somewhere else.

Chapter 19

James forced himself to breathe and slowly opened his eyes.

The pain was still there, and it pulsed stronger than ever.

He heard the sounds of a wild forest around him, smelled the scent of the earth and the animals... the world at the dawn of the age of mankind.

He was here, and yet he was not.

When he looked down at his hands, they were transparent, and his feet made no imprint on the springy forest turf.

He was an intangible spirit, a ghost.

A spectator.

Out of the trees, a man came. Or perhaps, In James's time, he would have been only a boy. But in this age of predators and short lives, he was already a man.

He carried a wooden bucket, crude and simple, filled with murky water, and he slipped out of sight between two other trees.

Something was familiar about the boy, and James decided to follow him as he went into a small clearing.

There was a woman lying on a pile of furs. Her fair hair was braided in a long plait down her back, and she wore a simple, sleeveless dress of dun fabric.

She lay with her eyes closed, and James saw that she was young, perhaps in her mid-teens.

The woman was wounded; an elder man crouched beside her, in the process of cleaning what looked like the bite of an animal on her arm.

The elder man had features strikingly similar to those of the boy. And, come to think of it, to those of James...

The older man wore a headdress of bones and

feathers fastened to a wolf's skull, and his face was painted with a charcoal-like substance.

His long, dark beard swayed as he fixed his eyes on the boy.

"*Wuthin's aug,*" he snapped. "*Ick sagte the; cookend!*"

"*Ick konde nea enen vurra maack!*" the boy protested.

"Pah!" the old man scoffed.

The boy cowered, but the man just gave a grunt.

"*Oppa den gron,*" he murmured as he tapped the ground beside him.

The boy knelt down next to the woman and placed the wooden bucket on the ground, then sat down beside the elder man, his expression full of concern.

He leaned over and stroked the girl's brow with a gentle hand.

But the elder man just focused on the pail of water.

He closed his eyes and concentrated, his painted, savage face turning into a mask of the deepest effort. Then he raised two gnarled hands and spoke.

"*Vanvlooy tod cookend.*

"*Furanderinghe, obergange. Vurra.*

"*Vanvlooy tod cookend.*"

And just like that, the water in the pail began bubbling as if the hottest flames in the world licked at the bucket.

159

"Damn," James muttered, but his voice was lost in the ages.

Slowly, the vision faded, but the faces remained for some time in the ensuing darkness.

The man and the boy could have been his father at different times in his life, and the girl bore a resemblance to the pictures he had seen of one of his aunts, back when she had been a young woman.

They were his ancestors.

Chapter 20

"James?" Sara asked.

James blinked and shook his head, the vision fading. "I... I think I just *saw*."

Sara nodded. "You did," she purred. "You are truly of the House of Harkness."

He moved his mouth, lost in thought for a moment. "It... it goes back a ways."

"It does," Sara purred, her tail swooping excitedly. "I know it's a bit much, but do you remember the words?"

He cleared his throat. "I... I do."

"Write them down," she said, offering him a pen. "Before they fade from your mind."

He swallowed and nod, then jotted the words down in his Grimoire.

The act felt like more than just writing; it was as if he sealed something away and made it permanent, and as if he finalized his claim on both the Grimoire and High Magic.

"What... What's the spell called?" he muttered.

"Word of Boiling," Sara said, a reverent tone in her voice as she watched over his shoulder, her full breasts poking against his back.

He wrote down the name, then the words, the sense of mysticism and mystery sweeping him along.

This was amazing.

He was becoming a mage — a true artist of the arcane. It was intoxicating.

"Can I try it?" he asked.

She nodded. "Of course."

He placed the pen on the table and turned to the basin of water, his heart racing.

He closed his eyes and pictured the cauldron full of

water, the flames licking the pot. And as the sharp sensation in his head mounted, he raised his hands — like his ancestor had done, and spoke the incantation:

"*Vanvlooy tod cookend.*

"*Furanderinghe, obergange. Vurra.*

"*Vanvlooy tod cookend.*"

He suddenly felt cold, and he sensed the rush of power as the spell took hold of him. It was a simple spell, a simple incantation, but it was another step on his path of High Magic.

And when he opened his eyes, the water was boiling.

"Fuck..." he muttered.

Sara made a happy hop and clapped her hands. "You did it, James!"

"I did," he said. "But I couldn't have done it without you."

She smiled proudly. "Thank you. But... I must admit there is some self-interest involved..."

He turned to her; eyebrows raised. "Huh? What do you mean?"

She grinned and gave him a playful poke, her left ear twitching. "Now you can make me tea..."

He laughed and shook his head, surrendering to the sense of wonder and mystery that came with his exploration of this road of magic.

It was really happening.

Chapter 21

They left the cellar together to return to the cabin.

Despite the excitement energizing James, calling upon the ancestral memories of his Bloodline and casting his new-learned spell had drained a lot of energy from him.

Sara realized this without even asking him, and the sweet cat girl just offered that they withdraw to the cabin to relax.

Music to my ears, James thought.

And he did make her tea, although he boiled the water the old-fashioned way for now, feeling a little too much of that strange combination of jittery and tired that makes you mistrust your own hands.

James put the kettle on the fire, and he sat down to take a break.

He leaned back into one of the armchairs in the living room and looked around the cabin. It was a very rustic cabin, not unlike the ones he had seen in the wilds of North Dakota.

Sara hopped onto his lap without asking and just cuddled with him, shutting his eyes, and a soft purr rose from the base of her throat. Her left ear gave her signature twitch as she got all comfy.

He was enjoying the moment, but he was also thinking about his dreams and visions. He had never been a man of unfairly blessed talents, and he'd always worked hard to compensate, content to put in elbow grease to achieve what others got by mere luck alone.

But his recent experiences with magic were opening doors that had never been opened before.

It was a newfound feeling, like he had finally located the key to the lock of a treasure chest. And he wanted to keep exploring the treasures that lay beyond.

But what he had just experienced in the cellar, with Sara's help, was something that he knew would never be repeated. He had become a High Mage, and he was a mage in the truest sense of the word.

A High Mage of the House of Harkness.

What kind of responsibility was that? Was there a purpose or a goal he needed to pursue or fight for?

Honestly, he didn't feel like that. He liked the cabin; he liked Tour.

Why not just stay here? At least for now.

The whistling of the kettle on the fireplace roused him from his considerations. Sara stretched lazily in his lap and patted him on the thigh.

She hopped off with all the grace of a cat and looked at him curiously with big yellow eyes as he made them a pot of tea.

"Tea will do you good," she purred. "It'll help restore your strength."

He nodded, but he wasn't sure how true that was. Magic had been draining on him, but it had been exhilarating too. He felt invigorated and more powerful than he had in his life, and he hoped he could continue to use the newfound powers.

"Will you go work in town again tomorrow?" she

asked.

He glanced at her over her shoulder.

"For Lucy," she added with a purr, drawing out the name like it was a delicacy she wanted to taste for as long as possible.

He chuckled. "What do you know about Lucy?"

Sara smiled. "I know enough to say that she needs a strong man to help her, and she is also in desperate need of a man to satisfy her."

He smirked. "You're getting mighty specific, aren't you?"

She shrugged. "I know you are handsome, and I know you have a way with women. I can tell that Lucy is a special woman."

He grinned as he placed the teapot on the low table, then looked at her over his shoulder as he retrieved two pewter mugs from the kitchen.

"It feels like you're trying to say something," he teased.

She leaned against the table and crossed her legs, looking up at him curiously.

"Do you like her?" she asked.

"Of course, I like her," he said. "Lucy is a great woman."

"She has a daughter."

James blinked. "She does?"

"Hm-hm," Sara purred, watching James with great care. "She wouldn't be much of a 'MILF' if she didn't, hmm?"

James laughed and turned to face her. "What the... How do you know I call her *that* in my mind?"

Sara stuck out her tongue, wagging her tail playfully. "We cat girls have our secret ways."

He chuckled and shook his head. "All right, fine. Tell me about Lucy's daughter."

"I know Lucy's daughter," Sara said, her yellow eyes full of mystery. "But don't ask Lucy about her. Not yet... In time, you'll come to meet her, I believe. She is in touch with the forest."

"'In touch with the forest'," James echoed. "What does that mean?"

"You'll find out," she purred. "For now... I think it's good that you are seeing Lucy. Lucy has... lost something along the way. Her connection. Like many of the women in Tour. You can bring her back and make her happy."

James blinked, confused. Was she just telling him that she didn't mind him dating Lucy?

Sara giggled as if she guessed his thoughts. "When she loosens up a little to her own origins, perhaps she can come over." Sara licked her lips and sat on her knees in the armchair. "We could have fun, the three of us."

The way she said that woke James's cock up. He had gone three rounds with Lucy, but he felt like he could have a taste of Sara too, especially now that his mind was exploring all the dirty things that Sara's words awakened in him.

He grinned. "I guess we could," he agreed.

She purred her approval. "Now, come sit with me, please," she said in her sweetest voice. "And bring the tea!"

He laughed and picked up the two mugs, handing her one as he sat down in the armchair. She hopped onto his lap, and he stroked her supple back, winning more sweet purrs from her.

But his need was roused, and his eyes drifted to her nice round ass in her tight yellow dress and the cute, restless tail.

He smiled to himself and kissed her on the neck. "I'm glad I have a cat girl," he said. "And I'm even gladder it's you."

"I am glad I have you, too," she purred, leaning her head against his chest.

Chapter 22

James rose early. Sara had spent the night with him, but the cat girl had already left the cabin come sunrise.

James would've loved to wake up with her and share a breakfast, but he expected she had her reasons. She was furtive, perhaps even a little secretive, but they would get to know each other better as time passed.

Hopefully, they would also get to spend their

mornings together.

James still hadn't done any shopping. Lucy had paid him four hundred bucks, but he simply hadn't found the time to spend any of it.

Besides, the cabin had no fridge or freezer. It was going to be a challenge to store his food.

He dressed and went outside, hoping to see Sara somewhere, but the area was empty. He shrugged and decided to start the day by getting some water.

The bucket was empty, and he headed over to the well to fill it. Once he had fresh water, he washed up, drank, and ignored the rumble of his stomach.

He was nearing his last set of clothes, so he decided to play it bold and loaded up his dirty laundry before getting behind the wheel and driving down to Lucy's.

He whistled as he drove, keeping an eye out for Corinne as he passed the barn and saw the farmhouse in the distance. But he didn't spot her, and he continued on his way.

He pulled up in front of Lucy's store and parked, then slung his duffel bag with dirty laundry over his shoulders. The sign on the door still said the place was closed, but he walked up and knocked, anyway.

He heard a rustling sound, and a moment later, the door opened.

Lucy looked at him, her eyes bright with surprise. She wore a summer dress with a floral print that hung down to her thighs, and a pair of scuffed cowboy boots underneath. Her blonde locks were tied into a loose ponytail with a ribbon that matched the color of her dress. The overall effect was very cute.

"Well, hello you!" she said, a big smile on her lips.

He grinned. "Good morning, Lucy."

"It *is* a good morning," she said, her smile growing wider. "I hope you're hungry."

"I am, actually. I forgot to do some shopping."

"Well, let's go inside." She beckoned him in but remained half in the doorway with a coy smile on her lips.

That meant he had to squeeze past her, and he didn't mind one bit.

In passing, she smiled up at him as their bodies pressed together, and he could feel her familiar curves through the thin summer dress.

He hopped on the opportunity and kissed her on her lips, savoring her sweet taste and slight hint of lavender of her perfume, then stepped inside.

She followed, smiling, and closed the door behind them.

"I can make you some coffee," she offered. "And I

can whip up some pancakes in a pinch!"

"Oh, that sounds perfect!" he said.

She looked at his duffel bag and narrowed her eyes. "Is that laundry?"

He nodded. "I don't have a machine... I was wondering..."

She chuckled. "Put in on the counter! I'll get to it this morning."

"Thanks, Lucy."

She winked and turned away, leaving him to it.

He unpacked the duffel bag and laid out his dirty clothes.

As promised, Lucy brought him a mug of steaming coffee when she returned, along with two plates full of pancakes smothered with strawberries and whipped cream. She placed them on a table and offered him a seat.

He smiled at her. "This is so nice, Lucy."

"I had some strawberries and whipped cream left," she said with a wink.

He ate his pancakes quickly and drank his coffee. The meal was simple but tasty, and it chased off the morning grogginess with fervor.

Lucy watched him eat with a smile as she prepared the store for business. She served him more coffee after he'd finished eating, then sat down across from him.

The summer dress with its cheerful print brought out the bubbliness of her character. She wore no makeup, save for eye shadow around her big blue eyes, which gave her a natural beauty that was hard to find in the city.

"So," she began. "You're up for another day at Rovary's?"

He grinned. "I guess that's my plan. It's honest work."

She giggled and leaned back in her chair. "And can I tempt you with dinner after?"

"You bet... but I need to do some shopping, too. Some stuff that'll keep without a fridge or freezer."

She placed a finger on her plump lower lip. "Well, seeing as I run the store, so I could pack you up some things." She thought about it for a moment before shrugging. "But why don't you stay here tonight? I'll make you breakfast tomorrow!"

That idea sounded good. He hadn't been on a sleepover date in forever, and he liked the idea of spending a full night with Lucy. Maybe he could learn a little more about her and the mysterious origin Sara alluded to. He was sure she would prove an interesting partner.

"Sure," he said. "That sounds like fun."

She smiled and patted his hand. "Good!" she said. She got to her feet. "I'm gonna go get dressed for the day, but I'll come by Rovary's by the end of the afternoon to pick up the lumber."

"Thanks again, Lucy. I really appreciate this opportunity."

She waved him off. "No thanks necessary! Go kick some tree ass!"

He gave her a peck on the cheek, chugged back his coffee, and headed out into the fresh morning air.

Chapter 23

James was settling into a habit of doing his work at Rovary's lot.

He took the old axe from the toolshed and ran his thumb along the edge of the blade before sharpening it with the whetstone provided.

That was a skill he'd picked up while hunting with his father, back when the man still spent time with his kids. It had been years since they went hunting together.

Once he finished, he shouldered the hatchet and found some of the shorter pine trees. The woods were quiet around here today. James didn't mind; he enjoyed being out in the wilds by himself.

His mind wandered as he swung the felling axe in rhythm to a song in his head and listened to the rustling leaves in the wound.

It was a peaceful moment, one he wanted to cherish.

And then something darted past, almost causing him to jump. Startled, he turned toward where the creature had come from, only to find nothing there. Not even a hole or bush or anything that might have obscured his vision.

He shrugged. "Must've been an animal," he muttered to himself.

He didn't detect any other signs of movement until he got closer to the next set of trees. There, he spotted some motion. It seemed too big to be an animal—something must be moving in the brush near those trees!

He walked up slowly, watching for the source of the movement, and saw the bushes swaying slightly. Something was definitely there, but not what he'd expected.

"What the...?" he whispered, raising his gaze from the shadows of the undergrowth.

There was a dark figure in the tree. It was humanoid and crouched on a big branch, most details robbed from view by the shadows under the canopy. But the shape was clear enough; whatever it was, it had wings — large with feathers in many blue hues.

And it was female...

A toned and limber figure, but the curves were unmistakably feminine. She was a bird-like woman squatting on the branches, studying him. She had scales, too — although they covered only her shoulders and arms and legs; the rest was soft and feminine.

Behind the branch swished a lizard-like tail.

James gulped audibly, heart beating like mad. His hands began to sweat.

This was a dream.

He was asleep in his bed and about to wake up. It couldn't be real.

And yet... he'd made water boil with magic just last light — under the watchful eye of a cat girl.

"Whoa there!" he yelled as she spread her feathered wings with a hint of menace. He took a step back. "You're not a bird," he said. "You can talk, right?"

She tilted her head as if listening, then spoke to him. "I hear you, Mage." Her voice rang with melody, and he somehow knew a song from her would make the stars come down to listen.

"Who are you?" he asked.

The girl cocked her head to the side and looked at him. "Do I need to introduce myself? I am Astra. What is your name, Mage?"

"My name's James Beckett," he answered. "Why don't you come down here so we can talk in person?"

"Why should I do that when I have a perfectly good perch already?"

He shrugged. "It's polite..."

Only a slight smile betrayed that Astra cared little about being polite. She said nothing, so James considered her for a few more seconds before walking around behind her and placing his hand on the tree trunk.

It felt smooth against his palm; the tree was slender.

"Are you sure this tree is strong enough to hold you?"

She grinned. "Mmm... very much so. I'm not heavy." Then she sat there quietly, waiting for him to ask another question.

"Were you watching me?" he asked.

"For a little while now. Ever since you first came to these lands."

He paused. "Why didn't you speak to me sooner?"

"Because I did not know who or what you were until today. You've been coming here every morning, but only today did I sense a lingering aura of true magic that rang strong enough to identify you as a Mage."

She lifted her chin proudly. "You practice High Magic. It has been long since we saw a true Mage in these parts. You will be the first in many years."

James struggled to believe she'd been watching him all this time.

How had he missed her presence?

But then again, maybe she could shift into the form of a bird, like Sara shifted into cat shape?

He would never notice Astra in that form. She might simply have cloaked herself like that, knowing that James wouldn't look up if a bird flew overhead.

He shook his head and chuckled. "Well, it's nice to meet you."

"Hm," she hummed, still a little standoffish.

"So," he said, crossing his arms. "Anything I can help you with? Any reason you're watching me?"

Astra studied James for a moment, as if she were still making up her mind about whether she could trust him.

In the end, she gave a little squawk, nodded, and said., "I am your new neighbor, Mage."

"A neighbor?" he asked. "That's news to me."

She laughed. "I live in the Eltrathing Tree," she said. "I've always lived there. The tree holds a fraction of the magical essence of the Cahay, my people, and my ancestors planted the seed of the tree when we first arrived to these shores — aeons ago."

"Cahay? What kind of creatures are Cahay?" he asked.

Her wings rustled as she spread them out for him, a proud display of beauty, and he was mesmerized by it, as well as by her own beauty. She had a trim and toned figure — but very feminine.

"Most are bird-like beings of great wisdom, strength, power... but also cunning."

She leaned forward, perched on her branch, folding her wings behind her. Her voice sounded so musical to his ear that he almost swayed to it. "We are an ancient race from before men even knew fire," she said.

James took a step back from the girl. "Ancient? Before men? What age are we talking about? Like, dinosaur age?"

She nodded. "My kind was around when the world was still young. I believe you would call us prehistoric. My kind came here to these lands, however, at the same time humans did, though few of them know we exist, especially in these days. But we've remained hidden, mostly because of our powerful magic, and the danger of those who would use it."

He scratched his head. "What do you mean, dangerous magic?"

"Well, you must realize by now, Mage, that High Magic offers great power to the wielder. We are no different from any other species on this earth — except for one thing..." she said with a soft smile. "We descend from the greatest and most powerful mythical beasts of old..."

It seemed as if everything else faded away as he heard what Astra had said just seconds ago... 'except for one thing.'

He considered it for a second, contemplating her exotic appearance. Then what she said hit him like a sledgehammer...

The greatest and most powerful mythical beasts of old.

The scales, the tail, the wings.

"You're related to dragons?"

Her eyes flashed briefly before they returned to normal. "Very good deduction! That's right," she answered simply.

"A dragon! Like a dragon from old stories? Are there more dragons here on Earth? In this country, even?"

He glanced up at the tree, as if they could all come down at once.

She nodded. "I have not seen many... but there must be some around. Our kind... we move unseen. We have learned to hide ourselves from humankind through magic and subterfuge. There are other creatures of myth and legend soaring above the clouds." She pointed upward toward the sky.

He was astonished by that statement, but he didn't let his excitement show.

Instead, he asked, "So, are you saying that I might get a chance to meet a dragon?"

"There is always that possibility," she replied with a slight grin. "The patient eye sees many things, Mage."

He laughed and shook his head. "Okay, I will. But I'm not known for my patience."

She tilted her head again, looking at him like he was the most interesting creature she'd ever encountered.

"So I imagine," she finally said, then spread her wings in majesty once more. "Take care, Mage," she said in her melodic voice. "High Magic has risks of its own. Be sure not to fall into its many traps."

With those words, she gathered strength as if she was about to leap into the sky.

"Wait!" James called out, winning another glance from her. "Will I see you again?"

She grinned. "I said we are neighbors, did I not? Neighbors run into one another."

And with those words, she leaped out of the tree and soared up. She flew low, almost touching the tree tops, leaves and needles shaking in her wake.

And then, just like that, Astra was gone... like a daydream.

James stood there for at least a minute, scratching the back of his neck.

He had so much to learn; so much he didn't know yet...

Chapter 24

James was still thinking about Astra when he resumed his work chopping wood.

He was getting better at the work. The first few times, he had been inefficient, but today was different.

He guided the blade with skill to cut deep into the wood, perceived the best angle, and had discovered the best pace for himself. He swung faster and harder, and he was hitting a lot heavier.

And it was good to be alone.

It made him feel more relaxed when he worked in private. He felt his heart beat more quickly and his breathing became quicker when he worked in front of people; but out here by himself, there was no need to concern himself with others.

It was all about the task at hand. And without supervision — no managers breathing down his neck — he could be at ease without having to worry about his movements being too quick or too slow. And that — ironically enough — made him work faster.

It also gave him a chance to think things over without feeling rushed to finish the task at hand.

He could concentrate better without someone standing there watching him and giving him directions every few seconds.

It was also quiet; no sounds from the town distracted him or interfered with his concentration. And that gave him time to consider how he should handle his new neighbor; or maybe neighbors, since there was a good chance that Astra wasn't the only one living in that tree...

As he swung the axe for the next strike, he glanced up at the tree again just to make sure that she wasn't still there, watching him. But it seemed that she had truly disappeared.

She had been very nice to look at, and she understood exactly how to flaunt it... but she might also be dangerous... and she certainly was mysterious.

What is her game? James asked himself.

And why hadn't he heard of such creatures before? Cahay, cat girls, dragons... Did they all live in the shadows, unknown to normal people?

Or was James going crazy?

He pushed the thoughts away to focus on his work. He wasn't going to finish chopping all the wood today by himself — and he needed to do as much as he could before Lucy would come to make the pickup.

Still, he wondered how long she wanted him to keep doing this. The money was fine, but there would come a time when she'd have enough lumber. And then what?

He'd need to find other work. That would take some time since he didn't know anyone else in this town who might hire him.

He thought about that as he continued his work. If only there was someone he knew who might give him a recommendation... Or maybe Corinne had some work at her farm? Perhaps she needed some help around her place?

He turned the thought over in his head as he worked through the afternoon. Maybe he should go talk to Corinne after Lucy picked up the wood... or, well, after they had supper...

With the prospect of having supper with Lucy on his mind, he continued working with a smile on his lips.

James ate his sandwiches in the shade under a large tree, looking out over a peaceful clearing in the forest.

Here, out in the wild and unhurried, everything tasted better. Even a drink of water was a delicacy.

It was so silent out here that it made him feel as if he was floating through space and time — with nothing and no one bothering him. It was just him and nature — and he liked that.

He could sit here and relax... for hours if he wanted to. He never realized that he had been so overstimulated and in need of peace... until now.

"It's peaceful out here," he said to himself out loud as he took another bite of his sandwich, confirming his own thoughts about the place.

Still... work remained to be done.

He finished up and rose from his comfy spot with some reluctance. Time to get back to work. He reached for his shirt, which was lying on a rock nearby, and put it on. It was already dirty.

He grabbed his axe and headed toward the trees, where he would continue to chop wood. He tried to walk slowly, but the muscles in his arms and shoulders were stiff and sore from the long hours of work.

The sun was getting lower, and he would have to hurry to get at least as much as he chopped down yesterday.

He set his jaw and began working, putting the axe to the younger, more sprightly trees and felling them. He took his time, settled into the rhythm of chopping, his cuts now skillful and well-placed.

Whenever he felled a tree, he dragged it to the pile near the toolshed, very thankful for the workman's gloves that made sure he got no splinters, cuts, or scratches from the unworked wood.

James continued like that with the peace that hard workers and athletes understood well — some called it 'being in the Zone.' There was only his work, the strain of his muscles, the air in his lungs, and the satisfaction of making the body do what it was made for — tame the world around it.

The sun was sinking into the western horizon as he noticed headlights coming down the trail to Rovary's.

Lucy.

It had been a long day, but he had done a good job. And now his stomach growled. It had been a while since lunch, and his legs were like jelly.

He had to force his feet to move and carry him toward the toolshed. He could hear the sound of the truck's engine as it pulled into the yard, and a moment later, the door opened and Lucy stepped out of the truck.

"Hey, James!" she called him as he walked toward her. "How was your day?"

"Good, I guess," he replied, wiping the sweat off his forehead. "I managed to get plenty of wood cut."

"You're a hard worker," she said with a smile. "But you look tired. Are you alright?"

He shrugged. "I'm fine. Just a bit hungry. It was a long day."

"I know what you mean. It's almost dinnertime. Let's load up the wood, and you can follow me home! I have a great meal in store for you."

He smiled. "Thanks, that sounds nice."

They stacked the wood onto the flatbed of Lucy's truck, and then they started driving back to the general store, with James following her in his old sedan.

The sun was setting, and he was tired. He had worked hard all day, and he needed to rest. He didn't know what kind of meal Lucy had planned, but he hoped that she had something good in store for him.

And as he thought about food, he almost fell asleep at the wheel. He had to roll down a window to let the fresh air kick him in the face.

He was a lot more tired than he thought. But then again, the past few days had been crazy. He hadn't slept much, but he'd done a lot of... well, other things.

When they finally arrived at Lucy's house, he parked his car next to her truck and followed her up to her front porch. As he approached, she opened the door and welcomed him inside with a warm smile.

"Come on in, James. I hope you are hungry. I, for one, am starving!"

He grinned and nodded. "Same here."

She led him to the bar that separated her open kitchen from her living room and gestured for him to sit down.

James watched her go into the kitchen with delight, admiring her perfect body in the flimsy summer dress, so sexily finished off with the cowboy boots. Her house was nice and clean — as it had been yesterday — with soft notes of lavender drifting to his nostrils on occasions. Being here again felt like coming home.

He yawned as she leaned against the bar, winning a grin from her. "Coffee first?"

He chuckled. "Please! It's been a few busy days."

"That it has," she said. She looked at him. "You look like you haven't been sleeping well."

"I've been... busy."

"Is that so?" she asked with a smile. "I thought you stayed at your cabin. Isn't it peaceful and quiet?"

He nodded. "It is... but..."

"But what?"

He smiled and waved it away. He didn't want to tell Lucy about Sara, even though Sara seemed to know Lucy. After all, Lucy would probably think he was crazy if he told her about a cat girl living in the cabin with him.

"It's nothing," he said. "I guess it's just stress from the entire situation. My father passing away, me moving out here to the sticks..." He grinned at her. "No offense."

"None taken," she said. "I like living in the sticks. So..." She eyed him for a moment and licked her lips. "Maybe you need a massage to help you relax? What do you say we have dinner, and then you have a quick shower, and I'll massage you after? I have quite the pair of magic hands."

He laughed and winked. "You have magic hands, huh?"

She blushed and looked at the floor. "Well, it's not a superpower. It's just that I use my hands a lot, and they have gotten pretty strong and flexible from all the work. I'd bet I can knead your muscles like a pro and make you feel better. Come on! Let's go eat, and then you can take a nice, long, hot shower and relax."

"Sounds like a plan," he agreed.

Chapter 25

Lucy cooked them some good but simple food: baked potatoes with salmon and some veg. But she'd livened up the potatoes with fresh parsley, rosemary, and thyme.

As for the salmon, it was so fresh it was almost still swimming. And salmon that fresh doesn't need anything. She just baked it in the oven until it was nice and juicy. She served the vegetables cold but well-seasoned, crisp and fresh, and the whole meal went down perfectly with a glass of natural water.

They enjoyed some light conversation during dinner, with Lucy telling a little more about her childhood.

"My family is from Tour," she explained. "One of the original families that settled here, and I was born here. But my father and my mother... well, they kind of eloped. They were from two families that didn't get along at all, and their marriage was frowned upon. So they moved around a lot, and I was basically raised on the road."

She gave a disarming smile. "They were free spirits, and we never stayed long in one place."

"Being free and moving around sounds nice," James said. "Although it can be hard on a kid."

She nodded. "It was. I never made any real friends or connections that lasted." She fell silent for a moment.

"So what happened next?" James asked.

"Well, they both died..." Lucy said, sadness passing over her face. "It was an accident. We crashed after they evaded a drunk driver without his headlights on. By rights... I should have been dead too, but I somehow survived. Unharmed. The firemen and police called it a miracle, and the doctors agreed."

James looked at her, his heart filling with sympathy for this beautiful woman who lost her parents as a little girl.

"I'm sorry," he said. "I can't imagine how hard that must've been."

Lucy sighed. "Thank you. I never blamed them for anything, really. There are nights... when I get angry at the drunk driver." She shook her head and looked up at him with a smile.

"But what's the point?" she continued. "I'm alive, and I'm very thankful for it. Every day. And I'm thankful that they were with me for so long."

"So, that's how you ended up in Rovary's general store?" James asked.

"Hm-hm," she hummed. "Uncle Rovary took me in. He was a good man. He had a big heart, and he liked to help people. Although an uncle can't substitute a father and a mother, he was always there for me whenever I needed him. And he was a wonderful storyteller, so I've heard a lot of stories from him."

"A storyteller, huh? That sounds interesting..."

"Oh, he was the best! I wish I had a talent like his. I tried to write a few short stories, but they just weren't good enough. I might have a knack for stories, but it's not coming out yet. I love reading. I read a lot. It's all I ever do when I get some free time."

"I could tell by the books," James said with a grin.

Bookshelves lined nearly half of the living room walls.

She chuckled. "Yeah, that makes sense…"

They shared a brief silence, and James had the fire of curiosity within him. Sara had told him that Lucy had a daughter, and he was curious to know about Lucy's relationship with her child.

But he sensed that it was a sensitive subject; talking about her past seemed difficult for the otherwise so bubbly blonde.

No, he would ask her some other time.

With subtlety, he changed the subject to books, and Lucy was happy to elaborate on her passion for thrillers.

They had even read some of the same books — mainstream stuff, mainly — but Lucy was so passionate about reading and spoke so enthusiastically that James decided he'd read some books she recommended, just to get to know her better.

When James finished eating, he felt truly rejuvenated. His mind was clear and sharp, his body relaxed, and his stomach full. He had to admit, Lucy had some skills in the kitchen.

"Thanks, Lucy," he said as she began cleaning up. "Can't I at least help you with the washing up?"

Lucy came out of the kitchen with a small bottle of something in her hand as she shook her head. "Nope. I'll do the cleaning and the washing up... this time."

She held up the bottle. "This is a special massage oil," she said. "Get yourself cleaned up and lie down on my bed. It's the door at the end of the hallway to your left when you leave the bathroom. I'll be waiting to massage you."

"That sounds like heaven."

She shot him a wink. "Go! You worked hard; you deserve some relaxation."

James showered, dried off, and then realized he had nothing clean to put on. However, Lucy had seen it all, so what did it matter?

He shrugged, wrapped the towel around his waist, and headed over to the bedroom, where he found Lucy lying on her bed. She wore only a tight t-shirt and a pair of spandex booty shorts that outlined her perfect ass and cupped her pretty pussy.

She was facing away from him, her blonde hair flowing down her back and over the bed in waves. Her long legs stretched out as she lay on her side, a book open on the bed in front of her.

He regarded her in silence for a moment, drinking in the beauty of her as she lay there in the candlelight. He really was a very lucky man to have her.

He smiled and walked up to the bed. "I don't have anything to wear," he said.

Lucy looked up at him, her eyes taking him in, and she smiled. "That's okay. You're fine." She reached out and patted the bed as she moved over. "Just lie down."

He did as she said, his eyes burning on the soft flesh of her thighs and the way those tight clothes hugged her perfect curves. She had him acting up. Already, his cock stirred under the towel.

She placed her book on the bedside table and then sat up, her breasts bouncing as she did so — she wore no bra under the tight shirt.

"I'm going to start by massaging your neck and shoulders... to get the tension out. This will loosen your muscles and make it easier for me to massage the rest."

"Sounds good."

She grinned. "I hope you like the massage oil."

"I can't wait," he said. "Is it lavender?"

"It is. I'll tell you; it smells nice and calming. I like lavender a lot."

He laughed. "I noticed!"

She chuckled and continued. "But I'm not sure if it's your type of scent."

"I think it's perfect. It smells like you."

"Oh? I smell like lavender?"

He nodded. "It reminds me of you. I think it's lovely."

She blushed and bit her lip. "That's sweet," she said. "And you have no idea how nice that is to hear. Now, let's see what we can do about those tense muscles."

He nodded, and she began rubbing his neck and shoulders, sitting on her knees beside him on the bed.

Her gentle touch soothed him, and she took care not to push too hard, which he appreciated.

He closed his eyes and breathed in the aroma of the lavender. It was relaxing, and he could feel himself starting to unwind. He had forgotten about his aching muscles and the stress from his day.

As she worked, she began humming a melody that was familiar, but he couldn't place it right now. She started working on the muscles in his shoulders. The way her hands moved and her soft humming soothed him was almost like a meditation.

He opened his eyes and watched her sideways as she worked, not noticing him studying her.

She was so beautiful, so bright and cheerful, so full of life. And he wanted to keep her all to himself. He loved the way she made him feel — like he was the most important man in the world, and that everything he did was perfect. He'd never felt so special.

But he also wanted to make her feel the same way. To prove what she meant to him. That she was beautiful, inside and out, and that he loved even the parts she believed others found strange.

She was so focused on her work that he was surprised when she suddenly stopped and looked down at him.

"What's wrong?" he asked, opening his eyes and glancing at her over his shoulder.

It was as if she hadn't heard him. Her eyes were a little hazy, and she just leaned left, draping herself over his back so that their faces aligned.

Then, catching James by surprise, she kissed him on the lips — full and passionate.

James's eyes widened as Lucy kissed him. There had been a slight hint of awkwardness after last night, but the warmth flowed back in now.

He kissed her back, and she felt soft and warm. Her lips were full and sensual.

She broke the kiss after a few seconds and smiled at him. "Sorry," she said. "I didn't mean to stop massaging you."

He nodded; his eyes fixed on her. "Don't apologize. I liked it."

"Really?"

"Yes."

She blushed. "I didn't mean to... I just... I got carried away. I didn't know if... after yesterday, you know..." She cleared her throat. "If we're a thing... Are we a thing?"

"It's okay," he said, reaching up and touching her face. "I liked it. And I like you. I want to be a thing if you want to."

Her cheeks turned a deeper shade of pink, and she looked down. "Very much... yes."

"'Very much yes' sounds good," James joked, throwing her a wink.

She laughed, and her deft hands returned to their work, kneading his neck and shoulders, but the air was charged differently now, and she leaned forward. "Do you... do you mind if I sit on you? It's, uh, easier that way."

"Sure," he said, his voice a little hoarse. "I'm happy if you're comfortable."

She climbed onto his back, straddling him below his butt.

Her weight felt good on him, pressed his groin into the soft mattress, and his rod responded to the pressure. His heart beat faster, pulsed in his throat. He wanted her.

She sighed, and he understood she was getting swept up, too.

She reached down and began massaging his upper back, running her fingers around his shoulder blades before slowly inching down his spine.

He arched his back and groaned as her fingertips kneaded muscles that had been sore without him even knowing.

"Lucy, that's... so good." he muttered, wanting to say more, but he was lost to the pleasure of her touch.

"Just relax, my love. Let me do all the work."

She kept working, her fingers kneading his skin. He sensed the tension leaving his body, the knots melting away.

"Lucy, I..."

"Shh," she said, leaning down and kissing his shoulder. "I know. Just enjoy it."

He had never been so relaxed, and he was eager for her to continue. She took her time, moving her hands down his back and sides, then up and around to his shoulders.

"How do you feel?" she asked.

He groaned. "Good. So good."

She moved down to his waist, and her fingers were light as feathers as she removed the towel.

She gave an appreciative hum as she studied his backside, then shimmied down to work on his ankles and legs. She slowly worked her way up, kneading the tension from his muscles.

Lucy wasn't as gentle there as she had been with his shoulders, but his legs welcomed it. He groaned as her strong fingers dug deep.

"Lucy," he said, his voice thick. "This is great... You're killing me here."

She smiled, her fingers continuing to massage his thighs, then rose to pour out more oil. "Whoops," she purred when she spilled a significant gob of oil over herself. "I'm getting all slippery here!"

He looked over his shoulder to see the oil all over her

tight shirt. The fabric was thin, and he spied her nipples clearly through the wet shirt. Some of it had trickled down her delicious midriff to stain her tight booty shorts.

"Hmmm," she purred, rubbing the oil out. "I do love the feel."

James's cock was straining, and his mind emptied at the sight of that delicious woman and her lusty teasing.

He couldn't help but notice the label on the bottle as she placed it on the nightstand; it doubled as lube.

Damn...

She returned to him, her hands gently gliding over his body. He heard her breath grow thick with need, and he sensed a heat rising in his chest.

She worked her way up, caressing him everywhere as she went, until her fingers tickled the insides of his thighs.

When she spoke, her voice was heavy and husky. "I think it's time you turn around..."

Chapter 26

James turned around, his eyes wide and mouth open.

Lucy was straddling him, her legs spread apart, her tight shorts stretched over her hips. The oil had trickled down to outline her plump pussy lips in her booty shorts.

He stared at her, and his cock twitched, drawing her eyes.

Lucy bit her lower lip as she studied it. "I was going to wait for you to ask me," she said, her voice low. "But I can't wait anymore. I'm so horny. I need you."

He grinned at that as she propped up on her elbows. He watched her pull her shirt off, revealing her glorious breasts. She was so beautiful, so perfect, and he wanted her so badly.

She slid her hand between her legs and touched herself, a soft moan escaping her lips. "Baby," she purred. "Will you please fuck my ass tonight? I want to feel that big cock in my tight little hole."

Hot damn...

With those words, she reached down with her oily hands and grabbed a firm hold of his cock, jerking him off as she shot him a naughty glance with her big blue eyes.

Her ass... Such a dirty request...

James had wanted to pilfer that round MILF ass ever since he first saw Lucy. The thought of slipping his cock into that tight, forbidden hole and pumping his hot cum in there was almost enough to make him shoot his load now.

"Please, baby," she begged, kneading her breasts with one hand and tugging on his cock with the other. "I need to be your little anal slut tonight."

He propped up further, his hands on her thighs as he kissed her neck and shoulders, then moved down to lick at her nipples, teasing her with his tongue and making her shiver.

"I'll fuck your tight ass," he whispered into her ear. He grabbed the bottle of oil and poured a few drops into his palm. "I'll fill any hole you want me to, baby."

She gasped, and her fingers flew down to her clit. "Oh God, I'm so ready! Please, I need you now. Fuck me. I want it so bad."

"Hmm," he grunted, head spinning with desire. He grabbed hold of her with a wicked grin, then flipped her off him and onto the bed, right next to him.

Lucy gave a cute little yelp as she landed on her tummy. In less than a second, he hopped on top of her, hands itching as he placed them on the waistband of her spandex booty shorts.

"Tear them off," she crooned, looking at him over her shoulder. "Rip them apart."

He gripped the sides of those slutty shorts and pulled hard. They tore easily, revealing a plump, oiled-up ass ready to be pummeled. The sound of the fabric ripping was music to his ears.

Lucy arched her back as he threw the shorts to the floor. "Hmm," she purred. "Are you gonna use my tight ass, baby?"

He knelt down and ran his fingers along her cheeks, reveling in the way her cheeks tightened, his eyes fixing on her tight little rose.

"Mmm," she moaned, rolling her hips and reaching around to spread her cheeks.

James bent down and buried his face in her ass, smelling her musk and the oil. He slipped an oiled-up finger into her tight hole, and she whimpered and wiggled under his ministrations. She was lubed up and ready for it.

"I want that cock in my ass, James. Make love to me. I need it."

He grinned, and without hesitation, he pushed two fingers into her tight ass.

She yelped with pleasure and arched her toned back, pushing her butt up for him. He reached around and massaged her tits, then slid his fingers down and rubbed her clit.

She shuddered in response, and he felt her body tense up.

His hand gave her plump, trembling ass another squeeze, then moved to her wet pussy. She was soaking, and he loved the way it felt.

He slid his fingers inside her and began to pump both

of her holes, loving the way she quivered and sighed with every thrust.

"Oh, James, I'm so close. I need it so badly. Please... please fuck my ass while you make me come!"

He kissed her shoulder, then let his eyes feast on that quivering ass as he pummeled it with his fingers.

It was time to give her what she wanted...

James's cock, glib and oily, stood at firm attention, more than ready to claim his dirty price — Lucy's ass.

With a grunt of need, he hovered over her, grabbing his dick and lining it up with her tight little pucker.

She moaned with delight, pushing her ass up slightly, and slipped one hand under her body to continue rubbing her own clit.

It was a beautiful sight.

James bit his lip as he pushed the tip of his cock against that oily but tight asshole. He felt the resistance before her ass gave a little, opening up to him, and his tip slid inside. He groaned; his mind awash with lust as he watched his cock slip in to explore that tight, slick tunnel.

"Oh, yes!" she cried. "So good! Fuck me, baby. Fuck my ass!"

He pulled back and pushed again, burying his cock deeper with the next thrust.

He was rewarded with an even louder scream, and he began to pump his cock into that tight hole, listening to her moans and groans.

Seeing his big rod slip between those quivering cheeks and into that forbidden hole while she lay on the bed, dominated by him, was a delight. And it was even better that she enjoyed it so much, moaning and mumbling his name as he laid claim to her tight ass.

"Oh, God!" she cried. "I love it. Fuck my ass. Make me yours. I'm all yours, baby. I'm all yours."

He was going to have her now. He leaned down and kissed her shoulder, then started pounding her ass with long, deep thrusts.

She screamed in pleasure, and her whole body shook.

"Yes! Yes! Take my ass, James. I'm so close. Give it to me, baby."

"Mmm," he growled, staring down at her gorgeous ass bouncing under his fierce love.

He leaned down, grabbed her by the hair, and rammed his cock into her, going balls-deep. She screamed, and he heard her come, her body bucking with the intensity of her orgasm. He groaned and thrust, making her body jolt with his thick cock.

And he couldn't hold it in any longer.

"Fuck," he groaned. "I'm gonna cum."

"Yes!" she cried out. "Cum in my ass! Make me your little anal slut!"

She loved to talk dirty, and it turned him on like crazy.

His balls tightened, and his orgasm came hard. He slammed his cock into her and grunted with delight as he fired his first rope of hot, sticky cum into her tight little ass.

"Ahn," Lucy moaned, reaching around to spread her ass cheeks for it, body still trembling with the aftershock of her orgasm. "I can feel you, baby! Hmmm, fill me up!"

He couldn't stop. He was so horny. And her ass was so perfect. He continued to pump his cum into her, his eyes locked on the sight of her beautiful ass bouncing as he pummeled her.

"Oh, baby," she purred. "I want more! Fill my ass."

His cock twitched, and he gave a sigh of delight as he shot his last load into her tight, slippery hole.

He had emptied his balls completely, but the sight of her sweaty, oily body quivering under him, the tatters of her spandex booty shorts still clinging to his hips, was enough to make him want to go again.

He stayed there, straddling her, his cock still twitching with his last dribbles of cum.

"That was amazing, baby," she purred. "So hot."

He gave a grunt of agreement, then pulled out, watching her stretched asshole brimming with his cum for a moment before rolling to his side.

She had folded her arms below her head and smiled at him, then lifted her head to kiss him. He responded, and his lips parted, his tongue eager for hers. He sucked on her lower lip before he pulled away with a delighted sigh.

"Hmm... You fucked me good, baby," she said. "I'll walk funny for a bit after this dirty adventure."

James chuckled and gave her oily ass a resounding slap, making her yelp. "If it's up to me, you'll walk funny for the rest of your days."

She laughed and rolled over, nestling in James's arms. But her naked, oily body pressed against him roused his hunger and his need again.

Lucy would get no rest just yet...

Chapter 27

This time around, James spent the night at Lucy's, just as she had asked him to.

He was eager to see Sara again, but for now, he just wanted to sleep. And Lucy's warm body felt too good against his.

He slept with Lucy cuddling against him, and they were both pleasantly exhausted.

When morning came, a rosy light heralded it, limning the white drapes in front of the window of Lucy's bedroom.

"Good morning," Lucy yawned, kissing James on the cheek. "Did you sleep well?"

"Yeah, I did," he replied, yawning. "You?"

"Perfectly," she replied, sitting up and stretching. She looked so lovely in the morning light. Her face was smooth, her eyes bright, and her hair shone with luster.

"We should get up," James said, leaning over and giving her a kiss. "We've got work to do today."

Lucy giggled, then sat up and kissed him. "Okay, lover boy. What are you doing?"

"More lumberjacking," James said. Despite the massage, his muscles were still sore. He flashed a glance at Lucy. "And you're gonna do some storekeeping, right?"

"Ugh," she moaned, rolling over. She took the sheets with her, and James drank in her shape under the thin covers, which outlined every inch of her curvy and delicious body. Her blonde hair draped over the pillow as she lay there on the white sheets in the gentle glow.

"I think you're going to be very popular with the customers," he teased, crawling into the bed and kissing her shoulder.

She giggled, and he nuzzled her neck. "Hmm. I only ever get women in the store," she muttered.

"You'll be popular, regardless," James said, squeezing her butt through the sheets. "And I bet I can convince the girls to give you more business, too."

"Hmm," Lucy purred, reaching back and grabbing his cock. He groaned as she squeezed him, her hand moving to her slit, rubbing herself.

James chuckled. "What are you doing?" he asked, watching her as she stroked him.

She threw a naughty look over her shoulder. "What does it look like I'm doing?" she replied. "I'm getting myself another helping."

He chuckled, letting his hand roam over her round ass. "Well," he muttered. "I suppose it's still early... We have some time."

With a broad grin, Lucy rolled over and hopped onto him.

It was an hour later when James emerged from the shower, sweat and bodily juices rinsed off.

A stack of neatly washed and folded clothes lay

waiting for him in Lucy's tidy bathroom, and the clothes smelled of lavender. He took a big whiff, then got dressed and headed out into the living room with the adjoining kitchen, lured by the aroma of bacon, eggs, and fresh coffee.

Lucy was busy at the stove, wearing nothing but a loose-fitting t-shirt. The top was damp and clinging to her breasts, and James stared at her in delight and wonder.

"Hey!" she called out, laughing. "What are you staring at?"

"Your tits," James said simply, standing in the doorway.

Lucy laughed. "Good!" she purred as she set a plate of steaming bacon and scrambled eggs on the table, then poured coffee for both of them.

James sat down and dug in, and Lucy joined him, eating heartily and drinking coffee. It was good food, and enjoying breakfast with a scantily clad blonde MILF was the best way to begin the day.

"So," Lucy said after they had finished breakfast. "How do you enjoy the lumberjack life?"

"Not bad," James replied, taking another bite of his second piece of toast as he looked up at her. "And the money's good."

She chuckled. "Yeah, I have your money for yesterday in the store. Another two hundred dollars."

James narrowed his eyes. "Who's paying this much for just some wood?"

Lucy smirked. "I have my ways," she murmured, sipping her coffee.

James grinned. "I bet you do. But I have to say, I'm a little surprised that you've got a customer willing to pay so much for a little lumber."

"Oh, it's not the lumber," Lucy said with a chuckle. "It's the trees."

James frowned. "What do you mean? I thought we were cutting down those trees."

"Oh, we are," Lucy said with a shrug. "But that's not why people pay so much for the wood."

"What is it, then?" James asked, eyeing Lucy warily.

"The trees themselves," Lucy said, grinning.

James scowled. "I don't get it."

"No, silly," Lucy giggled. "Neither do I. I have a customer who pays money for the trees so long as they are freshly cut. Unworked, with the limbs still attached. She picks them up in the morning, usually around seven o'clock."

James stared at Lucy. "Are you serious?"

"Yes, of course," Lucy said with a grin.

"So, how many does she need?" James scooped up some more scrambled eggs. "Can I do this job forever? Infinite money?"

Lucy laughed. "No, she said she almost has enough. Two more days should do it."

"Then what?" James asked, munching on the last of his eggs. "What does she want with all those 'fresh' trees?"

Lucy shrugged. "I tried to ask, but she wasn't very talkative. I learned early on that it's best not to ask too many questions."

"Why?" James asked.

"Because," Lucy said with a sly smile. "It's not always for the best to know everything."

"So, who's this mysterious customer?" James asked.

Lucy's eyes sparkled. "I think you'll find out soon enough."

Chapter 28

After breakfast, James greeted the morning sun with a broad smile on his lips.

Lucy had packed some lunch for him, and the day's work was ahead of him. The sky shone clear and blue, with dawn's rosy glow already diminishing.

He had half a mind to hang around to catch a glimpse of Lucy's mystery customer, but he decided against it.

She insinuated they would meet at some point, and James didn't want to violate her trust or come across as a nosy creep.

And so he headed to his old sedan. The engine didn't turn over until the third try, but after that, he headed on his way.

He drove up to the old logging site. He parked, then grabbed the axe from the toolshed and began chopping at the nearest tree.

It was a young pine tree, and he worked quickly to fell it. Then he went to work on the next tree, and the next.

Soon, his muscles ached, and he stopped to rest for a moment. He was sweating profusely, but it was good to work hard.

He took a swig of water from his canteen, then resumed work. He felled a few more trees before it was time for lunch. He was glad he had brought some food from Lucy's. He ate and took a break. After that, he continued working.

As the afternoon wore on, the air cooled, and James found himself in the shade of the trees, his shirt soaked through with sweat.

He had burned through the aching in his muscles, but he hadn't had the best rest ever, having spent most of the night pounding Lucy into submission, going through a veritable Kama Sutra's worth of sex positions.

His lips curled into a smile at the thought. Now, with a full stomach and in a cool breeze under the shade of a tree, he felt fatigue tugging at him. His eyelids became heavy, and they closed almost on their own.

Within a moment, he drifted away.

James was dreaming.

He was near a house, an old house with a wide porch. There was a swing on the porch, and he sat on it, slowly swaying in the wind.

The door creaked open, and a woman stepped out onto the porch. She was old, bent, and wrinkly, with a tight bun of gray hair. She walked over to James, then sat down on the swing beside him, but she didn't seem to acknowledge his presence.

When James looked down at himself, he noticed he was weirdly transparent, as he had been when he dreamed of the druid who cast the spell to boil water.

Another Bloodline memory...

The woman leaned back on the swing and sighed.

By her dress and the general appearance of the house, James guessed this memory went back a century or so. The woman took a moment to regard the house, and James followed her stare to find out that a large part of it had been damaged.

It was a wooden house, and it looked like some kind of explosion or fire laid waste to it. A stack of raw and unworked lumber lay close to the house, almost as if someone had carelessly dumped it there. Nails, varnish, sandpaper, and other materials rested near a workbench nearby.

After a while, the old woman rose to her feet.

"My son is dead," she whispered to herself. "And I will never see him again." She stood silent for a second, then repeated it again, as if it were a mantra to get herself to accept that single, horrible fact.

James didn't know what to say. She probably couldn't even hear or see him. And so he remained silent.

"My son is dead, and I will never see him again."

James watched the woman walk away. She moved slowly, like an old crone, but he knew she wasn't really old; sorrow and hardship had taken their toll. Her face was wrinkled, her hair thinning and gray, and her body was frail.

She repeated her mantra a couple of times as she stood on the porch, and she did indeed seem to draw strength from it.

In short order, she looked up at her damaged house, and her expression hardened. In that moment, James recognized the Beckett features — the sharp eyes and firm jaw of his father.

"Best get to it," she muttered.

She ambled over to the pile of lumber, her going slow, and took a breather before she raised her hands.

Then, she shut her eyes and concentrated deeply, waving her hands as if she conducted an orchestra.

When she spoke, her voice was much more powerful than when she had been mourning her deceased son. In fact, her words thundered across the grounds.

"*Vanhoudt tod plancka.*

"*Bawerckinghe, maacken. Kraft.*

"*Vanhoudt tod plancka.*"

And as she spoke, the timbers — in their loose and unorganized piles — rose one at a time.

They rotated gently in the air as they were stripped by an unseen force. That force removed the bark, the branches, and cut the timber into boards.

The resulting boards were sanded down by an unseen force, then given a coating of varnish and set down gently to dry.

In short order, she prepared the entire stack of lumber, casting the same spell over and over again.

Of course, she had more work to do — she would need to remove the ruined sections of wood wall without letting the house collapse, to say the least, but James sensed he would not see that part.

Already, the vision faded as he turned lighter and drifted away.

But the words of the spell remained at the back of his mind as darkness overtook him.

Chapter 29

When James woke up from his nap, a figure flitted at the edge of his vision.

He was still in the forest, in the shade of the tree where he had been chopping wood, and the sun shone in the sky. But he was no longer alone.

He blinked and turned his head to look. On a thick branch above, a familiar shape squatted, a grin on her plump lips.

Astra.

"Greetings, Mage," she said, grinning down at him. "You look peaceful when you sleep."

"What are you doing here?" James asked, his voice hoarse from sleep. Then, to himself, "How long have I been sleeping?"

Astra regarded him with amusement as she sat perched on her branch. She shifted her weight slightly, giving James a chance to ogle her delicious curves and fine alabaster skin.

She was fit with defined muscles, and the loincloth and slutty straps that covered her full chest hid very little from his hungry eyes.

"I always roam these skies, Mage," she said. "And I sensed some magical activity." She eyed him with curiosity. "It came from you. What were you doing?"

"I had a dream," James said. He stood up and stretched, his body aching all over from the exertion of the day's work.

"Was it a good dream?"

James smiled. "Yes, it was."

Astra cocked her head at him. "Tell me about it."

"Well, I suppose I would call it an ancestral memory..."

Astra's gaze intensified. "Did you learn a spell? Tell me."

James looked up and shielded his eyes from the sunlight. "If you want to talk to me, come down."

Astra tilted her head. "Why?"

"Because I prefer being at eye level with people I talk to."

Astra shrugged, then jumped down from the branch.

She struck her wings once to soften her descent and landed lightly on the grass, making not a sound. Then she walked towards James, her hips and dragon tail swaying in a way that made him want to push her down against the springy turf.

And it seemed she understood her effect on him, as she studied him from under heavy-lidded eyes, an amused and seductive smile on her plump lips.

James returned her smile, but inside, he felt his heart pounding.

Astra stopped a few feet in front of James and folded her arms under her ample breasts. James's eyes trailed down to those and her toned abs.

There was something about a woman whose stomach could double as a washboard...

"Now," she said. "Tell me about your dream."

James felt the blood rush to his cheeks. He cleared his

throat. "Well, it was a memory, but not my own. I think it was from at least a century back. An old woman grieved the loss of her son, then used magic to cut raw timber into boards."

Astra nodded. "I see. What did she do with the boards?"

"She used magic to strip away the bark and branches, then to sand and varnish the boards. After that, the dream ended. But I supposed she used the boards to repair her house."

Astra leaned in, and the musky scent of her swirled out to meet James's nostrils. She smelled wild and fresh, like pine trees in an icy northern wind.

"Did she speak words of power?" Astra asked.

"Yes," James answered, his voice barely a whisper. "She spoke the words over and over again. It was an incantation."

"What were the words?"

For a moment, James hesitated. Was there harm in telling her? She had a certain hunger and eagerness about her.

In the end, he decided he should not take any chances with High Magic; he knew too little of it, and perhaps this bird woman — this Cahay — had ill intentions.

He should talk to Sara about her — and about sharing

spells in general.

"I'm sorry," he said. "I believe the words were meant for me alone."

Astra's eyes widened. "How so?"

James thought fast. "They were a memory from my Bloodline, the House of Harkness. I don't know if such things are even mine to share. I shouldn't tell you."

Astra stared at him, her eyes narrowed. Then she chuckled. "I like to hear secrets, Mage. They're a gift, a privilege, a rare thing, even for me."

She extended a hand — her nails were long, almost claw-like — and a shiver passed through James as she trailed that sharp nail across his left pectoral muscle, stopping an inch short of his nipple. "The Cahay gather secrets," she said, her voice a purr. "Shinies of the heart and the mind. Can I not persuade you, Mage?"

His cock jolted in his pants as she inched closer.

His fantasy of pushing her down into the springy turf and fucking her into submission suddenly seemed a lot more within reach. He swallowed and tried to clear his mind.

"I'd rather keep the secrets to myself," he said, trying to maintain some measure of dignity.

Astra regarded him with her sly smile. "But I am here. I can see the desire in your eyes. Your body tells me that you want to share with me. I see it in the way you stare at my breasts. I see it in the way you lick your lips when you watch me."

James couldn't help himself. He stared at her breasts, and he didn't try to hide it. Her nipples were hard, poking against her flimsy strap, her skin was smooth, and her hips were...

Astra smirked, and James bit his lip.

Then he gathered his strength. "I'm sorry, but no," he said, his voice seemingly distant.

She made a face, but only for a moment. She stepped back, withdrew her teasing finger, and eyed him with what looked like respect.

"Very well, Mage," she said. "Keep your secret. But if you change your mind, you know in which skies I roam."

She spun and hopped up, wings batting as she took to the air and soared over the canopy, leaving James with a hard-on and his mind spinning.

Chapter 30

It took James some time to recover from the encounter with Astra. His mind overflowed with questions about the nature of High Magic.

Could he share spells? *Should* he?

Perhaps he could trade with Astra? She might teach him what she knew, and he could teach her what he knew.

He was hungry for more knowledge, for more spells, because he now began to understand that spells simplified life.

If he had a few more of these construction spells, he could build whatever he wanted! He would fix up the cabin, add whatever he wanted, and even raise new structures from scratch.

But first, he needed to talk to Sara.

He returned to work, cutting down more trees. Lucy had said that, after today, there was work for one more day. That was another four hundred dollars, which meant he made one thousand dollars in just five days.

It was crazy; someone was overpaying him dearly.

But at least he could afford to get the groceries he needed, maybe do a little work around the cabin. He liked that prospect, making the place more into his own home. He loved the idea of fixing the house, putting his stamp on it, making it his.

James paused to wipe the sweat from his brow. It was hot work, but it felt good to be active, to be moving. The sun beat down on him, and the heat seemed to soak into his bones. But that feeling was good.

It made him feel alive.

The sun was well on its way down when he was stacking logs near the toolshed and heard the familiar hum of Lucy's pickup truck as it came down the dirt road that led from the Highway to Rovary's lot.

He straightened himself, wiped his forehead, and waited while Lucy parked.

Lucy stepped out of the cab of her truck; her blonde hair pulled back in a ponytail.

She wore a white t-shirt, a pair of close-fitting jeans, and brown work boots. James smiled and walked towards her.

"Hey, James!" she said. "How's it going?"

"I'm good, Lucy. How are you?"

She gave him a naughty grin. "A little tired, baby. You know why."

James laughed. "I sure do!"

Lucy took off her work gloves and folded them, placing them in her back pocket as she eyed the stack of lumber.

"Good haul," she said, and her blue eyes flicked over to him. "So... do you feel like coming with me again tonight? I'll make you dinner."

He grinned and walked over, giving her shapely ass in those tight jeans a squeeze.

"I'd love to," he said. "But I really need to get back to the cabin. I'll follow you to the store to get some groceries. But I should get home after that."

She pouted. "Hmm... I was looking forward to playing with you again."

She stepped close and pressed her lips to his, kissing him deeply, her tongue pushing against his lips, searching for entrance.

He wrapped his arms around her and held her close, his lips parting to let her tongue inside.

She tasted of mint, and her hands ran up his arms and across his shoulders, pulling him closer to her. She kissed him hungrily, and his cock strained against his jeans.

"You sure?" she asked, breaking the kiss. "We could have a *lot* of fun tonight."

"Tempting," he said, then shook his head. "But no, I really should get back to the cabin. I got to get used to my new abode."

She nodded, and her expression turned to disappointment. "Some other time?"

"Of course," he said. "I'm not done with you... I don't think I ever will be. And hey, I could cook you dinner sometime at the cabin! I'll show you how to build a fire and make a nice meal."

She brightened. "That would be great. I could help, too."

"Sounds fun," he said, giving the blonde MILF

another pat on the butt. "By the way," he added, "can I borrow this axe? I'll bring it back with me tomorrow."

She raised a dark blonde eyebrow. "Sure... but why?"

"I want to do some work around the cabin," he said. "I'm not sure what yet, but I'm going to clean up the place, make it more livable, maybe build a small shed out back for tools and such."

Lucy's mouth dropped open. "Wow, you've got big plans," she said. "I thought you were just gonna stay there for a couple of weeks. I didn't know you were going to live in the cabin."

"Well, I am," James said. "And I want to get the place fixed up so I can do whatever I want. You can come over and we can hang out once I've got things in order."

"I'd like that! If you need anything else from the shed, feel free to borrow it."

"I appreciate that," James said. "Now, let's get these bad boys loaded up." He nodded at the stack of logs. "I'll follow you into town and be your friendly customer today."

She chuckled and winked. "Best customer I've had in months."

Laughing, they went to work, loading the logs on the flatbed of Lucy's truck.

It took them a little under half an hour, and there was still some daylight left.

With a satisfied nod, James hopped into his old car and followed Lucy's taillights down the old forest path until they came to the highway. From there, he followed her north into Tour, up Main Street, until they came to her store.

By then, evening was closing in. It was time to do some shopping and then head back to the cabin.

James followed Lucy into her store. There were a few other patrons, women from Tour, and although he greeted them, he was not here for conversation.

He set out to find food that would keep for a while despite being unrefrigerated.

There were canned goods, mostly from the nearby factories, along with pasta and potted sauces. James made his pick from those, then also chose a couple of sausages, a bag of potatoes, and some veg that would keep outside the fridge, like cucumbers and tomatoes, for a salad. He also took a limited supply of bacon and eggs; without a fridge, he'd have to eat those tomorrow morning.

The general store also sold cutlery, so he bought a set of good cooking knives, as well as some plates, some utensils, and a set of strong pans.

"Need a hand?" Lucy asked, approaching him with a cart.

James smiled at her and nodded, loading everything he picked into the cart.

He finished up by getting toilet paper, some potato chips and other snacks, and some simple household products anyone would need, like soap and cleaning supplies.

"Thanks, Lucy," he said as he went over to the register. "This is all I need."

She smiled at him as she rang his items up. It totaled to a little over one-hundred-and-fifty dollars — the pans and knives weren't cheap — and she subtracted the expenses from his pay for that day, handing him a fifty.

"There we go," she said with a wink. "Looks like you made a good day's work. Let's hope the next one is even better."

He grinned. "I certainly hope so. Thanks for the help."

"My pleasure," she said. "So, I'll see you tomorrow?"

"You bet! I'll head straight to Rovary's and see you at the end of the afternoon."

"Good night, then."

"Good night."

Chapter 31

The drive home was quiet. James wasn't tired, but he was content to drive in silence.

He had made a good day's work, and now he was headed to his new home.

He drove north out of town to Forrester Trail and passed the barn when it was already getting darker. He was about to zoom past when he noticed a light flicker inside the barn. The door was open.

That's weird, he thought.

James stopped the car, turning the engine off. He climbed out of the car and walked towards the barn, his boots crunching on the dry grass.

He glanced around the lot and found no one else, but he kept a watchful eye as he approached the barn.

Inside, James found Corinne leaning against the wall near the ladder to the hayloft.

She wore a dirty but tight-fitting t-shirt that showed off her fit body, her tight jeans hugging her curvy ass. Her red hair was tied back in a ponytail.

She was contemplating something and didn't even notice James enter. That gave him a moment to enjoy the view. Out of her usual overalls, James had a moment to truly appreciate how fit the farmer's daughter was. The sprinkling of freckles on her cute face finished the job.

"Hey there," he said, making her snap out of her contemplations.

"Well, howdy yourself!" she called out when she saw him. "If it ain't James Beckett!"

He laughed. "The one and only," he said with a smile.

"Come to steal my hay, huh? Sneaking around in my

barn?"

He laughed. "No, I'm just passing through. I wanted to check up on you; I was wondering if you were doing okay."

Her smile faded. "Well, that's nice of you. And since you asked: no, not really okay. I mean, it ain't easy out here. I'm trying to build up the farm and make a living, but it's hard. I'm struggling to make ends meet."

He nodded. "Anything I can do to help?"

She sighed. "Well, it's hard with this wild... fox, or whatever, going after the chickens."

"What?"

"A fox, or a wolf... I don't know what kind of creature it is, but it's been coming out at night and killing our chickens. It's really terrifying. I just want it to stop."

"It's probably just a wild animal," he said. "Maybe a coyote, maybe a wolf. You might ask the local hunters if they've seen anything."

"I appreciate the help," she said with a grateful nod. "But not many people from Tour are in the hunting business. And meanwhile, this thing has been coming out and killing my chickens. It's gotta be stopped."

"I can come by tomorrow evening and help you out," he said. "I could stand watch. I'm a good shot. And if I can't hit it, maybe a few gunshots will scare it off."

She bit her lip. "You'd do that? That would be awesome! Thank you!"

He nodded. "Sure, no problem. Thing is, I don't have a rifle. Do you have one I could borrow?"

She touched her lip as she thought, her plump lips pouting in a cute way. "Uh, I think so," she said. "But I'm not sure it works. I haven't used it in a while."

"Well, have it ready tomorrow evening, and I'll have a look."

She grinned, placed one hand on her hip, and threw James a seductive grin.

"Say, ain't you working for Lucy? You got time for little old me?" She licked her lips, and her posture drew his eyes to her luscious hips and the way her big breasts strained against the fabric of her shirt.

He cleared his throat. "Yeah, I've got time," he said. "I mean, I'm working for Lucy, yeah, but tomorrow is the last day. And I'll come over and help you catch this killer fox or whatever."

"Aw, that's sweet," she said. "I'll make sure I've got something good for you to eat."

He laughed. "Don't worry about that."

"Now, now," she said, wagging her finger. "It ain't proper to have a man come and help without giving him something to eat. You come have dinner with me

244

tomorrow evening, and I'll set you up by the chicken coop with a rifle and a full belly. How's that sound?"

He chuckled. "I can't argue with that."

She straightened herself, pushing her chest out, and James caught a glimpse of the puffy nipples of her large breasts, poking against the fabric of her shirt.

She held the pose for a moment, and James couldn't take his eyes off her. He wondered if she had freckles down there, too.

"Sounds like we got ourselves a deal," she said. "I'll see you tomorrow, then."

"Sounds like a plan," he said, smiling. "See you tomorrow."

He gave her a last smile, and it took some effort to physically remove himself from the premises.

Corinne had flirty ways, and he was pretty sure she had been sending him signals from the moment they first met. And even though she said nothing about payment, he could afford a night of volunteer work at Corinne's farm.

In fact, he was looking forward to it.

Chapter 32

James parked his car in front of the cabin.

He went inside and surveyed the place with joy. He loved the layout; there was a living room with a stone fireplace and a small kitchen. A narrow hallway connected the living room and kitchen to a single bedroom.

The place had no electricity. During the day, the

windows let the light in. At night, he had to rely on oil lamps. His cabin was a cozy little home, but he hadn't had time to decorate yet.

Let's see if Sara is in, he thought to himself.

He opened the hatch to the cellar and headed down the stone steps.

James felt the coldness of the surrounding stone. He reached the bottom and looked around. The stone walls were clean and smooth. The air smelled musty.

"Sara?" he called out.

"Over here, James," Sara said, her voice echoing in the cellar.

He heard her from behind the wall and walked around, finding her crouching on the floor, her back to him, as she seemed preoccupied with something on the floor in front of her.

"Oh, hey, sorry," he said. "I didn't mean to surprise you. Looking at something?"

"Yes, I am," she said, her voice a low purr.

"What are you looking at?"

She looked over her shoulder as he walked up to her. There was some blood around her mouth and a playful twinkle in her big, yellow eyes.

On the cold basement floor lay the mangled remains of a mouse.

"Oh!" James muttered, taking a step back.

She shrugged and gave a cute grin, baring her canines and her sharp, white teeth. "It is... a matter of nature," she purred.

"I see," James muttered, trying to look past her.

In some weird way, she was still hot.

Even hotter perhaps as she squatted on the basement floor, tail swishing, with blood around her lips and just a slightly crazy predator look in her wide, yellow eyes.

The tight shirt and Daisy Dukes she wore, yellow and stained with blood, showed off her perfect body, and the savagely hot element to her personality got James all riled up.

Fuck, James thought... *I didn't expect I'd find this interesting.*

She grinned, and her left ear gave its characteristic twitch. "I haven't seen you come in last night," she said, cocking her head. "Did you sleep at Lucy's?"

There was no judgment, anger, or annoyance in the question — only curiosity.

James was happy about that. She had told him she didn't mind sharing him with other women; but saying and doing were often two different things.

He smiled at her and nodded. "Yeah," he said. "I did."

"And did you have fun?" she asked, a little edge of naughty in her voice.

"Oh yeah, definitely," he said.

She purred and came over on all fours. She crawled toward him, and James didn't hesitate to reach out and touch her soft hair, letting his hand run over her ear.

She gave him a hungry smile, and it took everything in James to keep his hands away from her. Her breasts were heaving as she rubbed her head against his leg. Her thick thighs looked inviting as she smelled him for a moment.

She made a low, guttural noise and hopped to her feet, leaned in close, her breath on his face, her tongue licking his cheek, and her scent filling his nostrils.

"Her scent is on you," she purred. "Lavender..." She drew out the word in a way that made James's cock twitch. "But something else too, hm?" She gave a predator's grin. "A bird? Or a lizard?"

Astra...

He nodded, licking his lips for a moment as his gaze dipped to her luscious cleavage.

Blood had dripped down it, and he was a little disturbed at how turned on he was.

"That was what I wanted to talk to you about," he said, his voice hoarse. "There was a woman — Astra."

"Astra," she purred. "The little Dragonkin girl... You should have spoken to me about her right away, but I suppose it's better late than never."

She moved closer, pressing her breasts against him. "What did she want?"

He nodded. "She knows I'm a mage. She wants me to tell her my spells."

"Hmmm..." Sara said, leaning her head back, her eyes half closed. She stared up at the ceiling.

"She's very bold, isn't she?" Sara muttered. "I can't say I blame her. I'm not so shy about the subject either. But she and I..."

She clucked her tongue and a dangerous light flickered in her eyes. "Well, let's say birds and cats don't get along. She is haughty, arrogant... I do not like her."

"She's a little different from you and I, I guess," James said, his cock twitching again at the dangerous blaze in Sara's eyes.

"Mmmm," she purred, her voice husky. "Yes, I suppose she is. I haven't heard of her in years, though. It's interesting that she's just reappearing now. Perhaps she sensed your presence."

Sara extended a claw-like finger and trailed it along James's chest. "Perhaps she wants a taste," the cat girl crooned.

"It might be the magic," James said. "She told me as much.

Sara's tail swished. "Mmmm... Well, she already knows some spells. She is a spellcaster herself."

"I thought she was a Dragonkin," James said. "Or a Cahay, as she calls it."

"She is, of course, but she's also a spellcaster. She and I have... clashed before."

She was still running her long nail across James's chest, her yellow eyes fixed on the way her finger pushed into the fabric of his shirt.

"You fought each other?"

"Hm-hm," she purred, then looked up at him. "I'm hungry."

He blinked at the sudden change in subject. "Hungry?"

"Did you bring food?"

"Uh, yeah," James said, nodding. He jerked a thumb in the ladder's direction. "I bought enough food from Lucy's store."

"Good," she said, then gave a cute smile. "We will eat first and talk later... perhaps more than talk."

She gave him a wicked grin, then sashayed past him, her tail swirling around his leg for a moment as the savage scent of her — tinged with the iron scent of blood — pervaded his nostrils.

She is crazy hot, he thought as he turned to follow her.

James sat down on the couch, putting his hands behind his head, glad to exchange the dampness and darkness of the cellar for the warmth of the living room.

Outside, the sun was setting, bathing the room in the last orange light of the day. It was peaceful, quiet, and homely, even though the cabin was small.

"I'll make us some dinner," Sara said.

An advantage of the place being so small was that James could watch her as she worked in the kitchen, opening and closing cabinets. He smiled as he studied those luscious curves, her tail swishing around as she prepared the meal.

Every now and then, her left ear gave that characteristic twitch.

"Hey, Sara," James called.

"Yes?" Sara replied.

"Why is your left ear twitching?"

"It twitches?" she asked.

"Yes," he said.

"Well, I was concentrating," she said, setting to work boiling water for some pasta. "Maybe that's why?"

He chuckled. "Might be."

He watched with a smile on his lips as she went to work boiling the pasta and cutting the fresh vegetables to make a sauce. "Need any help?" he asked.

She grinned at him over her shoulder. "Help? Why would I need help?"

He laughed. "True, you seem to be doing just fine."

He continued watching her for a moment before heading outside to get some firewood for a fire. He took a modest supply from the awning to the side of the cabin, as well as a couple of smaller branches and dry inner bark for tinder, and headed back inside.

Sara had put the water on to boil. She was standing next to the stove, smiling at James as he crouched beside the fireplace and arranged the wood and the tinder.

When he got things where he wanted them, he struck a long match and used it to light some of the inner bark.

Pretty soon, the aroma of a fresh fire made its way to his nostrils. He used the poke to meticulously arrange the firewood so that it would catch the flame, then settled back on the couch.

"I should get a spell for that," he said when he caught Sara looking.

She studied him with her big yellow eyes. "A fire spell?"

"Yeah," he said. "I bet I could do it."

"Of the Eleven Elements of Magic, Fire and Lightning are the most difficult," Sara said. "You're probably right. I try to stay away from those spells, apart from those with basic utility."

"Really?" James asked, surprised by this.

She nodded and grinned. "I am a cat girl, after all. We have nine lives, you know, but I'd rather still not waste any."

He smiled. "Fair enough."

"But your spell to boil water is a Fire spell," she purred, "and I have no doubt you can master more fire spells." She smiled at him, a smile that made his heart skip a beat. "You should seek the memories of your Bloodline to learn them."

"How would I do that?" he asked.

"Well," she began, stirring the pasta as she put a pan on the fire for the sauce. "First, you write down everything you know in the Grimoire..."

James perked an eyebrow. "That helps me learn new spells?"

She grinned at him. "It helps you remember the ones you already understand."

He chuckled. "Fair enough. Where is it?"

She licked her lips, then raised her dainty hands. Her left ear twitched for a moment, and then she began chanting.

"*Vanealders tod heer.*

"*Brengang, bestansvlack. Rhuimte.*

"*Vanealders tod heer.*"

She raised both her palms, and a moment later, the Grimoire appeared on them, weighing them down.

"That's amazing," James muttered.

She smiled. "As your familiar, I can store and summon your Grimoire."

Smile still on her lips, she strutted over to him. Her tight shirt and Daisy Dukes outlined the perfect contours of her figure, and the bloodstains still on them didn't bother James one bit.

"It's a spell that belongs to the Element of Space." She bent down, her arms going around him, and placed the Grimoire on the table, her face close to his.

"Write down the one you learned today while I finish cooking," she said as she leaned forward to place the book on the table, offering him a sight of her generous cleavage. "And also write down and memorize the

words to call your Grimoire. It should prove useful."
She followed up with a quick kiss.

"Hmm… sounds good," James said around her kiss,
feeling her soft lips press against his. There was the iron
taste of blood to her still.

She broke away, her grin a little wicked. "You mind
the blood, don't you?"

"No," he said. "I like you just fine."

She licked her lips and her tail swished, giving him a
glimpse of her long, muscular legs.

"I like you too, James Beckett," she purred as she
returned to the kitchen.

He took a moment to examine the Grimoire.

It was a simple tome, with a leather cover, a thick
spine, and pages of coarse, creamy paper. The symbol
of the Eleven Elements of Magic adorned the cover.

Inside, there was the introduction of High Magic,
followed by the two spells he knew: Word of Familiar
Binding and Word of Boiling.

He turned a page and jotted down the words to his
Board Crafting spell.

In addition, he wrote down how he had discovered
the spell. While the process of revisiting the memories
of his ancestors of the House of Harkness seemed of
little interest to the magic itself, it still interested James.

By the time he had finished, Sara was draining the pasta and putting the final herbs in the sauce: basil, thyme, dried oregano, parsley, and red pepper flakes.

James's mouth watered at the aroma that drifted to him.

"Time to eat!" Sara purred.

Chapter 33

They sat down at the small table in the living area. It was all they had.

I'll need to get some proper furniture and some point, James thought. *Something that fits in the cabin.*

Sara had retrieved pewter plates from the kitchen and brought them to the table. She set them down and placed a bowl of pasta on each of them.

"There we go," she said.

"Bon appétit!" James said, mouth-watering at the aroma of the freshly made sauce.

"Thank you," Sara said, smiling at him. "You too!" She picked up her own spoon, but before she could use it, James grabbed her hand and kissed it.

The touch of her smooth, warm skin sent a thrill through him, and he felt the urge to press her body against his.

She smiled at him, a look in her eyes that told him she could feel it as well. "Don't distract me," she purred. "Food first!"

He laughed, then scooped up some pasta with his fork and ate. It was piping hot and delicious, with a balance of herbs that gave it some zest without drowning out the taste of the meat and the tomatoes.

"Hmm," he hummed. "Delicious."

"It is, isn't it?" Sara agreed.

"So," he said, "you were telling me about learning new spells from my Bloodline's memories?"

She nodded. "You got a lot of memories to draw from. As far as I understand, you're the only descendant of the House of Harkness with the aptitude for magic. But I know little of your house's history."

"I'm not sure either," James said. "I have a brother.

Some aunts, too. So, I'm not the only one in the family."

"Yes," Sara said, her tail swishing for a moment. "But not all descendants possess the affinity for magic like you do. I suspect that is what drew you to me in the first place."

She watched him with big yellow eyes as she took another bite of pasta.

"To you?" James said. "I only inherited the cabin."

She grinned. "Such things happen for a reason. It's fated."

"You sound like a fortune teller."

She chuckled, and her tail flicked. "Maybe I am one." She winked at him.

"Maybe you are," James said and laughed before taking another bite of the pasta. He loved the taste of it, and he loved the way Sara's eyes sparkled when she smiled.

She brushed a strand of hair out of her face. "So," she said. "Calling upon the memory is much like what you did for the Boil spell. You direct your intent toward a certain effect, and when you feel the magic loading in your body, almost causing physical pain, you..."

She considered this for a moment, her left ear twitching.

"Well," she continued. "You direct your mind

inward. Like changing focus. The mana you gathered will trigger the Bloodline, and you may see someone in the past who achieved what you desire."

"How do I know if I've been successful?" he asked.

Sara shrugged. "Oh, you'll just *know*." She looked around the room and then back at him. "Once you do, you'll have to put the knowledge into practice."

"I think I understand," James said. "It's like a puzzle. I've got all these pieces, and I have to put them together. I can't just stand there and stare at the pieces. I have to actually build the picture."

"Exactly!" Sara said. "If you've done it right, the spell will activate." She smiled. "It's a wonderful feeling. And then, when it's done, you can call on the knowledge whenever you need it."

"That's awesome." James grinned. "So, I imagine the effect and search the Bloodline's memories?" He took another bite, watching Sara expectantly.

She nodded and licked her lips. "Do you want to try? What would you like to learn?" Sara asked. "What is a power you would like to have? A spell you would want to cast?"

"Well," he said, "I think I should start small. I'd love to learn how to cast a spell to produce a small flame — something to light the fireplace."

"You want to become a fire mage?" she asked.

"Well," he mused. "Not like that. I want to master more magic than just fire. But it sounds like a practical thing, you know? Just like the Boil spell. I could have used that one for the pasta, by the way." He gave her a wink.

She chuckled, her tail swishing playfully. "I know," she purred. "But I like to cook, and waiting for the water to boil somehow relaxes me. Besides, you'd have to maintain the spell for several minutes; that can be straining."

James nodded. "Fair enough."

"But a spell to light the fireplace," she continued. "That should be possible. We can try after dinner."

"Thank you," James said, and he leaned in to give her a kiss on the cheek.

She turned her head real quickly, and her soft lips met his. She purred her satisfaction, gave him a meaningful look, then attacked her food with vigor.

James noticed that she did her best to make sure she had as much meat in the sauce she scooped up as possible.

He had to smile at that; the cat girl's love of food, especially meat, was endearing to him.

With a grin, he dug into the remainder of his plate,

already looking forward to learning his next spell.

After Sara and James finished their meal, they moved to the living area.

They sat down at the small table, Sara nestling herself comfy on James's lap. His loins stirred as she wriggled her shapely ass around to get snug, and he got a few peeks under her short, tight dress, admiring her round ass in her pretty thong. As she sat, her tail wrapped around him with a soft promise.

"So, I guess I should start with the simplest spells," James said, his voice husky as he pushed away temptation — for the moment.

"Pure fire spells with limited effects are easier to cast," Sara said. "The smaller the flame, the easier. Let's try to trigger your Bloodline memory by starting with a candle."

She veered up and reached for a candle on the table, her shapely ass pushing into his face as she turned.

She placed the candle in front of him, squeezing the wick between her thumb and forefinger.

"Okay, let's start with that." She hopped down and

flopped on the floor, looking up at him with big eyes, her left ear twitching once. "Do it!"

"Fire," James muttered to himself.

"Focus on the effect," she purred. "Imagine a candle burning. Your intent must be there."

"Okay," James said. "I'm imagining a candle. It's lit. The wick is burning."

"Good," Sara said, still holding the candle. "Now, imagine the flame growing. Imagine it getting bigger, hotter. It's all you can see."

"Okay," James said.

He focused on the image. He imagined the candle, lit and burning. Power gathered within him. It felt like a flame in his stomach, a slow, simmering warmth. "I feel the mana," he said.

"Good," Sara said. "Now, let the energy grow until it almost hurts you."

James sensed the heat inside him grow. It was almost painful. The energy swirled, becoming a single point of white-hot fire. The energy became a ball, a sphere of power that spun and grew. The light of the fireball swirled around his mind, bright and yellow.

"Inward now," Sara purred. "As we did before. Focus your intent on your Bloodline, your ancestors. Call on the memories of your family and let them trail down into the ages past. Your clan, your house — the House of Harkness. Remember them."

He gave a single nod, sweat beading his brow as he diverted the energy to his memories. A throbbing pain surfaced; it burned in his head.

"The pain is part of it," Sara said. "It's a good sign. Now, visualize what you're trying to accomplish. The flame has to burn brighter, hotter. Let the fire expand and spread. Let the flame burn brighter, hotter, and the power grows."

"Hrmm," James groaned.

"And now think of the ancestors who achieved this!" she purred, and he could hear her shifting her weight excitedly.

"But..." He groaned. "I don't know who achieved this before."

"No, no, not a face. Just visualize the fire in different places, manifesting. See it in a hut, in a hovel, in a castle maybe, in a small house. Keep visualizing while calling upon the memories of your family."

It was like running an internet query — just keep trying different combinations. He tried to imagine the fire in different locations: a forest, a cave, a beach, a field.

Then, on a whim, a ship...

And just like that, he fell through time and space into another ancestral memory.

Chapter 34

James found himself on a ship.

Wood creaked and groaned as the waves rocked it, and the wind whistled through the rigging. The ship's sails billowed and flapped.

The sky darkened overhead, and storm clouds rolled in. The sea rose, and the deck shifted as the winds picked up.

A young woman stood on the deck of the ship. She wore a dark cloak with a hood that hid her face from view. She closed her eyes and breathed in and out, focusing.

Then she opened her eyes, and they were the same piercing green eyes that James saw in the mirror every day.

"Come on," she said — to herself; there was no one else here.

Lightning shot forth, lashing the sky in all directions as the rain came down in torrents. She drew in a breath and exhaled with a sigh. A gale wind tore at the sails, and the ship lurched to one side.

The wind whipped her hair around and tossed the ship about, but she remained standing with great stability and sped toward the galley's aft castle.

James found that he stood stable on the deck despite the storm. He stepped forward. As he did, the ship listed further, and a man slipped past, his scream fading quick as he went overboard.

This was serious.

James followed the woman with the green eyes as she struggled to reach the aft castle. The rain pelted down, and lightning tormented the sky.

She ran across the deck, her hands stretched out to

grab whatever she could, and she stumbled several times, her legs shaking under her as she rose time and time again.

The wind buffeted James's body, and he leaned back against it as he kept up with her. But despite it all, the wind failed to disturb him. He was once again a ghost in this memory of his ancestors.

Finally, she made it to the castle and ducked inside. James followed her and entered as well, stepping through the door the moment she closed it. He was a ghost in that sense of the word, too.

The woman was alone in a small room. In some distant corner, an ancient gray cat shivered.

"Now, where is it?" the woman muttered to herself.

Then, the ship listed starboard, and she lost balance. James shot forward, extending a hard to help her, but even if he could've, he would've been too late.

She bounced against the wall like a rag-doll, and the crunch was so hard that nausea rose from the pits of James's stomach.

A moment later, she hopped to her feet again as if nothing had happened.

Huh, James thought. *That's a nifty trick...*

He wondered if she had some kind of spell to protect her, or if she was just lucky.

"Here we go," she said, ambling over to the desk bolted to the floor.

She pulled open a drawer and retrieved a grimoire that was similar to his. On the cover were the emblems of the Eleven Elements of Magic: Time, Space, Fire, Lightning, Force, Water, Air, Life, Death, Blood, and Earth.

She flipped through the pages, searching for something.

"Ah!" she said.

Then, a sudden gust of wind blew out her lantern. Total darkness enveloped them, lit up only for a moment as lightning raked the sky. In that moment, James saw her wide, green eyes again.

"By the..." she sighed, and he heard her fumble with the lantern, opening the little door.

A moment later, her words thundered through the small cabin.

"Vanluket tod flamma.

"Furanderinghe, verneetigung. Vurra.

"Vanluket tod flamma."

A flame sprang to life, hovering half an inch above her extended forefinger as she stuck it into the lantern and touched the wick with it. The oil on it caught, and the warm light spread through the cabin.

"There," she hummed, hanging the lantern back on its chain before turning to the grimoire. "Now for the *real* magic..."

And like that, the vision faded.

James felt his feet becoming lighter, as if he floated up, and a sharp spark consumed the surrounding scenery.

Once again, darkness washed over him, and the world faded fast as he returned to his own time and age.

Chapter 35

James's eyes shot open. His heart hammered in his chest, and his entire body shook.

He straightened his back in the chair, sweat beading his brow and his breath coming in ragged gasps.

"Sara," he croaked. "That... was intense."

Sara lay curled up in a little ball beside his chair, her tail upright like an antenna.

She sat up and stretched, looking at him with those yellow eyes. "Did you find it?"

He nodded.

"Good," Sara purred. "You did good. Now, what do you want to try next?"

"I don't know," James said. "That was pretty intense."

"Do you remember the words?" she asked, her left ear twitching. "It would be wise to write them in the Grimoire."

"Yes, yes, I remember them."

She smiled. "Good. Try summoning your Grimoire! Have you memorized those words?"

James nodded.

She clapped her hands. "Try it! Visualize the Grimoire!"

James focused on the Grimoire in my mind, seeing the leather-bound tome before me, covered in the emblems of the Eleven Elements.

When James had the image firm in his mind, his intent focused on it, he spoke the words of magic.

"*Vanealders tod heer.*

"*Brengang, bestansvlack. Rhuimte.*

"*Vanealders tod heer.*"

As James spoke, he raised his palms, and the

Grimoire appeared in them.

Sara gave a pleased purr. "Good work," she said.

James's lips curled with no small measure of pride as he felt the weight of the Grimoire in his hands. He actually did it, just like that, and it was getting easier, too.

"You are a natural," Sara said.

He let out a long breath, relaxing. "I guess I am."

She sat at his feet, her hands on his legs as he scribbled down the magic words of his brand-new spell and some details about how he acquired it.

Again, he doubted the details of his ancestral memories were relevant to the magic itself, but he wrote them down anyway, just in case and because it interested him.

"This is a nice one," she purred. "A powerful spell, and one that will prove useful to you."

James frowned. "How so?"

"Fire is the key to life," she said. "You will need it often and for many things. It may bring heat to cold places and light to the dark. It may also destroy those who threaten you, but you must use it wisely and sparingly in that manner. Respect its power."

He nodded. "Thank you, Sara. You are a great help to me."

"Of course," she purred. Her yellow eyes flicked to the candle. "Now, you can light the candle."

He looked down at the candle. The wick rose from the top, almost as if it were challenging him.

Sara looked at him with big yellow eyes blazing with admiration as he leaned forward. He had to glimpse at the words in the Grimoire one more time.

Then he focused on the wick and imagined a happy little flame dancing at the end of it.

Power surged in him, crackling in the channels of his body, and the vision of the flickering flame grew stronger still.

He spoke the words.

"Vanluket tod flamma.

"Furanderinghe, verneetigung. Vurra.

"Vanluket tod flamma."

The wick burst into flame. The wax melted away, and the flame grew higher as it danced its merry jig.

Sara gave an excited yelp and clapped her hands. "See?" Sara said. "A natural!"

He smiled. "Thanks, Sara. You're the best."

She pouted at him as she rose to her knees, trailing a slender finger along the outside of his thigh.

"If that's so," she purred, "then you should reward me properly."

James followed Sara's finger as it trailed along his thigh, a need blossoming in his breast.

"A proper reward, huh?" he muttered, his voice going husky. "That sounds fun."

Sara stood, her tail twitching as she gave him a naughty look, still pouting like a little girl who hadn't had a cookie in days.

"You've been giving Lucy all of your time," she crooned.

"I know," he said, grinning.

Her finger trailed up to his bulge, already hardening, as she watched him with yellow, blazing eyes.

"What dirty things have you been doing to her?" she purred.

He grinned wider. "Oh, just the usual. She loves it."

Sara purred in delight. "She does, doesn't she? Well, then, I must enjoy you and her both soon. I expect you will be quite the active lover."

"You would... *enjoy* us both?"

She licked her lips as her fingers trailed up. A shiver passed through James as those dainty fingers pricked his tightened ball-sack through his pants.

"Oh, yes," she purred. "I would."

He bit his lip and glanced down at where her hand was now stroking, teasing.

"Hmm," she purred as it stiffened under her ministration. "You..." Her eyes widened, and she chuckled. "You even used her ass!"

James swallowed. "Uh, what? How do you..."

She laughed. "Familiars sense these things." She licked her lips. "Did you like it? Do you enjoy using that forbidden hole for your pleasure? Did you revel in pushing her down into her bed and pounding her little rose until you filled it with your seed?"

The naughty light in her eyes — the filthy little promise there — made James's heart pound.

And it didn't help that she kept stroking his cock through his pants.

"Well?" she insisted.

"Yes," James whispered. "I loved it."

"Good," she purred. "I'm sure she did, too. Lucy is a woman of dirty little secrets. A lustful beauty lurks under those innocent blonde locks."

"Hmm," James grunted as she ran her finger up and down his shaft. "Do you... hmm... Do you know her well?"

Sara chuckled, a light tinkle. "I know everyone in Tour." Her other hand moved up to play with James's belt buckle. "Cat girls have their secret ways, remember?"

James chuckled, peering down at this gorgeous creature on her knees before him, her tail swishing, her cute ears perked up, and that wide-eyed curiosity and playfulness in her gaze.

"I'll keep that in mind," he said.

She giggled, then unbuckled his belt with a deft hand before looking at him with pouting lips.

"But you can't give other girls something that you haven't given me," she crooned. "I cannot accept that Lucy has enjoyed pleasures with you that I did not."

James swallowed, his cock nearly bursting from his pants. "You mean..."

"Hm-hm," she hummed. "You must do it to me too."

James's mouth went dry. He nodded slowly. "Of course," he rasped.

"Good boy," she purred, pushing up and kissing him.

Her soft tongue slid into James's mouth, and he felt her hot breath against his as she kissed him. His hands roamed over her body as they embraced, her firm breasts pressing against his chest, her slim waist beneath his palms.

Their kiss deepened, tongues dueling as James pulled Sara closer to him, crushing her to his body as he tasted her sweet lips and the delicate flavor of her flesh.

When they broke apart, James gazed down at her, drinking in her beautiful features and the way her eyes glowed with desire for him.

"Come," she purred, pulling him to his feet.

James followed, heart drumming in his chest.

Chapter 36

Sara pushed James down on the bed, then stood before him, cocking one hip and placing her hand on it. "Are you ready?" she asked.

"Yes," he answered.

Sara smiled. "Then take off your clothes."

He obeyed, kicking off his boots and stripping away his shirt and pants.

The cold air hit him as he sat naked on the bed, but he paid no mind to it, only staring at Sara, who was still clothed in the tight yellow shirt and Daisy Dukes that outlined her perfect curves.

Her nipples were stiff now, and they poked at the fabric in a way that made his hands itch to touch them.

He watched as she hooked her thumbs under the straps of her skimpy top, revealing more of her skin, making her big breasts bounce enticingly.

She peeled off her Daisy Dukes, letting them slip down to her ankles, and stepped out of them, standing before him wearing nothing but a pair of high heels.

"Damn..." James groaned, enraptured by how her silky black hair spilled down her shoulders and the cute and perfect little triangle above her delicious pussy.

With a naughty fire in her yellow eyes, she turned around, showing him her ass. It was round and plump and inviting, bouncing a little as she shifted her weight on her heels.

He could already feel himself hardening even further between his legs.

She turned back to face him, looking over her shoulder at him with that wicked smile on her lips, as she placed her forefingers under the curve of her ass cheeks, pushing them up for him while her tail lifted up, showing her tight crack.

"Do you want this?" she purred.

"Yes," he breathed.

With her eyes still on him, she bent over to retrieve something from her crumpled-up shorts, giving him a perfect look at her inviting asshole and plump pussy lips as she balanced on her high heels, her big breasts swaying as her tail swept from side to side.

At length, she retrieved a glass bottle of lube and tossed it at James.

"Will you do it for me?" she purred.

"Of course," he muttered, voice nearly gone. He took the bottle and opened it, pouring some onto his fingers. "Bring that ass over here," he said.

She bit her lip and moved toward him, click-clacking on those sexy heels, before settling on the bed beside him.

As she did so, she leaned forward and sniffed him with a sigh of delight. Her scent filled his nostrils — sweet, with a hint of muskiness.

He reached out to cup one of her tits, then ran his thumb along the edge of her taut nipple, feeling its hardness.

Sara mewled, closing her eyes as she arched her neck back.

"You like that?" he asked.

"Yes," she purred, arching her back. "I love it when you play with my nipples."

James squeezed her tit, rolling it in his palm, then moved his hand down to squeeze her other breast to her moans of delight.

Her tail curled around his legs. "Hmm... Keep... Ah, keep doing that."

He grinned down at her as he continued to fondle her tits, squeezing and kneading them as she lay there on the bed with her head thrown back and her eyes closed. His free hand slid down to stroke the outside of her thigh, then slipped between her legs to find her heat.

She mewled with pleasure, spreading her legs for him as she sat on her knees on the bed.

He felt her wetness against his fingers as he stroked her slit, sliding his finger inside her tight cunt.

Her clit was swollen beneath his touch, and he pressed down on it with his fingertip, watching as she shuddered, her tail gripping him as her ears folded back.

"Ah!" she gasped. "That's good. Keep doing that, James."

"You're so wet," he murmured. "And tight."

She bit her lip as she ground on his fingers. "Hmm,

James... Please, use your other hand to oil me up. I... I want to feel your fingers in both of my holes."

"Oh?" he asked, smirking and with a teasing edge to his voice. "Are you sure?"

She pushed out her tight little tushy. "Don't tease me, James," she purred. "I've been craving this since we first met. You make me feel so... dirty. Just don't get any on my tail."

He chuckled. "Well, if that's what you want..."

James reached over and grabbed the bottle of lube while Sara jiggled her round ass for him.

He poured a glob of sticky goop over her ass, winning a mewl of delight from Sara as the cold stuff splattered on her luscious rump.

She shivered and squirmed as the glob slipped into her tight little crack, and James's cock bucked in his pants as he placed his hand there, spreading the stuff on her butt cheeks.

Then he repeated the process, working it in between her ass cheeks before coating her puckered hole.

Sara groaned, arching her back as he spread the

slippery fluid. Her asshole twitched at his touch, and he grinned down at her as he coated it thoroughly. He pulled his fingers away to admire his work — a round, slippery ass glib with lube.

"Good girl," he whispered, looking at her round rear end with admiration.

It was so smooth and soft, and he could already imagine himself pushing his rod into her little pucker, making it yield to him.

All the while, he kept massaging her tight little pussy, and Sara was close to begging now, panting and grinding against his fingers as they worked their way through her folds and up to her clit.

"Please," she breathed. "I need more."

"I'm not done yet," he said with a grin.

"But I am!" she cried. "I can't take much more! Please!"

"Then beg nicely," he suggested. "Tell me how badly you want my cock in your ass."

Sara stared up at him with wide eyes, biting her lip as she struggled to control herself. "Please," she finally managed. "Please fuck my ass while you rub my pussy, James. I'll do anything."

His smile grew wider as he watched her struggle for words. "Anything?"

"Yes!" she whimpered. "Anything!"

"You'll be my little slut whenever I want it. Say it."

"I'll be your slut," she moaned. "I'll do whatever you say. I'll suck your cock every day, if that's what you want."

"And what else?" he asked. "What will you do for me?"

She looked up at him, face flushed with arousal, sweat beading on her brow.

She took a deep breath, then lifted her head to meet his gaze. "I'll let you cum in my ass whenever you want," she whispered.

"Hmm," he hummed, placing his hand on her round ass. She quivered with need as he slipped his finger into her crack and teased her tight little pucker as he rubbed her swollen clit.

"Say it again."

"Ahh! James! I'll let you cum in my ass! Whenever you want!" she cried out.

"Good girl," he murmured. He slid two fingers into her pussy and began pushing them in and out of her slick tunnel while he fingered her ass.

"So greedy," he grunted, giving her butt a squeeze. "You like having my fingers inside both of your holes?"

"Yes!" she gasped. "It feels amazing!"

"Mmmm," he murmured, rubbing her clit faster and harder than before. Her juices were flowing freely now, dripping down onto his bedsheets.

"Ah! Ah! Ahhhhh!" Sara cried out, shuddering hard as she squirmed on his fingers, gasping as she tried to catch her breath. "I'm... oh... I'm going to come."

"Good girl," he muttered, smiling down at her as she writhed on his hands. "Come for me…"

He kept pumping her pussy and fingering her tight little rump as she came all over his fingers, crying out and shaking with pleasure as wave after wave of ecstasy washed over her body.

Finally, when she had calmed down enough to speak, she turned to look at him with those big yellow eyes, panting as she smiled at him.

"Did you enjoy that?" he asked, kissing her cheek.

"Yes," she purred. "It was... amazing."

He pulled his fingers out of her little pucker, and it sucked on them as they plopped free.

Her hole was wider now, and she would be ready to take his cock in her ass.

There was no need for words; her eyes said it all as she begged him for it.

With a grin, James rose to undress.

Sara remained kneeling, looking at James over her shoulders, cheeks flushed, as he removed his clothes.

His cock was thick and long and throbbing. The tip of it glistened with precum, and she licked her lips hungrily as she looked up at him.

"Are you ready?" he asked, moving toward her.

"Yes," she replied, voice trembling with anticipation.

He scooted up behind her as she pushed her ass out.

She was still on her knees, toned legs folded under her, wearing nothing but her high heels.

He grunted his appreciation at that glib, open asshole, and placed his hands on her hips. Then he leaned forward to kiss her neck, tasting the sweet scent of her skin, his cock slipping into her crack like a hotdog snug in its bun.

She shivered, leaning back against him as he kissed her throat.

"Oh, yes..." she breathed. "Please... put your cock in my ass and pull my tail."

James grinned as he pressed his cockhead between her cheeks and slowly pushed into her tight little anus.

Sara moaned softly as he sank into her, inch by inch, until his balls touched her soft buttocks.

"Hmm," James groaned. "You took it all in one go, you eager little anal slut." As he spoke, he grabbed her tail, wrapped it once around his fist, and gave it a single tug.

She gave a low meow as he bottomed out inside her, then sighed in relief as he pulled back.

"Ah, James," she crooned. "It's so good to feel your big cock filling my ass." She gave her ass a little wiggle, making the luscious flesh jiggle, and he almost shot his load.

But he wanted it to last...

He pushed in again, making her yelp and stretching her tight little sphincter before pulling out completely, watching her pink rosebud twitch with lust as he did so. He gave her tail another pull, and she meowed with tortured need.

Sara was breathing hard now, sweat forming on her brow as she looked back at him with wide eyes.

"Do it," she whispered. "Use my ass."

"Say please," he suggested.

"Please," she gasped. "Please fuck my ass. Please fuck my ass hard!"

He laughed as he gripped her hips and plunged his

shaft deep into her bowels.

He could feel her muscles gripping him tightly as he drove himself into her depths. Her ass rippled around him, squeezing him in waves as he pumped his cock into her tight little rectum.

"Oh!" she cried out. "Oh god! It feels so good! Fuck my ass!"

"Good girl," he said, smirking down at her. "Keep begging for it. Tell me how much you want it."

She whimpered as he thrust his cock deeper into her ass, pushing past the barrier of her sphincter and sinking deep inside her.

She squirmed beneath him, gasping and moaning as he began fucking her ass roughly, grabbing her waist and pounding her rump with abandon.

"I love your cock in my ass!" she mewled, shuddering as he buried his entire length inside her. "Fuck my ass! I'm yours forever! Take me! Take my ass!"

Her ass was so tight around him now, gripping him like a vise.

He couldn't wait to cum inside her, and he knew he wouldn't be able to hold off for long. He grabbed her tail and tugged it hard, causing her to yelp and arch her back as she came apart in his arms.

He could no longer contain the load in his balls, and he roared as his cock erupted inside her ass, pumping jets of hot semen deep into her bowels.

"Ohhhh!" she gasped. "I can feel your cum filling my ass! Oh god! Yes! Give it to me!"

He held onto her tail as he emptied himself inside her, groaning loudly as his balls spasmed and sent more and more seed shooting into her tight pucker as she quavered and trembled.

Finally, when there was nothing left in his balls, he let go of her tail and pulled out of her ass.

His spent cock slipped from her gaping hole with a slurp, leaving a wire of thick white cum that connected the tip to her stretched orifice.

Sara collapsed onto the bed, panting heavily as she stared up at him with those huge yellow eyes.

She looked exhausted, but satisfied, and that made him smile.

He collapsed on the bed beside her, and she snuggled up warm against him.

Sara and James basked in their post-coital warmth for a

bit before James turned to her with a smile on his lips.

"And?" he began. "Was it everything you hoped it would be?"

"Yes," she replied. "Thank you."

"Thank *you*," he groaned. "It was perfect."

With a smile and a purr, she nuzzled up against him, placing soft kisses on his shoulder.

"Hmm," she hummed. "You're very virile, you know," she said, her left ear twitching once. "You've been doing a lot of fucking..."

He chuckled and shook his head. "Don't worry about that," he said. "I'll save enough for you."

She giggled softly as he leaned over to kiss her cheek, then moved down to scratch behind one of her ears.

"Hmm," she purred. "That's nice." She looked up at him with big yellow eyes. "What will you do tomorrow?"

"Tomorrow?" he asked. "Lucy has one more day of work for me. And I promised Corinne I'd help her guard her chickens at night."

"Ooh," she crooned. "Corinne!" She grinned at him. "I bet you'll get along well with her. I knew she had the hots for you."

He blushed at that. "Well... maybe."

"You should ask her out," she suggested. "You two

are so cute together."

"Are we?" he asked. "I mean, I think she's pretty cool, but I don't really have much in common with her."

"That's not true," Sara insisted. "You both like the outdoors. You're both passionate lovers. You're both adventurous. If you put your minds to it, you could find a way to connect."

He smiled. "I guess that's true."

"Of course it is," she said confidently. "And if you want to impress her, why don't you take her on a date? A real date! A picnic! She'd love that!"

"Hey, that's a pretty good idea." James nodded. "Yeah, I could do that."

"Good!" she exclaimed. "Now, I'm going to get myself cleaned up." With that, she hopped up to her knees and kicked off her heels.

James chuckled, giving her glib ass a wet smack as she veered up from the bed. He then lay back on the bed, hands behind his head, and stared at the rafters.

Slowly, sleep descended on him, and he slipped away to the sweet sounds of Sara softly singing to herself as she cleaned up.

Chapter 37

James got up early and washed up before heading outside to cut some firewood for the next few days. Thanks to the axe he borrowed from Lucy, he could top up his own supply.

And it was nice to be out in the early morning air, with only the sound of his axe hitting the logs, and the occasional bird calling for mates.

It was peaceful here. Quiet. And the air came fresh and wholesome — his lungs were alive with it.

When he returned to the cabin, he found Sara still fast asleep in the bedroom, curled up under a blanket on the bed. The sun was rising now, shining through the window to light up her sleeping form.

She looked so pure and beautiful, it almost hurt to look at her.

He crept into the kitchen quietly, making sure not to wake her, and made himself some eggs.

When he focused on the stove, he grinned broadly. He envisioned a fire blazing out from his finger, like it had with the woman on the ship, then spoke his magical formula as he felt the mana blossom in his core.

"*Vanluket tod flamma.*

"*Furanderinghe, verneetigung. Vurra.*

"*Vanluket tod flamma.*"

The flame sprang to life, and he opened the valve of the propane, lit it, and waved his hand to extinguish the flame. The feeling was more than a little amazing.

Within a minute, the aroma of eggs and bacon filled the cabin. Like any feline, Sara was awake at once and came traipsing into the kitchen with curious, wide eyes.

"Oooh," she purred. "Bacon!"

James grinned. "Want some?"

"Hm-hm!" she hummed, moving up to clasp his arm, a steady purr rising from the base of her throat as she watched him cook.

He cooked two eggs for each of them, along with several strips of bacon.

They ate with relish, savoring every bite, and joked and laughed as they enjoyed their coffee.

Afterward, they sat down on the chair in the living room and cuddled together for a few moments before James decided he had to head out for work if he wanted to finish today.

"Time to go," he said.

Sara snuggled up against him, wrapping her arms around his waist and resting her head on his shoulder.

"I'll miss you," she said. "But I know you have to work."

He smiled and kissed her on the back of her head, between her cat ears.

"Hm-hm," he hummed. "And I'll be heading straight to Corinne's afterwards. I should be back after sunrise."

She giggled softly. "Oh yes! That's right." She turned her head slightly to look up at him. "I can't wait to see you again in the morning. I'll clean up a little and make sure the cabin is nice and cozy when you return."

"Hm, that sounds amazing." He leaned over and

gave her another kiss.

She kissed him back, then hopped to her feet to see him off.

A minute later, he was in the driver's seat of his old sedan, heading down to Rovary's for what he supposed would be the last time for now.

James arrived at Rovary's a little later in the morning than he normally did, so he was eager to get to work. There was a lot of chopping and splitting to do, but he didn't mind. In fact, it was kind of fun; he was getting better at it, too.

He found himself whistling as he set his axe to the first small tree, striking it hard enough to split the wood deeply. His muscles flexed as he swung again and again until he'd brought the bole down to the ground.

Soon, he was working steadily, swinging his axe with a smooth rhythm as he chopped his way through the woods.

He paused occasionally to grab a drink from his water bottle or take a quick break to give his arms some rest. But mostly he kept going, enjoying the feel of sweat trickling down his body as the heat of the day grew stronger.

After an hour or so of this, his stomach began growling loudly, and he realized how hungry he was.

He stopped for lunch and took a few minutes to eat a BLT-sandwich he had prepared that morning and some fruit while he rested against a nearby tree.

As he finished eating, he looked around at the trees all around him. It was quiet here. Peaceful. And he couldn't help but think about how much he liked being alone like this. No one else around for miles. Just him and nature.

He thought about Sara. About what she had told him last night. How she wanted him to ask Corinne out on a date.

He would like that, and he expected Corinne was open to it as well.

Sara had been right; Corinne was his type, really — strong, independent, adventurous, and passionate. Someone who loved the outdoors.

Maybe they could connect somehow?

He'd ask her tonight.

He stood up from his spot by the tree and stretched his arms above his head. Then he shook out his legs and arched his back.

The muscles in his arms burned pleasantly as he worked them, and he felt his chest expand with the effort.

With a grin, he walked over to the nearest tree, hefting his axe. He struck it three times in rapid succession before dropping it. With a grunt, he put aside his axe and dragged the felled tree along. He tossed it onto the pile he had already built and went back to take down another one.

An hour passed, and he was sweating profusely now. His shirt clung to his chest, sticking to his skin, and his hair was soaked with sweat. He was puffing as he lifted the axe high in the air once more. He brought it down hard, splitting the trunk of the tree.

Then he paused to catch his breath. Sweat dripped from his forehead and ran down his face as he wiped it away with his arm.

When he looked up again, he saw a figure perched on the branches of a mighty oak tree, watching him.

Astra was back…

A grin touched James's lips. "Astra," he said, tipping

his head. "How are you?"

She jumped down lightly from the branch and landed gracefully next to him, blue hair falling in waves behind her as her wings folded. Her purple eyes were bright and curious.

"I'm well," she replied. "And you, Mage?"

He shrugged. "Good." He glanced at her, then back at the surrounding trees. "You know... chopping wood."

She laughed softly at that and stepped closer, wrinkling her nose. "Hmm," she hummed. "You have been with Sara. I catch her scent on you."

He nodded. "Yeah. She and I share my cabin." He grinned at that.

"Yes," Astra murmured. "The cabin... You love it there, don't you?"

"I do," James agreed. "It's quiet and peaceful out there."

"Yes," she purred, stepping close to him again.

She smelled like wildflowers with an earthy musk, warm and comforting.

Her purple eyes drifted over him, inspecting his physique as she shifted her weight, giving him an ample eyeful of side-boob under her halter top.

"So many things can happen out in the woods," she

said, voice laden with promise.

He chuckled. "Well, it can. That's true!"

She smiled widely. "Have you thought of my offer?" she crooned, extending a hand to run a long-nailed finger over his chest, plucking at the button of his plaid shirt.

Again, his need stirred at the touch of this exotic creature, but he found it easier to keep himself in check than he had last time.

Perhaps it was because this wasn't just any woman, but someone who radiated something unknown. Sara and she had history, and he would not be too quick to trust Astra.

"I have," he admitted after a moment.

She raised an eyebrow and gave him a sultry glance from under long lashes. "And?"

"And... I'm not sure if I should accept your offer yet," he said. "I mean, we're not even sure where it will lead or what it means for us. Besides, I don't want to 'trade' for affection. I want to earn it."

She perked a blue eyebrow. "You are a peculiar one."

He chuckled. "Maybe so. But I will not *trade*... Maybe we should get to know each other better? We can talk on occasion. I would also like to know why you and Sara don't get along."

She shrugged her fair shoulders. "Dragonkin and cat girls don't get along."

"Why is that?" James asked.

"Because they are different species," she explained simply.

"That's silly," he replied. "There's no reason for that kind of prejudice."

"Silly?" she repeated with a chuckle. "Mage, the Cahay have been around for millions of years. My people never got along with hers. It's always been that way."

"But…" James frowned. "But that's ridiculous!"

Astra shook her head. "No. There is a good reason for it. A grudge runs between our kinds that goes back to the dawn of time, when her kind first emerged from the forests."

"That old, huh?" James said. "And what do you mean by 'her kind'?"

"Yes, the Fae. All creatures such as her — cat girls, fox girls, wolf girls — they are all Fae."

"Oh, and bird girls are so different?"

She drew herself up, an angry light in her eyes. "I am not a 'bird girl'…"

He held up his hands and smiled. "Look, I meant nothing by it! The whole thing just sounds absurd to me."

"Our history is absurd to you?" she said, voice low and dangerous.

Well, this is going great! he thought.

"Of course it isn't," he replied calmly. "And I'm willing to learn about it if it'll help me understand why you two aren't getting along. Like I said, we need to get to know each other."

She relaxed slightly, but still looked a little flustered. "Fine," she said after a few moments. "What do you propose?"

James chuckled. "Well, how about we start with some dinner? And maybe a walk? You can tell me more about yourself."

"A walk?" she murmured. Then she glanced at him. "Why would I walk? I have wings."

He chuckles. "Well, I don't. So unless you want to carry me up there…" He gestured vaguely in the air.

"Hmm," she hummed. "You would ride me, Mage?"

James swallowed, then broke out laughing.

She perked an eyebrow as he rumbled his laugh.

He wiped away the tears that were forming in his eyes and nodded. "Yeah, let's start with dinner and a walk. If it goes well, I'll ride you."

The joke seemed to go over her head. As a different

species, James expected her sense of humor might differ to.

She frowned. "Now? You want to do this now?"

He chuckled. "Well, I need to finish chopping these trees," he said. "And I already got plans for tonight. Look, maybe you can visit me at the cabin, and we can choose a day together? I could show you around."

"The... cabin. Is that not where Sara lives?"

"Hm-hm, but she'll leave you alone at my request. You don't have to fear her."

She stiffened again. "I don't 'fear' her."

He waved it away. "Fine, fine... you don't. But you said your home is not far from here, right?"

"Yes," she replied after a moment.

"Then why don't you come over to the cabin soon, and I'll show you my place?"

She hesitated for a moment before releasing a sigh. "I suppose it wouldn't hurt to see what you're offering."

"Good," he smiled. "You'll be welcome at my house."

She nodded and lingered for a moment, somewhat awkwardly, until she cleared her throat.

"Very well," she muttered. Then she turned and flew off into the sky, leaving James standing under the tree next to his felling axe.

He smiled and shook his head, then got back to work.

He still had a few hours left in the day before Lucy would come pick everything up, and he wanted to make sure she had a good supply and could complete her client's order.

Chapter 38

The light of the day was fading when James finished cutting down what would be the last tree in today's pile.

He'd spent most of the afternoon working on clearing out the glade, and now he stood outside the toolshed, overlooking the day's bounty while he waited for Lucy to arrive.

He heard the sound of her truck first. It pulled into the driveway and stopped behind his car. He saw her step out of the driver's side and walk towards him.

She wore a sleeveless shirt with a high collar that covered her neck and shoulders, which gave way to a short skirt below. Her hair was tied up into a bun, showing off her elegant features.

She gave him a broad smile, one that she reserved especially for him.

"Hello there!" she called brightly.

He grinned back at her, leaning on his axe. "Hey! How are things with you?"

She came up to him, stood on her tippy toes, and placed a warm kiss on his lips.

The slight lavender hint of her perfume enveloped him, and he reached up to touch her cheek, letting his fingers slip through her silky blonde locks.

"Hmm," she moaned, pulling back and fixing her blue eyes on him. "Can I tempt you to come over tonight? I'll cook up something really special."

"I'd love that," he replied. "But I'm afraid I've made plans."

"Hmm," she purred, still in his embrace. "That's a shame."

Her tight body against his was enough to reawaken

his lust, and he was sorry he couldn't take her up on her offer.

He wanted to progress things with Corinne, but there would be more time for Lucy soon — hopefully for both of them, in fact.

He smiled and gave her another warm kiss. "Maybe next time, you can visit me?" he said. "I'll cook you a meal."

"Oh," she cooed, giving him a playful poke. "That sounds nice."

Then she stepped back and looked him over. "You look like you've been working hard all day."

"I have," he replied with a nod. "How about you? You must have worked very hard, too."

"Well," she murmured, smiling slightly as she ran a hand through her hair. "It was a busy day, and my customer is eager for the final shipment."

James grinned. "Oh, the mystery customer!"

She laughed, giving him another playful poke. "Shush, you!"

He laughed along and gave her another kiss, which she answered with fervor. "Well, let's load up your truck," he said after they broke apart.

They walked together to the pile and began moving the lumber onto the flatbed of Lucy's truck.

Once everything was loaded up, Lucy drove back to town, while James followed in his own car. When she arrived at the shop, she parked the truck, and they met in the lot.

The sun was setting, and James had to admit that Lucy was more beautiful than ever in its rosy light.

She huddled against him, burying her soft hands under his shirt. "Hmm," she purred. "You sure?"

He laughed, taking a whiff of her delicious scent. "You're making it awfully hard to say no..."

She grinned up at him, a mischievous twinkle in her eye. "I'm committed," she crooned. She giggled and wrapped her arms around him, pressing herself close.

"Hmm, so am I," James agreed. "But I can't let Corinne down."

She looked up at him with her big blue eyes. "Ah, Corinne, is it?" she said.

He smiled and nodded. "I hope you're not jealous," he said. "It doesn't change the way I feel about you."

She shook her head. "I'm... well, I'm not sure, actually."

She bit her lip and stared down at the floor. "I mean, yes, I want you to be happy. And the idea of sharing you... it's kind of exciting. But I don't know how I should feel about it." She looked up at him. "What will people think?"

James shrugged his shoulders. "You worry too much about what people think," he said. "The truth is that most people won't even care. And even if they do, what would it matter to us if we're happy?"

She nodded slowly. "I guess that's true... I just feel weird about it."

He smiled and gave her a kiss on her forehead. "Think about it for a while, okay? Maybe ask yourself what you think is most important to you? How *you* feel, or how *others* feel."

She sighed and leaned into him again. "I suppose that makes sense," she murmured.

They stood there for a moment in silence, enjoying each other's company.

Finally, James broke away from her embrace and took her by her hand.

"Come on," he said. "I'm going to be your last customer for the day."

She smiled; one blonde eyebrow perked. "Oh, what are you buying?"

"I need an axe of my own," James said. "And a hatchet for some finer work, as well as some tools for woodworking like a saw and carving knives..."

"That sounds ambitious," she said, curiosity in her

big blue eyes. "What are you planning?"

"I want to expand the cabin," James said. "I'd like to build a workshop out back, for starters."

"That sounds like a lot of work," she mused.

James grinned. "I have a few tricks up my sleeves," he said, thinking of his Board Crafting spell. It would save him a lot of time, even though he intended to use logs for the walls.

"How long will it take?" Lucy asked.

He thought for a moment before answering. "A couple of weeks, maybe? I'll have to buy supplies first, but once I get started, I think it will go quickly. Thanks to you, I don't have to worry about money for a while."

She smiled and squeezed his hand. "I'm glad to hear that," she said.

Then she pulled him towards the door. "Well, let's get you set up. I should have most of the things you need!"

Chapter 39

With the trunk of his busted-up sedan full of tools and equipment, James drove north up Main Street and out of Tour toward Corinne's farm.

It was the same road that led to his cabin, and he was becoming intimately familiar with the surroundings. He knew every bend in the road, every hilltop, and every tree along the way.

The sun caressed the world with its last rays, but the air was still warm and pleasant. The sky was clear and deep blue, the clouds high above floating gently across it.

A gentle breeze blew through the open windows of the car, and James felt refreshed, if a bit sweaty from a hard day's work.

He relished the fresh breeze and let his fingers tap the wheel as he hummed a song to himself, feeling good.

Soon enough, the clearing with the old barn appeared, flanked by some tall pine trees. He slowed down as he drove up to the large gate and the partially overgrown fence that marked Corinne's grounds.

As he got closer, he could see that the gate had been left slightly open, which meant that she was expecting him.

He drove up the lane, past the barn that led to Corinne's farm. The farmhouse stood at the far end of a long driveway, flanked by old trees, which made James think the farmhouse had been here for a while.

Still, it was small and in dire need of repair; it looked like Corinne had spoken the truth when she said that times were hard for her.

He parked his car in front of the house and stepped out into the cool evening air. He stretched his arms and closed his eyes for a moment, savoring the feel of the wind on his skin.

Then he opened his eyes and walked up to the door. After knocking twice, he waited for several moments until he heard footsteps approaching from inside.

The door swung open and revealed Corinne, looking more beautiful than ever.

She wore a stained shirt, tied up with a knot to reveal her toned stomach, and faded Daisy Dukes that revealed her smooth legs, tanned from working outdoors. Her ginger hair fell loosely around her shoulders, framing her face in beautiful fire.

She gave him an awkward smile as she reached up to brush the stray strands behind her ear. "Oh, damn," she muttered. "Is it this late already?"

She sighed and gestured down at her stained outfit. "I wanted to clean up before ya got here..."

"It's fine," he replied. "I just came from work myself." He looked her up and down. "Besides, you look beautiful."

She gave a shy smile. "You mean that?"

He nodded and took her hand in his own. "Very much so."

She blushed and turned away, leading him inside. "I've got a kettle on the stove," she said. "I'll make us something to drink."

Corinne bustled around the kitchen, making tea for them both.

The kitchen was big, but old. It would not surprise James if the farmhouse had been in Corinne's family for several generations.

There was a large table at the center, and Corinne had parked James on one of the old wooden chairs in dire need of replacement.

The tablecloth was a checkerboard affair that would have done well in the seventies, and most of the cutlery and other stuff wasn't much more modern.

Still, James didn't mind; he liked earnestness in people, and Corinne wasn't hiding anything from him. This was who she was, and she made no point of putting on appearances.

Corinne seemed nervous as she moved around, and James couldn't blame her — they'd never spent much time alone together, and it was obvious her house wasn't exactly in the best shape.

And she probably felt a little scruffy in her outfit, too,

completely unaware that her stained shirt and old Daisy Dukes made her every part the sexy farmer's daughter.

He sat at the table and watched her move around the room, admiring her lithe form. She was all curves and smooth, freckled skin, and he wondered what it would be like to bury his face between those luscious thighs.

He tried not to stare at her ass in those tight Daisy Dukes as she went about preparing their drinks, but he failed miserably.

She finally set two cups down in front of them and handed one to him. "Here you go," she said.

"Thanks," he said. "So, how are things?"

Corinne's normally so bright demeanor was quavering, and he could tell she was close to breaking out in tears.

It took her a moment to compose herself before she spoke again. "Things aren't good," she said quietly. "I'm barely keeping my head above water. I can't pay the bills anymore... I'm going to lose the farm if I don't find a way to get some money soon."

James put his cup down on the table with a clink and leaned forward, putting his elbows on the table. "What happened? How did things fall apart?"

She bit her lip and looked down at her hands. "I didn't have any insurance," she murmured. "And then

316

there was the accident..."

"Accident?" James asked.

She nodded. "My tractor broke down last year. The engine needed expensive repairs, and since I don't have any insurance, I had to pay for it myself."

"That sounds expensive," he said. "How much did it cost you?"

"A lot," she whispered. "I borrowed from a bank... but I can't really make the payments. The harvest was bad." She sighed. "And now this damn fox or whatever is at my chickens."

A wet sheen covered her green eyes as she wiped her cheeks with the back of her hand. "Eggs were doin' good until that bastard came along... Now I can't meet the demand."

James reached out and placed his hand over hers. "We'll deal with the fox tonight," he said. "What else can I do to help?"

She swallowed away the lump in her throat and threw him a grateful look. "I... I could really use a hand around the farm. But... I have no money to pay with. It all goes to the bank."

He nodded and squeezed her hand. "I understand," he said. "You don't have to pay me. I'll help you for free."

Her face lit up with relief. "Really? That would be wonderful! If you're willing to help me out, I promise I'll do everything in my power to repay you!"

He smiled and stood up from the chair. "Don't worry about it. I'd be happy to help you, Corinne."

She beamed a smile, some of her worries washing away. "Well, at least let me cook dinner first," she said. "Then we can talk more about your plans."

"Sounds great," he replied.

Chapter 40

Corinne got to work with fresh ingredients, chopping up vegetables — carrots and celery — while she gave James a knife and let him peel potatoes at the kitchen table.

It was nice and easy to cook together, and James didn't mind the job at all.

"It's all from my farm," Corinne chirped, some of her

good cheer returning. "Fresh and biological. I try to grow it all as my ancestors have grown it all for..." She touched her plump lips for a moment. "Well, for over a century, I guess!"

James nodded and continued peeling. "It smells delicious."

He cut into a potato and inspected it before splitting it in two and tossing it into the pot.

"So... what sort of stuff do you usually grow here?" he asked.

"Hmm... Well, I plant broccoli, horseradish, peas, onions, and parsley in spring. Those can take a beating, so it doesn't matter if there is a brief cold snap. Once I'm fairly sure we've seen the last frost, I'll plant potatoes — lots of 'em — parsnips, celery, carrots, and beets. When spring is good and well underway, I plant snap beans and cucumbers mainly. I have a greenhouse for tomatoes."

"What kind of herbs do you grow?" James asked.

"Basil, mint, oregano, rosemary, sage, tarragon, thyme, chives, dill, bay leaves, garlic, lavender, marjoram, lemon balm, and many others," she rattled off without missing a beat.

James laughed. "Wow."

She threw him a grin over her shoulder as she began

chopping up a batch of fresh tomatoes.

"Yeah, pretty much anything that grows in my garden will probably end up in one of my meals. What I have left, I sell in town — usually to Lucy. She gives me a fair price, and a few other folks from Tour come by on their own when I'm harvesting. That's how I get by."

"How long does it take you to harvest all this?" he asked.

"Oh, once the harvest begins, I get almost no rest at all." She chopped up some more tomatoes. "I start early in the morning and continue after lunch. By the time the sun sets, I'm ready for bed."

"That must be hard," he said.

She shrugged and turned back to him. "It's honest work, and I love being outside." She put her hands on her shapely hips and eyed the pot of peeled potatoes. "You about done with them there spuds, Mr. Beckett?"

I laughed and nodded, pushing the pot over the table to her. "All done!"

She grinned. "All right," she said. "Time to boil and mash these puppies!"

She placed the pan on the fire and added water from the kettle.

With all the vegetables cut up, she sashayed over to the table and poured them both another cup of tea.

James watched her with pleasure, reveling in the scene's homeliness. He could imagine himself spending more time with Corinne.

He really did want to get to know her better.

And he had a feeling that a good way to get to open up was to talk about the farm.

"So," he began. "I take it things used to be better around the farm?"

She laughed. "I don't wanna bother ya with all that!" she said.

"It's not a bother at all!" he said. "I'd love to hear."

She threw him a soft glance, her big green eyes still a little wet from the tears shed earlier.

"All right," she said. "If ya really wanna hear!"

Corinne took a sip from her drink and considered her words for a moment before she began talking.

"Things were fine until three years ago." She sighed. "My father died suddenly, and I had to run the farm alone."

She shook her head. "It was too much for me to handle. But I tried. I really did. It's just..." She threw up her hands. "The place needs more than one person."

"I'd imagine a lot of guys would love to live here with you."

"Hmm," she hummed. "Maybe. I never met anyone that struck my fancy. And I'd be damned if I'd settle for anyone I don't really love."

James gave her an appreciative look. "You shouldn't. Things'll come apart if you try with someone you don't like."

She fixed him with her deep green eyes. "Hm-hm," she agreed, running a slender finger along the edge of her teacup.

"So, what about James Beckett?" she asked. "I bet the girls are all knocking at your door."

He raised his eyebrows. "You think so?"

She smiled knowingly. "Oh, yeah."

"Well, they're not exactly lining up," he replied.

As she looked at him with a knowing grin, he wondered how much he should tell her. She probably didn't know that Sara existed and — like Lucy — would probably know nothing of magic. Telling her here and now might only make her think he was crazy.

He decided to keep quiet for now.

"What about Lucy?" Corinne asked.

He ran his tongue over his teeth, considering what to

say, but she broke out laughing.

"Oh, come on, James!" she called out, pulling at her bottom eyelid. "I'm not blind, you know?"

James laughed along with her. "Fine! Fine! You caught me!"

"Good," she said with a wink. "She's a nice woman." There seemed to be some dejection in her tone.

"Well..." James began, rubbing his chin thoughtfully, wondering how to approach this. Encouraged by Sara, he was convinced that having multiple girlfriends would be best for him.

But how was he going to broach that subject with Corinne?

He'd only just told Lucy, and now he needed to see if she would be on board.

Corinne had a broad smile on her plump lips, one ginger eyebrow still raised. "Well, what?" she prompted him, a teasing edge to her voice.

He smiled. "Lucy's definitely nice," he said. "We're exploring things, seeing how we feel about each other."

"That sounds interesting," Corinne said. "Exploring is fun."

The little twinkle in her eye told James that the fat lady hadn't sung just yet when it came to his chances with Corinne.

He grinned and casually shrugged his shoulders. "So," he said, changing the subject, "Have you lived here in Tour all your life?"

"Ha!" she yelped, throwing a potato peel at him. "Changin' the subject ain't allowed!"

He laughed, swatting the peel away. "You're ruthless, Corinne," he joked.

She grinned and flopped down in the chair opposite his, elbows on her table to afford him a generous look down her freckled cleavage. She was a delight — a naughty little delicacy.

"Did you and Lucy... ya know?" She wagged her head, wriggling her eyebrows.

He laughed. "What's that supposed to mean?" he asked, mockingly imitating her wagging and wriggling. "What is that?"

"Oh! You're gonna make me say it?"

He nodded. "I'm gonna make you say it."

She leaned in. "Did you have sex with Lucy?"

"I don't kiss and tell."

"Pah!" she exclaimed, tumbling back in her chair before fixing him with her green gaze, coppery eyebrow raised. "I guess I'll just have to ask Lucy herself."

"You do that," he said, leaning back.

Corinne fluttered her lips, frustrated because he

wouldn't spill the beans.

She hopped to her feet and checked on the potatoes, and James swore she was making a bit more of an effort to sway her generous hips as she walked.

Fantasies of having a tumble in the hay — literally — with this country girl once again surfaced in James's head.

He pushed them away for now. She was definitely flirting, but he wanted to take a gentle approach.

Even though her booty in those Daisy Dukes was making it very hard...

"So, let me try this again," James said after a while. "How long have you been living in Tour?"

She turned around with a wooden spoon in her hand, holding it like a baton. "I've lived here my whole life," she answered.

"Really? How old are you?"

She smirked. "I'm twenty-two years young."

He nodded slowly. "That must be hard sometimes."

She gave him a quizzical look. "Why would it be hard?"

"Well, you live alone on a farm." He gestured toward the garden outside. "It's hard work to do alone."

She shrugged. "My dad taught me it's best to just work hard and not whine too much." She paused, thinking for a moment. "Besides, I love being alone. It gives me time to think."

"Do you ever get lonely?" he asked.

"Sure. But I'm used to it by now." She smiled. "And there's always the chickens to keep me company."

He chuckled. "So, where did you learn all this stuff about farming?"

"Oh, well," she said with a shrug. "I grew up watching my father do everything. I learned by doing."

James nodded. "That makes sense." He studied her as she went about her business, chopping vegetables and stirring pots.

Her movements were smooth and graceful, and watching her work was a joy. He could get used to a life with Corinne in the kitchen.

"I bet you made your father very proud," he said.

She stopped what she was doing and looked at him over her shoulder. "I sure hope so," she replied, smiling warmly. "I know he'd want me to follow in his footsteps."

She turned back to the pan and continued working.

"And it helps that following in his footsteps is exactly what I want to do."

James nodded. "Good." He sat quietly while she worked, listening to the sounds of her chopping and the bubbling of the boiling potatoes.

Moments later, the delicious aroma of freshly cut onions, garlic, parsley, and basil filled his nostrils, and he felt his mouth watering.

"And you?" she asked, shooting him a glance over her shoulders. "What are your dreams? Whose footsteps are most appealing to Mr. James Beckett?"

He smiled. "Love, family, happiness... Those are the things I want. I'd be perfectly content living in my cabin if the company is good. Perhaps a little adventure now and then, but nothing too heavy. Peace and quiet will do for me."

She giggled. "Wow! That sounds really nice! I wish I could get some peace and quiet. But there's always something to do next."

He folded his hands behind his head, gaze following her with a content smile. "Well, I don't mind hard work, you know? Getting up early, getting stuff done — that's pleasurable to me." He laughed. "I can't imagine how people manage their lives without doing any work!"

She grinned back. "You're right," she said. "If I never had any work to do, I'd probably go crazy." She shook her head. "But it's just that..." Her voice trailed off, looking down at the rattling pot with boiling potatoes.

"It's what?" he asked.

She sighed. "It's just that sometimes it seems like everyone else has it easy, while I'm struggling to survive."

"I understand what you mean," he said. "It helps when you're not alone, when you have someone to help you pull through the hard times, and someone you can help when they're having a rough time. It feels good to help someone you love."

Her face lit up like a sunrise. "Yes! Exactly!" she exclaimed. "We should all be more like that."

He smiled. "Well, let's see if we can make a difference in our own small way." He leaned forward and gave her a wink.

She chuckled. "Well, *you* have Lucy."

"Hm, maybe I have my eyes on more than just Lucy."

Corinne threw James a glance that betrayed more than a little interest.

"Is... is she okay with that?" she asked, genuine curiosity in her voice.

"She's thinking it over," James said.

"Ha... Wow, you're serious."

"Yep."

A slight flush crept up her cheeks as she considered it, and she looked cute as a button with her blushing, freckled face, slightly pouting as she milled over the ramifications of what James had said.

He chuckled. "The potatoes are boiling over."

"Oh gosh!" she fluttered, quickly turning back to turn down the fire. "I forgot to add a little butter. It usually does the trick. Well, they're done anyway."

James smiled and took a sip of his tea. As Corinne got to work to mash the potatoes, he gave her another appreciative look. He was pretty sure that she was interested in him and in what he was building.

With some luck and charm, she might just be aboard...

Chapter 41

At length, Corinne finished putting layers of vegetables, beef, and mashed potatoes in an oven dish, finally topping it all off with a layer of cheese.

"Cottage pie!" she purred, showing James the delicious end product, and the sweet aroma of beef, cheese, and herbs and spices made his mouth water.

"That looks great!" he said.

They spoke lightly while it baked in the oven, touching on things they had in common, most of which turned out to be related to the outdoors.

When the food was ready, Corinne served it up with a fresh garden salad, and they both dug in with relish.

"Hm," James said after taking his first bite. "This is really good! Spicy!"

She smiled. "Yeah, my dad taught me to make it spicy. He liked it that way."

"A wise man," James said, reveling in the sharp flavor. "This is great!"

She blushed slightly. "I'm glad you like it!"

James finished his first plate in no time, and Corinne helped him to seconds.

She was a little more of a modest eater herself, but she enjoyed watching James eat.

Together, they finished most of the cottage pie and the salad, and they shared a few more moments of companionable silence after that while their meal settled, broken only by James's repeated compliments for Corinne's exquisite cooking.

"So," she asked at length, "Do you think you'll ever settle down here?"

He smiled and gave a half shrug. "I like it here," he said. "The place is just what I was looking for. And now that I've found it, I don't want to leave. I can't speak for all time and all days to come, but I'm content here for now."

She nodded slowly. "Good," she said. "Because I kinda like you."

He grinned at her. "Well, I kinda like you too."

They shared a moment in silence before James decided to go for it. The cards were on the table, so why not?

"In fact," he began, "I'd like to take you out on a date."

"But... what would Lucy..."

"I think she'll be fine with it, Corinne," James said. "You know each other, and you get along."

"Yeah, but... wouldn't she think I'm, like, buttin' in or something?"

He considered this for a moment. "So, why don't we try this?" he said. "You talk to Lucy first. Ask her how she feels. Then, you think about how *you* feel. And when all of that is done and worked out, you come give me your answer." He smiled. "Unless you don't want to date me at all, in which case you can say 'no' right now."

She licked her lips, and a sly smile appeared on her plump lips. "No... I would like to date you."

"Well, then," he said. "It sounds like you have your answer already."

He stood up and held out his hand. "Shall we go do the dishes and then get to business?"

She looked at him curiously but took his offered hand and allowed him to pull her to her feet. Her eyes sparkled as she rose to her full height.

They shared a moment like that, peering into each other's eyes, sensing the heat between them rise.

When they broke eye contact, Corinne took his hand and led him towards the kitchen door.

"Here it is!" Corinne said

She handled the rifle with care as she placed the weapon on the table in front of James. She set it down gently, as though afraid the rifle might go off if she moved it any more than necessary.

James examined the weapon.

It was an old Winchester Model 1894, a lever action .30-30 caliber rifle.

The barrel and stock were scuffed, but otherwise seemed sound enough. The rifle had seen decades of proper care, and it showed. The weapon came with a box of cartridges, the brown cardboard so old it was barely rigid anymore.

"It used to be my dad's," Corinne said. "And his daddy's before him."

James nodded. "How long has it been since you've fired this thing?" he asked.

"Oh gosh," she said, flustered. "I haven't shot it in ages! I probably should clean it off and oil it up before I use it again."

"That won't be necessary," he said. "I've handled guns before."

He pulled the lever down and checked if the chamber was empty. She still moved smooth as butter with a gentle click.

"Bring out the oil and a piece of cloth, please," he said. "The rod, too, if you still have it. I'll clean her and make sure everything is in order before we go out to the coop."

She gave a happy nod, a big smile on her lips. "Sure."

He smiled back at her. "You okay?"

"Yeah," she said. "Just... Seeing you like that reminds me of when dad was still here." She made a face. "Not that you remind me of him or... like, anything *weird*. But... I..."

He raised an eyebrow.

"Foot in mouth," she muttered.

James laughed. "A screwdriver, too, please."

She grinned. "Yeah..."

James watched her hop off with a broad grin on his lips.

Corinne was growing on him for sure.

She returned a moment later with a maintenance kit for the rifle, and James got to work disassembling that rifle, an old cornerstone of the US, as far as he was concerned.

It was a classic design and one that never went out of style. A good shooter, reliable, easy to maintain — these were some of the reasons why the Winchester Model 1894 remained popular even after the advent of better technology.

He cleaned the bore and the action, although he found very little dirt — it had been put away in an excellent state.

Once that was done, James let it dry for a few minutes before applying some oil to the action.

"If I have a little more time, I'll disassemble her for you and give her some more thorough maintenance," he said to Corinne as she looked over his shoulder with big eyes. "But for now, this will do."

She nodded vigorously. "Great!"

She served him up a fresh cup of strong coffee while they waited for everything to dry.

"Here," she said, handing him the cup of steaming goodness. "You'll need it if you're going to sit through the night..."

James took the cup with a smile and nodded. She made a good cup of coffee — strong and plain. He appreciated a well-brewed espresso like most did, but there was still a lot he loved about good old American coffee, and it certainly did the trick to keep him awake through the night.

He did a last inspection of the old rifle after he finished his cup of coffee, then slung it over his shoulder, tucking a handful of cartridges into the breast pocket of his plaid shirt.

Corinne gave James an appreciative once-over as he stood up and stretched, and he winked at her.

She blushed slightly. "You look nice," she said. "Something about a man who carries a rifle with confidence."

"Well, I'm just happy I can help," James said. "And I'm glad you trust me to do that."

"Hmm, you look like you can handle it," she said, smiling.

"Well, I think it's time to head out," he said. "Can you show me the coop?"

She nodded. "You have a warm coat? It's bound to get cold."

"I do," he said. "We'll get it from my car on the way out."

She made a happy little hop. "Great! Let's go."

Chapter 42

Corinne and James headed out into the evening with a pair of electric torches.

The sun had set — except for a little strip of light in the west — and Corinne had been right; the temperature was steadily dropping. James took his fur-lined coat from his trunk before they headed toward the coop.

She led the way, her cowboy boots crunching on the gravel road. The dark green jacket she wore hung loosely from her shoulders, and it didn't cover her round butt in the Daisy Dukes.

"How old is the farm?" he asked as he walked alongside her.

"It's been in my family for five generations," she said. "It's a small farm, but it's always been big enough to support us. But now, it's a little *too* big. I can't do it all by myself."

"You have no siblings?"

She shook her head. "No. Just me. I'm an only child."

She shot him a grin over her shoulder. "Kind of a break with tradition as we used to have big families! My dad had seven brothers and sisters."

"And none of them want to help?" James asked.

She gave him a sly look. "Not really." She giggled. "I like to think of it as them being too busy to come visit. They moved to the city. Big careers and big money."

James laughed. "I guess that makes sense."

They arrived at the coop, and James surveyed it with a frown.

It was a big one, with plenty of chickens still clucking, although they would sleep soon. A wire-mesh fence encompassed the coop, and it looked sturdy and well-maintained, if perhaps a little old.

He perked an eyebrow. "Wait... How does a fox get in here? They don't fly or anything."

"I have no idea," Corinne said. "I inspected everything. It's almost like magic to me; I don't know how it works. The chickens just disappear. I don't know how that could happen. I thought at first that it maybe dug its way in, but there's no sign of any of that."

James nodded. "That's kind of strange."

She wrapped her arms around herself and shivered as a gust of wind cooled the air around them.

"Go on back inside," James said, seeing her shiver. "I'll stay out here for the night."

She gave him a smile that warmed his heart, then walked over to him. She got up on her tippy toes, then placed a warm kiss on his cheeks.

"You're the best," she said after she drew back. "I'll bring you some hot cocoa, a chair, and a couple of blankets."

James smiled, the warmth of her kiss still on his cheeks.

"That sounds great. I'll set up over there." He pointed at an old tree with a good view of the coop. A little out of the way and downwind of the forest. "That way, the fox won't smell me."

She nodded, her green eyes a little bigger. "Good idea! Okay, settle in, cowboy. I'll be back in a sec."

He watched her go with a grin on his lips before ambling over to the tree and setting up. There was a fresh breeze blowing, but his coat kept him comfortable.

He sat down and leaned back against the trunk of the tree. This was a good spot; he could see the coop clearly from here.

As he waited for Corinne to return, he thought about how much he enjoyed spending time with her.

She was a fun girl, and she was pretty, too. And unlike some of the women he'd known in the city, there was a warmth to her that reminded him of summer days spent by the lake, careless and free. Corinne was a country girl at heart.

When she returned with hot cocoa and a few snacks — biscuits, jerky, and a bar of chocolate — he was pleasantly surprised. He had expected her to bring him something simple, but she went out of her way to make sure he was comfy. She also brought him a bundle of blankets, a folding chair, and a lantern.

Still, she was shivering from the cold, so he took the tray from her and set it down on the ground.

"Thank you," he said. "This is perfect."

"Of course," she said. "Anything I can do. I'm really

happy that you're helping me out. I can finally catch some sleep without worrying about my chickens."

"If you need anything else, let me know," he said. "I'll be out here all night; you can call me anytime."

She gave him a warm smile. "All right. Thank you."

He smiled back at her. "Not a problem."

With that, Corinne left for the night, heading back to the farmhouse.

James watched her leave, a smile on his face, until the swaying beam of her electric torch went inside. When she was gone, he stretched and made himself comfortable in the chair, the rifle on his lap.

With care, he pushed a few cartridges into the feed system, but he didn't work the action just yet; he would do that only when necessary.

After that, he warmed his hands on his mug of cocoa and began his nightly vigil.

It was a beautiful night, not a cloud in the sky, and James could've counted the stars — they were so clear.

He sat on the ground next to the tree, leaning back against the trunk, watching the coop. It was a quiet night, the only sound coming from the rustling leaves. The chickens were all sleeping peacefully.

James had the lantern on and stayed vigilant, allowing his thoughts to stray a little as his eyes remained on the coop.

His mind drifted; he thought about Corinne, how she was such a sweetheart, and how he hoped to spend more time with her. He first imagined homely scenes with her in the kitchen, having breakfast together and laughing.

But his mind swiftly drifted to dirtier avenues. He imagined her naked body beneath him; her legs wrapped around him as he claimed her womanhood.

Next, his mind wandered to the image of her soft lips wrapped around his cock, her big breasts bouncing as she slobbered and gagged on his length. Then he imagined her riding him, her thighs squeezing his hips as she bounced up and down on him.

Soon enough, he saw Lucy and even Sara in that mental picture, and he imagined what it would be like to have all those sultry women in a king-sized bed, all to himself, pounding them in turn and filling them with his love. He saw them on their knees and backs, a welter of shapely legs and bouncing breasts for him to drown in, to breed, and to make his.

He would give Corinne that big family that he suspected she craved, and he could make Lucy a mother as well. Perhaps even Sara, although she was a bit of a wild one.

As he thought of his women in those ways, he became harder than he had been in a long time. But he enjoyed the fantasies and explored them further.

Until a rustling in the leaves roused him.

He perked up in his chair, peering at the chicken coop.

Something was moving; he spotted it through the mesh fencing on the other side of the chicken coop.

He couldn't make out what it was, but whatever it was, it was moving fast. It seemed like it was coming from the woods, so he grabbed the rifle and stood up, the stock of the weapon braced against his shoulder.

All of a sudden, the chickens were awake. The ones near the fence clucked in panic as the rustling intensified.

What the hell? James thought. *Is it in the coop?*

He stepped forward, lowering the rifle. At that very same moment, a slender figure broke free from the nearby trees and stepped forward.

Although it was dark, James discerned the details. The figure moved in a slightly crouched walk and was decidedly feminine. She was athletic and toned, with thick, luscious thighs, and supple breasts that jiggled a little with each sneaky step.

But what drew the eye most were fox ears and three fluffy tails…

A fox girl…

Astra had spoken of them. The Fae, she had called them — related to cat girls.

That was all James had time to consider before the fox girl saw him.

James's eyes widened; he couldn't help it.

She froze in place like a deer in the headlights, her eyes wide as saucers. Even in the dim moonlight, he saw one eye was green; the other blue. Her long, velvety hair was as red as the fur of a red fox with streaks of white in it.

She wore clothes that betrayed a life in the wild, made of furs and hides. Everything about her posture betrayed agility, speed, and quick reflexes.

"Stop!" James called out. "It's all right! I'm not going to hurt you."

She didn't move, just stood there with the moonlight shining on her, and James had a hard time not getting distracted by the ample cleavage offered by her scanty attire or the pale skin of her thighs revealed by her loincloth.

Hot damn, he thought.

He kept the rifle low so as not to pose too much of a threat, and he stepped forward. She took a step back, her multi-colored eyes wide, and seemed to crouch into a defensive posture. James watched her warily as he took another step.

"It's okay," he said.

Then she bolted like a scared deer.

He took a step forward, almost as if to run after her, but she vanished so much quicker than he could ever have kept up with.

She was gone, and all that remained were the chickens; they were still clucking.

After a few moments, he chuckled. "That is one quick fox girl," he said to himself. He couldn't help but laugh at the way she'd run away.

Then he thought about her again — her coppery hair with streaks of white, her big eyes, and those fluffy tails.

She was so different from anyone he'd ever seen before. He wasn't sure if she was human or not; maybe a wild spirit that had come to take the chickens? She was probably like Sara — a magical mix between human and animal.

Although he didn't understand Sara's nature very well yet, either. All he knew was that she was a familiar.

Maybe the fox girl was, too?

Before he could think much more on it, a new sound interrupted his thoughts: the soft tread of boots on gravel.

James turned around to see Corinne standing there with a lantern in her hand. She peered into the darkness, her brow furrowing at the sight of him.

"Are you okay?" she asked. "I heard something."

He smiled, letting the rifle hang at his side. "You were supposed to get a good night's rest," he said. "But yeah, I think I saw our culprit."

She perked a ginger eyebrow, shifted her weight to her right leg. "That's great!" she said. "But you didn't shoot it?"

He chuckled and shook his head. "Nah," he said. "It's a woman. Not a fox."

"A... woman?"

"Well, maybe a mix between a fox and a woman," James mused, peering at the edge of the forest where he'd last seen her.

"I don't understand," Corinne muttered. "A fox woman? I've never heard of anything like that."

James turned back to Corinne with a smile. "Some kind of magical creature," he said.

She frowned. "Are you okay? Was that cocoa bad?"

He laughed and shook his head.

He had considered telling her about magic earlier tonight but had decided against — for fear of her thinking he was a lunatic; he just wanted to get to know her a little better.

But now his hand was forced.

He glanced at the forest again, and he was pretty sure they wouldn't see any more of the fox girl tonight; she had fled in a panic.

"Let's go inside for a second," he said to Corinne. "I got something to show you..."

Chapter 43

James braced himself, then committed to his plan. He stretched out his hand and spoke the words.

"Vanluket tod flamma.

"Furanderinghe, verneetigung. Vurra.

"Vanluket tod flamma."

For a moment, Corinne looked at James as if he were totally crazy.

But when the flame sprouted a few inches from his extended forefinger, flickering and dancing, her jaw dropped.

"What the hell?" she muttered.

"Like I said, magic is real," James said. "And I'm a mage."

She looked like she saw a ghost. "No way," she muttered, craning her neck to look at the flickering flame from another angle, as if it were a trick she could see through.

"No way..." She continued to stare.

"I can do a few more things," James said. "I can make planks from timber, make water boil, or summon my Grimoire — that's my spellbook."

"No way," she said again.

He nodded. "And that's only the beginning of it," he added, his enthusiasm for his newfound art rising. "I'm sure there's much more I can learn."

She rose from the chair and walked around him, studying the flickering flame from every angle she could reasonably get.

As she did so, James sensed the tug of the magic on his energy. Maintaining the flame took some effort, but he wanted to give Corinne every opportunity to study the effect until she was satisfied that he was not tricking her.

"That is... I can't believe what I'm seeing."

James grinned. "Believe it," he said.

"But how? Why? How are you the only one who can do this?"

"I'm not the only one," he said. "It has something to do with my Bloodline — with my family. I think magic is in some way a hereditary trait. There are others like me; we're all mages."

She nodded slowly, looking at the flame with awe.

"That's amazing," she murmured. "I mean, really."

She turned to face him, her eyes wide and bright. "This is amazing!" she exclaimed again, with fervor this time.

He laughed. "Yeah, it is. I only just discovered it myself."

She reached out and held her hand close to the flame. The light danced over her fingers and then faded as she drew her hand back and waved it.

"Ow," she muttered. "It's hot. How come you're not burning?"

He shrugged. "I guess it's because it's my magic? I honestly don't know."

She licked her lips as she studied the flame a moment longer before swiveling her gaze over to him. "How did you discover this?"

"I found a book of spells in the cabin; I don't know how it got here. It found it in the cellar. And there was... a woman who explained it to me."

She perked a red eyebrow. "A woman?"

He chortled. "A cat woman... Just like your culprit is a fox woman. I believe they're some kind of spirits... Anyway, she became my familiar, and she has taught me many things about magic since then."

"A cat woman..." Corinne muttered. "Now that just sounds plain old crazy."

James grinned. "Not as crazy as it sounds," he said. "If you think about it, the world is full of all kinds of creatures, right? So why not spirits? I even met a Dragonkin in the forest."

"Dragons?"

"Dragons."

She shook her head. "I need to sit down."

She flopped in the chair at the kitchen table, and James dismissed his Flame spell as she took a drink from her mug of hot cocoa.

"This is a bit much," she muttered.

James chuckled. "That's fine; take your time," he said. "I was taken aback, too. But there is something about this place, Corinne, something about Tour that's magical. At this point, it hardly surprises me that there are more magical creatures in the forest. I feel like we might see all sorts of other things here."

"Do you... do you think they mean harm? Those spirits, I mean."

He shrugged. "I don't know. Maybe some of them. I'm not sure what their motives are yet."

She nodded, her eyes still wide with wonder. "This is all so unreal," she said. "And you're the one who discovered all of this?"

"I was the one who found the book of spells. But this has existed long before I did. I... I learn spells by calling upon the past, and I get visions of my ancestors — members of my Bloodline — casting spells in the distant past."

She was silent for a moment, and then said, "This is so weird."

He nodded. "I know. It takes some time to get used to the idea. I could introduce you to Sara? She could tell you more."

She swallowed and nodded. "Yeah, okay," she said. "That would be great."

Then she paused.

He understood what was on her mind; a little apprehension about meeting another woman in his life.

Especially if that other woman was a magical being like Sara.

When she didn't say anything more, James tried to put her at ease. "Hey," he said. "If you don't want to meet her, that's fine, too."

"No," she said, shaking her head. "Not that. It's just so weird, a cat woman..."

James chuckled. "I know what you mean. But you know what? I think you two would get along."

A lopsided grin appeared on her lips. "So, does Lucy know 'bout this cat woman? About all this magic business?"

James shook his head. "Not yet. I... I realize it sounds crazy. I wouldn't have told you tonight either if the appearance of the fox girl hadn't forced my hand. It's just... such a big thing, right? How do you go about telling someone?"

She inclined her head. "You can say that again... I reckon it's the strangest — and most interesting — thing I ever heard in my life."

"Yeah," James agreed. "I mean, I want to tell her. I think she even has a right to know, but I'm waiting for the right time."

When Corinne said nothing else, he just looked at her. She was staring at the glowing embers of the fire in the fireplace.

A beauty.

He smiled and remained silent, giving her some time to process it all.

After a while, Corinne looked up at James again.

She smiled, reached out, and touched his arm.

"This is like a dream," she said. "I can't believe it. I don't know what to do."

"You're not alone in that," he said. "This is a pretty big deal, Corinne. I'm not sure how to tell people about all this."

He sat back and grinned. "But it's also pretty damn amazing. There are no limits to this — at least, none that I've discovered yet. Imagine the possibilities: I can use my magic for so many things."

She perked up at that, the fire of enthusiasm returning to her green eyes.

"Do ya suppose you could help me fix up the farm with this magic of yours?"

"For sure," James said. "This is like a gift; I can use it to help you in so many ways."

She nodded and cleared her throat. "So," she said. "What about this Sara? Do you think we could go see her tomorrow?"

He shrugged. "Sure, if you want to."

"I think you should bring Lucy, too," she said. "She's a part of this, isn't she?"

James watched her for a moment, her intense green eyes blazing. As he mulled it over, he realized that her suggestion enamored him.

She was looking out for Lucy, her friend, and urging him to be open to her, which he wanted to be, but he had been a little apprehensive about her possible response.

"You think so?" he prompted her.

"Yeah," Corinne said. "Lucy has an open mind; ya know that. She'll be okay with it."

Then she grinned. "Besides, I would like it if she were there, too. She's a friend and a person I trust."

"You're right," James said. "Why don't I ask her to come over tomorrow — to the cabin? You can come too. I'll cook for you girls and introduce you to Sara."

Corinne nodded. "I'm open to it," she said. "I'm sure Lucy will be, too." Her eyes sparked for a moment. "In fact," she added. "The more I think about these powers of yours, the more excited I get! So much could be possible."

He grinned and placed his hand on her forearm. "All right," he said. "I'll invite her and put my cards on the table. We'll see how she responds. But for now, I think you should get some rest. That fox girl is not coming back tonight, I'm sure of that."

She licked her lips and nodded, her eyes on James.

For a moment, he considered making a move and asking if he couldn't stay the night.

There were plenty of fantasies he wanted to make into reality with this hot little redheaded farmer's daughter, but a part of him advised against it. She had just learned a world-shaking truth, and she needed time to process it.

If he played his cards right, there would be other chances.

He smiled and rose. "You know," he said. "I'm happy the fox girl came along. It's been a real relief to speak to someone about this — someone other than Sara, that is. I mean, she's sweet and understanding, but all this magic business is plain as daylight to her; she doesn't understand that it's strange to us."

Corinne gave a soft smile as she rose as well. "I'm happy about it, too. I'll need some time to think it over, ya know? But it feels good, and I'm a gal to trust her gut."

"Sleep on it," he said. "Things'll be clearer in the morning. Come to the cabin around dinnertime, and me and Sara will cook you up something nice. And there will be plenty of answers."

She nodded.

They stood in the kitchen, facing each other, and a moment of silence passed between them — not an awkward one, but a pleasant one, tinged with a little tension.

Corinne took a step forward — close enough to touch now — and smiled. "Thanks for coming," she said, opening her arms for a hug.

"My pleasure," he said.

James wasn't really sure how it happened, and he doubted Corinne knew, either, but their lips met as they hugged.

She was soft and vibrant with life in his arms, almost quivering as their lips touched softly. They explored each other for a moment, their bodies pressing close on their own accord, and Corinne's tongue — soft as velvet, warm and delicious — sought his as she arched her back to push her breasts up against him, a gentle moan escaping her lips.

James reveled in the feeling of her, her softness, and

even though his body responded with a needy fire, he loosened himself from the embrace soon enough.

He really wanted her to think about things and not rush into anything.

Besides, she had made it clear she wanted to know Lucy's thoughts on the matter of... well, sharing him.

"Thanks, Corinne," James said, his voice hoarse as he suppressed his need. "I look forward to seeing you tomorrow."

Her eyes were hazy with lust, but she swallowed and regained her composure. "Me, too," she said, her voice husky.

She walked him to the door, still holding his hand, and only reluctantly let go as he stepped briskly into the cool night air.

She remained in the doorway, framed by the gentle light from the hallway, as he stepped into his car, offered her a wave, and drove off.

As he lowered the window and let some cool night air in, he couldn't help but smirk.

To be continued, he thought.

Chapter 44

Sunlight filtering into the cabin awakened James, and he stirred and squinted his eyes before rubbing them.

Beside him, Sara mewled a lazy complaint.

The cat girl lay naked and curled up into a ball, nestled against him and radiating heat.

With a groan, he slipped an arm around her supple body, and she quavered in response, a low purr rising from her throat as her tail wrapped around him and her left ear twitched once.

He had pummeled her relentlessly when he came home yesterday, waking her from her sleep in his bed.

His need had been fueled in part by Corinne's kiss, and Sara's eager response had made him feel like a god. He was not a selfish lover; he knew how to control himself, but he couldn't resist the temptation of having a willing, beautiful creature spread out before him, her lithe body offering itself to his lustful gaze.

And as she wriggled against him now, a teasing mewling rising from her, his cock stiffened, and he buried his nose in her midnight black locks, smelling the wild, feral perfume of the cat girl.

Within a moment, he had her on her knees, mewling with pleasure as he pumped her full of his seed once more.

Afterward, they enjoyed breakfast together. Sara had taken a large button-down shirt of his, which looked very cute on her, especially with the top buttons open to reveal those luscious breasts that he so loved.

They were out of eggs and bacon — he had bought only a little since he had no fridge yet — but there was good bread, and Sara made a mean sandwich using tomatoes, cucumber, cheddar, and a delicious stack of beef jerky.

"This is great," James muttered around a mouthful of food. "I haven't had a sandwich like this in ages."

Sara nodded. "I need you well-fed and energetic," she purred, giving a little wiggle of her ass in his shirt.

Her tail poked out from under it, lifting the hem so that he got a nice eyeful of the curvature of her butt cheeks.

He grinned. "You sound like you have plans."

She shot him a naughty, yellow-eyed peek over her shoulder.

"Hmm," she just crooned.

He laughed.

"And what are *your* plans, my sweet?" she asked.

He took a bite, giving her ass a hungry look. "I bought a lot of tools at Lucy's yesterday. I want to start on getting the materials to build myself a workshop. And for tonight..."

She turned, one eyebrow perked. The shirt had sagged a little, showing a tasty pink areola as she perked an eyebrow. "Tonight?"

"I wanted to invite Corinne and Lucy over," he said. "Last night, I told Corinne about my magic, and she wants to meet you."

She blinked. "Ooh," she purred. "You told her?" She

twirled the butter knife at him, grinning with mischief. "Sounds like she's a special lady, then..."

He chuckled. "I think so, yeah."

"And Lucy, too?"

"Lucy, too."

"Hmm," she hummed, turning back to her sandwiches with such speed her butt cheeks jiggled from it. "Okay. That's a good idea. If you trust them, I will trust them too."

"Good," James said. "Then we can all talk and have some fun together."

He took another bite of his sandwich; it was so tasty and filling. He had to be careful not to overeat something so delicious. Then again, he had a full day of hard, physical labor ahead of him, so he might as well indulge a little.

"Corinne is interested in learning if we can use magic to help her around the farm."

"Ooh, farming," Sara purred. "That sounds fun. I'm sure there's something that High Magic can do to make it easier."

"Yeah, my thoughts exactly," James said and took another bite, washing it down with a mouthful of coffee.

He set the mug down on the table and wiped his

hand clean. "Then there's Lucy. She doesn't know yet, so we should handle her with a little care. I can imagine she'd be shocked."

"Don't be silly, my sweet," Sara said. "She likes you, and this will only make her like you more. Imagine finding out your lover is a real mage and can make your problems go away!"

He laughed. "Well, I'm not sure if it's that simple. But we'll see."

"Hmm," she said. "I think you'll find Lucy knows more than she lets on."

James perked an eyebrow and leaned in. "How so?"

"That's something she should tell you herself," Sara said.

"Hmm," James hummed.

"So, why did you tell Corinne first?" Sara asked, her tail giving a little swish as she mulled it over. "I thought you and Lucy were already very close. I would have imagined that you'd tell her first."

James nodded and sat back. "When I was guarding her chicken coop last night..."

"Hmm," she purred. *"Guarding her chicken coop,* hmm? Is *that* what you call it?"

He laughed, shaking his head. "Your mind is permanently in the gutter."

She gave him a naughty look over her shoulder and another wiggle of that shapely ass.

"Don't pretend you don't like it," she purred. "And don't pretend you're any different."

He grinned and nodded. "Fair enough... Anyway, it turns out some kind of fox girl is behind the disappearance of Corinne's chickens."

"A fox girl, huh?" Sara said, and chuckled.

"That's funny?"

"You'll see," she hummed, then turned around with another sandwich on a plate and a broad grin on her lips.

"You're being very mysterious this morning," James said, an eyebrow raised and a smile on his lips as he studied her.

"I'm a very mysterious girl," she purred, giving him a challenging look. "But I can guarantee you that tonight will be fun. That's all I can say, because the rest is up to Lucy to tell you."

I frowned. "You're not making much sense."

She placed the plate in front of him, then let her fingers trail over his chest on their way back up.

"Eat up, lumberjack," she said. "All will be revealed!"

He laughed, shook his head, and set to finishing his breakfast.

Chapter 45

With a solid breakfast as a foundation for the day's work, James gave Sara a kiss on the cheeks before he headed outside.

He breathed the fresh forest air — a lungful of relief — before he surveyed the land around his cabin.

If he wanted to build a workshop, he would need to clear some land first. Thinking about everything he had to do was a bit overwhelming. After all, clearing the land was quite a chore, but he'd have to level it, plan the walls, dig the foundations, and that would only mean he could get started.

And so he did what he did whenever he felt a little overwhelmed...

He just got to work.

After all, there was plenty he could do now. The axe he'd bought from Lucy was sturdy, and the first order of business was clearing out the area, starting with the biggest fish — saplings and young trees that had encroached on the cabin over the years.

He put his mind to it and set to whistling a tune as he once again found himself in the freshly scenting forest, chopping away at the trees like a man possessed.

As the day went on, James cleared more land. He stacked the trees he felled close to the cabin so he limb them later. He doubted this lumber would be useful for the workshop, but it would serve as firewood in a pinch.

When noon came around, Sara brought him lunch — a hearty and filling vegetable soup with toast and cheese — which he ate with gusto before heading back to work.

The sun was at its peak by then, and the clearing of

Country Mage

land seemed to be going faster than expected.

He took a quick break to drive down to Tour and get some shopping done and — of course — to invite Lucy.

He found her at her shop, dressed in a tight plaid skirt and a white blouse that struggled to contain her ample bosom. When he strolled into her shop, she perked up and her eyes shone with that special light she seemed to save only for him.

She leaned forward at once, always the temptress, offering him a delicious look down her blouse.

"Why, hello there, James!" she said. "I was hoping you'd drop in today! Did you have fun last night with Corinne?"

He grinned and walked over to the counter, leaning on it as she did. He placed his hand over hers and gave her a soft kiss on the cheek.

"It's nice to see you, too," he said. "Yeah, I think we solved her fox problem. For now."

She smiled. "Well, I really missed you last night," she said, running a finger over his biceps. "Dinner is less fun without you."

He returned her smile, a prickle going through him at the sultry blonde's velvet touch.

"It just so happens I'm here to remedy that," he said. "I told you I'd cook for you, so why not tonight? You can come over to the cabin."

"Romantic," she purred, her big blue eyes full of mischievous promise.

He grinned. He remembered what Sara had said about her, and he wondered about tonight, about the things that might be revealed during dinner.

"Romantic, indeed," James agreed. "Corinne will also be there."

She blinked. "Corinne?"

She bit her lower lip for a moment, considering the meaning of the redhead showing up as well. "That's... interesting."

Her finger remained on James's arm, and there was more than a little intrigue in her eyes.

"Hm-hm," James agreed. "It should be fun."

She smiled, a little color flushing her cheeks.

"You game?" he asked.

He realized there was a little pressure on the question. Only yesterday, they had spoken about a potential arrangement with multiple lovers for James. He wasn't sure if she'd thought it over.

She looked past him at the store, but there were no other clients.

"Hmm... I'm... I'd like to try."

He nodded. "That makes me very happy. Why don't

you come over tonight and we'll see how things go?"

She bit her lip. "Yes," she purred.

"There's only one problem, though," James said, his expression turning serious.

She perked an eyebrow, her smile fading. "Oh? What's that?"

"It won't be a surprise what I'm cooking," he said. "Since I have to buy it from you."

She laughed and slapped him on the arm. "Don't make jokes like that!"

He grinned and gave her another peck on the cheek before turning to his shopping.

He got all he needed, plus a couple of good bottles of wine, paid for it, and left again, followed by Lucy's hungry eyes.

Smiling, James drove back to his cabin.

Once James returned to the cabin, Sara helped unload the groceries and began the preparations for dinner.

It wasn't going to be anything fancy; just good steak, properly made, with fresh vegetables and homemade fries.

Sara got to work peeling and cutting the potatoes and cleaning the cabin for their visitors while James spent some more time working outside, setting the felling axe to what trees remained.

It wasn't until late afternoon that James took another break from his work; after all, he'd spent most of the day chopping wood and clearing land.

Figuring he had another hour or so before he'd have to fix dinner, he did some smaller work with the hatchet and shovel, clearing shrubs and bushes in the general area where he planned to build his workshop.

When the afternoon drew to its end, he surveyed his handiwork with no small measure of pride.

In one corner was a stack of lumber to be used for the fireplace. Beside it was a pile of branches, chips, and other discarded wood. Next to the cabin, he'd cleared the ground and left a large area that he'd planned to use as a workshop.

He expected he'd have to go at for perhaps another day or two before he would start on the planning and the foundation.

But it was enough for today.

He cleaned his tools, then bathed in the nearby creek. The water was cold but very refreshing, and James felt close to nature, close to where he belonged, as he washed himself in the clear and icy water that flowed down straight from the mountains.

As a North Dakota native and an avid outdoorsman, he was used to bathing in natural water. Of course, he'd love to install a shower and a bath in due time, but there was beauty in letting nature provide.

After his bath, he felt like a king, and he toweled himself down in the rosy light of sunset, the happy chatter of birds and the rustling leaves for company.

When he returned to the cabin, he caught the delicious smell of a wood fire. He entered, greeted by Sara who had, for the occasion, put on a skin-tight and excruciatingly sexy, short, black dress with matching stockings and heels. The hole cut for her tail was the cutest detail. Her hair was done up in a cute little bun, with a few strands dangling to frame her face.

He gave her a warm kiss and a pat on her shapely bottom as he made his way into the bedroom.

Wanting to look his best, he put on a pair of smart slacks, a black shirt, and a pair of dress shoes.

With all that done, he joined Sara in the living room and lit a few candles for a cozy and warm glow before he went to work on the steaks.

Sara shot him a loving glance, and they shared their homely delight with a profound sense of happiness, the only sound being Sara's happy humming.

A few minutes later, there was a knock at the door.

Chapter 46

James opened the door to see Lucy.

The beautiful blonde had wrapped her voluptuous self in an outfit that begged to be torn from her ready body. A tight halter top with no bra — her nipples poking at the fabric told the tale — and a skirt so tight it pushed in her luscious thighs, making James's head spin at the sight.

"Hello, you," she purred, throwing him a seductive glance from under long lashes.

She was beautiful without make-up, but she had applied some of it now — a modest amount of eyeliner and mascara to accentuate the blazing blue of her eyes and red lipstick that had just the right mix of sexy and classy.

"You look amazing," James said.

She smiled and flicked back some of her lush, golden locks.

"Thank you!" she said, looking him up and down. "So do you."

He smiled. "Not as amazing as you."

She blushed. "Oh, don't be so modest; you look really good in that outfit!"

She placed her hand on his chest. "Now, I'd like a kiss..."

He chuckled. "Now you're talking." He leaned in to kiss her.

As he did so, her soft breasts pushed up against him, and he felt himself getting hard.

She was so pretty and adorable, with her voluptuous figure and big blue eyes — and she made him feel like the luckiest man in the world. He didn't know if it was just her charm or if it was something else, but he couldn't help but lose himself in every kiss they shared.

When their lips parted, he sensed the heat coming from her body; she was flush with excitement.

"Come on in," he said.

He led her into the warm and cozy cabin.

Sure, it was small, but bathed in soft candlelight, with clean rugs on the floor, the log walls and homeliness of the quaint old place really struck home.

"Oh, it's beautiful!" Lucy exclaimed. "So cute and cozy!" She turned to look at him. "This is like a cabin from a fairytale."

James smiled and nodded. "That's exactly right," he said. "Now, let's get you something to drink."

At that moment, Sara came out of the bedroom and into the living room.

Lucy swiveled her eyes to the cat girl, smiled, then blinked as she noticed the cat ears, the yellow eyes, and the tail that gave a playful swish as she studied the curvy blonde with a playful pout on her full lips.

Lucy's mouth moved. "Wh..."

Sara came into the living room, got on her tippy toes to kiss James on the cheek, then flopped down on the couch with a playful grin, still studying Lucy, who stood wide-eyed.

"This is my friend Sara," James said. "She, uh, she

lives here with me."

Lucy looked up at him; her eyes were wide with surprise. Then she looked back at Sara. "Oh," she said. "Hello."

Sara chuckled in a way that made James raise his eyebrows.

She sprawled on the couch with all the laziness any feline could muster as she studied Lucy with a twinkle of joy in her yellow eyes.

"Hey," she purred. "Surprised?"

At that, Lucy's posture relaxed a little, and she snorted. "I guess not."

James blinked. "Uh, what's going on here? You two know each other?"

Sara licked her lips as her eyes roved over Lucy, who didn't seem as surprised as James would have thought her to be.

The blonde looked at me and smiled, her cheeks a little flushed. "I, uh, am kinda familiar with Sara's kind."

James had to make an effort to keep his jaw from dropping. "You are?"

"Yeah," she said. "My, uh, daughter... Kesha. She's a..."

"A fox girl," Sara purred.

"What?" James muttered.

Lucy gave a guilty nod. "Yeah. Kesha is a fox girl…"

James was still processing Lucy's confession as Sara rolled onto her back and glanced at him from half-lidded eyes.

"You even *met* her, James," she purred.

James barked an astounded laugh. "No shit?"

Sara laughed and swiveled a playful glance over to Lucy. "No shit, right?"

Lucy's cheeks were scarlet, and she gave a self-conscious chuckle. "Yeah… she's a forest spirit."

"Wait," James said, throwing up his hands. "You… *Your daughter* is a forest spirit?"

She nodded. "Uh-huh… I would've told you at some point, but… it… I was scared you'd think I was crazy."

"Well, James has a secret, too," Sara purred, playfully rolling onto her side, cheek propped up in her hand. Joy danced in her yellow eyes; she obviously enjoyed this — a lot.

Lucy looked at James, her blue eyes big. "A secret?"

"I… I'm a High Mage," he said, deciding to just throw

it out there.

Lucy's mouth dropped open. Sara let out a little squeal like a delighted kitten.

Lucy's mouth moved, but no words came out for a few seconds. Then she cleared her throat.

"A High Mage?" she said. "Like, a wizard?"

He nodded. "Yeah."

Lucy blinked and looked at Sara. "This is so cool!" She turned to James. "I knew it! I knew there was something different about you, James!"

"Yay!" Sara purred, clapping her hands. "She likes it!"

Lucy's eyes widened; she looked at James with a grin and a twinkle in her eyes.

"Of course, I like it," she said. "It's been decades since we had a High Mage in Tour."

"Wait, what?" James muttered. "You knew magic existed?"

"Yeah," Lucy said, her smile fading. "My parents... I told you about them, but I... lied. Well, not really, but... a little bit. They were the scions and only heirs of two competing Bloodlines here in Tour, and they eloped together. After they died, the Bloodlines reconciled and left Tour. There haven't been High Mages in Tour ever since."

"Except for spirits like me," Sara purred softly, playing with a stray thread hanging from the couch. "But we don't really count."

Lucy nodded. "Except Sara... And a few other spirits."

"Like your daughter?" James suggested.

Lucy's face reddened; her smile was tense. "Yeah. But Kesha and I... well, we don't talk. She... she is a complicated person, very serious, and she doesn't trust me. We have a... a sort of truce, but... we don't talk anymore."

The sorrow was plain to see on her face.

"Why doesn't she trust you?" James asked.

"I did something stupid. My intentions were good, but I screwed up."

She gave a wistful smile. "I'll tell you about it some other time, okay? For now, let's just say she left the house and moved into the forest to be closer to the wild. She's been living there ever since."

"Eating Corinne's chickens," Sara said, turning her attention back to the loose thread.

Lucy smiled and nodded. "That sounds like it could be Kesha... She's been out there for a while; I can imagine she's getting wilder."

James scratched behind his ears, considering the

wealth of information just shared with him.

It sounded like Lucy was really torn up over no longer being in touch with her daughter, and he wanted to help her.

At the same time, he was very relieved that the big reveal didn't turn out to be such a big deal to Lucy; she had known about magic for a long time.

Her parents had been High Mages, after all.

"But... If your parents were mages," James said. "Shouldn't you be one, too?"

Lucy blew out air. "If only... No, the aptitude doesn't always pass on. It's mysterious; sometimes, it skips a generation. Other times, it affects an entire generation. It can even fade from a Bloodline altogether."

Sara nodded in agreement, flicking the loose thread as her left ear twitched, her big eyes following the string as it swayed back and forth.

"Well," James puffed. "I don't know about you, but I could use a drink."

Lucy laughed. "Same here."

Sara licked her lips and looked at him, her eyes twinkling with mischief.

She flipped over and rolled onto her tummy, propping herself up on her elbows to look over at the other woman.

"Why don't you get the drinks, my sweet?" she purred. "Lucy can come sit on the couch with me."

James chuckled and nodded, looking once over his shoulder as the curvy and delicious blonde settled on the couch, still blushing a little.

Sara's gaze was almost predatory as she looked Lucy up and down.

Boy, James thought. *This is gonna be a wild night...*

Chapter 47

By the time James finished with the drinks, there was another knock on the door. When James opened the door, he saw Corinne, a slight blush on her face.

The freckled beauty had done up her unruly ginger hair and put on a summer dress with a floral pattern, although she still wore cowboy boots under them, the tips slightly turned inward as she tucked a stray lock behind her ear and gave James a bashful smile.

"Hey there, cowboy," she said.

He laughed. Apparently, the nickname was going to stick.

He leaned in and kissed her on the cheek before letting her in. "Welcome, Corinne," he said.

She stepped inside, and the other women gave her a curious look.

"Corinne, you already know Lucy," James said. "And I told you about Sara."

"Hmm," Sara purred, looking Corinne up and down, relinquishing the thread hanging from the couch to study her for a moment. "Only bad things, I trust."

James laughed, and Corinne blushed a little as she stepped into the warmth of the cabin, where the merry crackle-and-pop of the fire sounded.

James offered her a drink, then sat her down in the chair before sitting down on the couch between Sara and Lucy.

Sara leaned into him at once, nestling her head against James with a low purr in her throat, and James wrapped his arm around her.

Corinne looked at Sara with wide green eyes, her eyes dipping to the tail, rising to the ears, and coming to rest on the beautiful yellow eyes.

"Wow," she muttered at last. "I reckon you weren't lying, James," she said.

"Never," James said. "When I like a person, I don't lie to them."

Corinne's cheeks colored; she looked down at her drink and took a sip. She then glanced at Lucy.

"This is all so unreal, ain't it?" she muttered.

"Well," Lucy said, drawing out the word. "I'm actually a little familiar with all of this... *magic business*."

Corinne sat up. "What? No way!"

Lucy laughed, and James couldn't help but join in as some of the tension he had felt leading up to tonight slipped away.

These women were wonderful, understanding, and open-minded. He couldn't have found a better bunch.

"So, y'all are sayin' *I'm* the only in here who didn't know about all of this magic stuff?" Corinne said, looking at each of us.

"Pretty much," Lucy said with an innocent shrug.

Corinne looked at Sara, a smile on her plump lips. "And you?" she asked. "You're the one who can teach this?"

Sara gave her a bold look, taking her time to let her yellow gaze dip and study the redhead's yummy body.

It made Corinne blush a little, but she didn't turn

away, and James realized she was enjoying the attention.

"I'm James's familiar," Sara purred at length. "I can only teach *him*. Although with his talent, I believe he'll soon be the one teaching me. But so far as I know, only those of a certain Bloodline can become High Mages. Or maybe it's just those who have the aptitude—I'm not sure of everything. There are creatures in the forest that are more knowledgeable than I am."

"Wow," Corinne muttered. "That's a darn shame. I would've loved me a couple of spells to help me keep the farm clean."

"Well, James can help with that," Sara said, looking over at James as she snuggled up against him. "If he wants to?"

"Sure," James said. "We're practically neighbors, right?"

Corinne chuckled. "Yeah, I reckon we are at that."

"But I'd need a few more spells," James said. "Right now, my repertoire is very basic."

Sara ran a slender finger over his thigh, her eyes fixed on James's crotch in a way that made the other women blush a little. "You will," Sara purred. "Give it time."

Lucy and Corinne looked like they were holding their breaths, their gazes fixed on that adventurous little finger and the hardening bulge in James's pants.

The blonde blushed again, and James could tell that she was just about to open her mouth when Corinne spoke.

"So, um," Corinne said with a cough. "If it's all right with you, Sara, I'd like to know — is James your boyfriend?" She glanced at Lucy. "Or is he yours?"

That was bold of her! James grinned; he respected her being so straightforward.

"Why not both?" Sara purred before James had a chance to answer, a naughty light in her yellow eyes. "I'm not opposed to sharing the man in my bed."

James laughed and gave her a squeeze that made her start with a yelp; she was so much fun to tease.

Corinne and Lucy laughed at that, but both women's cheeks were radiant at this moment.

Time for a change of subject, he thought.

He gave Sara a pat on her thick thigh, then rose to his feet.

"Well, this man isn't opposed to sharing his *steaks*. But if we're going to fill our bellies tonight, we'd best get to it."

Sara got the hint and hopped to her feet with a naughty grin, and the two of them headed into the kitchen, leaving the two blushing beauties to cool down before the next round of teasing could begin.

With most preparations already made, James and Sara quickly served up dinner. The table in the living room was too small for four people, but that added to the rustic charm. Sara sat on the floor with her plate in her lap. Lucy sat on the couch; Corinne sat in the armchair, and James sat on the couch at Lucy's side.

"This is nice," Corinne said. "It's been a long while since I had a meal like this."

Sara looked over at her with a warm smile. "I'm glad you like it."

Lucy grinned. "It's so delicious!" she added. "All of this is so perfect, isn't it?" she said, looking around the room. "Not just dinner — all of it."

Corinne nodded. "I'll be honest: I'm kinda tired of eatin' dinner alone."

James grinned. "Honestly, this is my favorite part of the day," he said. "Good food and good company. This is all about relaxing for me. I hope you two will let me — *us* — cook you more meals like this. I want to get to know you better."

"Hmm," Sara agreed around a mouthful of meat — she was a bit of a gobbler.

Lucy smiled. "That would be wonderful, James."

Corinne smiled as well; her eyes flicked over to James, a slight blush appearing again. "If we have the chance, I'd love that."

James nodded and took a long drink from his wineglass.

"Then that's what we'll do," he finally said with a smile. "Let's not waste time; life is short, and we should always strive to enjoy it to the fullest with our loved ones. So, let's eat!"

Lucy beamed a smile and raised her glass. "Hear, hear!"

The others followed suit, and the glasses clinked before everyone dug in again.

They ate with succor, enjoying the meal.

As dinner progressed, Corinne and Lucy lost some of their anxiety and relaxed in the company of Sara and James, and they talked about a range of things: life in Tour, work, the farm, and things they enjoyed doing.

"This is really good," Corinne said with a smile. "If you have time, Sara, can you show me some of your cooking?"

Sara beamed a grin. "Of course!" she purred. "I'm so

happy that you like it."

James smiled at Corinne. "You know," he said. "Next time, we could try to cook with some fresh produce from your farm."

She chuckled. "Well, if y'all got your groceries from Lucy's, chances are you already cookin' with my produce."

Lucy grinned. "I buy a lot from Corinne. Girl drives a hard bargain, too." She cast Corinne an appreciative glance.

"Aw, shucks," Corinne said, waving it away.

Sara cleared her throat; she was still working on her third helping of meat, having disregarded most of the vegetables.

"A shame she doesn't have a ranch," Sara purred. "She could supply us with meat."

Corinne grinned at her, a little challenge appearing in her green eyes. "I'd say you get plenty of meat," she said, a naughty hint to her voice as her eyes flicked over to James. "You and Lucy."

James chuckled and sat back, eager to see where this would go...

Sara grinned, displaying her cute canines as her left ear twitched. "Hmm... Jealous?"

Corinne laughed, raising her hand with thumb and

forefinger held slightly apart. "Maybe just a teeny little," she said.

"I share my meat," Sara purred, keeping Corinne fixes with her exotic yellow eyes. "You want a piece, you only need to ask."

Corinne bit her lip. Her cheeks flushed, and she sat back a little, for the moment outplayed by Sara, who renewed her attack on her steak with vigor.

Lucy looked like she was about to burst into laughter.

James had to give it to Sara; she knew how to tease.

Corinne's cheeks were a lovely shade of red now. He couldn't help but smile at the cute display, especially when he saw that Lucy, sitting on the couch beside him, was watching the whole thing with a hungry fire in her eyes.

She leaned forward to put her near-empty plate on the table, offering Corinne and Sara a generous look down her tight halter top, a view both women appreciated for a moment.

And why not? Lucy's breasts were the perfect pair of MILF tits — firm and generous. One might drown in them.

"You know," the sultry blonde crooned. "*I* share my meat, too."

Corinne chuckled, her cheeks turning an even deeper

shade of red. "Yeah, but your plate is empty," she managed to say in a voice that quickly turned huskier.

"Is it?" Lucy purred.

And then, in a show that surprised even James, she placed her hand on the bulge in James's pants.

James almost spat out the mouthful he just drank from his wineglass.

Not that he didn't like the feeling — he loved it, in fact — but he hadn't expected such a bold move from Lucy.

Sara gave an appreciative purr from her spot on the floor, her big, yellow eyes fixed on where Lucy's slim fingers gently teased the growing bulge in James's pants.

James's gaze moved to Corinne.

The redhead's cheeks were so flushed that it almost blotted out her freckles, and James couldn't suppress a smile.

Still, the way she rubbed her thighs together as she sat in the chair and the way her stiff nipples poked against the fabric of her dress betrayed how she felt about all this.

Lucy's fingers continued to slide up and down James's bulge; his erection was like a steel rod now. He couldn't deny that he was enjoying this, too.

Sara sat on the floor with her legs crossed, watching Lucy and James with an eager look in her eyes. She licked her lips as she looked at Corinne; the tension between the four of them was palpable.

"So, what do you say about sharing?" Lucy purred. "How about a mouthful?"

Damn... James thought. *This is getting hot and heavy.*

Chapter 48

Corinne couldn't help but chuckle at Lucy's dirty joke, covering her mouth.

"A mouthful!?" she called out. "Lucy, that's so dirty!"

But Lucy licked her lips, her eyes hazy like those of a sultry temptress as her fingers played with and plucked at James's belt buckle.

And as if the sound of her pulling at his belt and

undoing it was some kind of magical chime, Sara gave a low purr, pushed away her plate, and crawled over to James on her hands and knees.

A gasp of pleasure escaped him at the sight of her, her tail swishing, her tight dress hugging her perfect body, and with her stockings and heels finishing the picture.

She was so fucking hot!

With effortless grace, Sara crawled over to him; she moved on her hands and knees like a cat. A purr of pleasure escaped her as she reached James's lap. She stopped just below his crotch, looking up at him with those big eyes that were so full of lust.

"Wait your turn," Lucy crooned, giving Sara a playful push with her bare foot as she undid the buttons on the front of James's slacks. Her big tits almost slipped from her skimpy little top, edges of her nipples already showing as she shot Sara a naughty glance.

Sara meowed at her, a blaze of defiance in her yellow eyes, but she licked her lips and watched as Lucy opened James's pants and pulled them down.

Two girls fighting over his dick...

At this point, James's cock was almost ready to make his boxers burst, and all three girls took in the sight with wide eyes.

"Hmm..." Lucy crooned. "There's plenty for us all."

Sara rose to her knees on his side, offering him a peek down her ample cleavage, while Lucy sat on his other side, massaging his rod through his boxers.

Across from him, Corinne sat with wide eyes, a soft mewl escaping her as she wriggled in her chair, all hot and bothered.

With a sigh of delight, Lucy lowered James's boxers and took his cock by the thick base, showing it to the other girls with no small measure of pride.

It made James so horny. The thought of Lucy licking his shaft made his balls ache with a need for release.

It still surprised him that she had been the one to take initiative... This was certainly a ringing agreement to share him with other girls.

Her lust — and her trust — had won it in the end.

The beautiful blonde looked up at James with her big blue eyes before lowering her head.

Her tongue ran up his shaft from the base to the tip, coating it in her saliva. She had a very talented tongue, and the warmth of her mouth on James's cock was like heaven. As she pulled back, a wire of spit connected the shining tip of his cock to her full lips.

"Delicious," she purred.

With a gasp of delight, Sara crawled up on the couch

beside him; her eagerness was written all over her face as she lifted her lips to James's and kissed him, pushing her delectable soft body up against his.

He could feel her heat through the thin fabric of her dress, which was now riding up her thighs, displaying a black lace thong with a garter belt that held up her slutty stockings.

She kissed James with a fervor that had him groaning with pleasure, and when she broke the kiss to look at him, her eyes were wide and hazy, blazing with need.

With a moan of desire, James grabbed her big tits and massaged them, winning a squeal of delight from Sara, who immediately pulled down the collar of her dress to let those delicious tits bounce free, so that James could play with her nipples, pulling at them and squeezing them, all to the tune of Sara's needy panting.

All the teasing came up now, and he felt the need rise within him as warm lips kissed his shaft, and his hands kneaded full and firm tits.

He already knew this was going to be a night to remember.

As James kissed Sara, squeezing her breast while Lucy licked his cock, Corinne let out a gasp.

"Oh, damn," she whispered. "You, uh, y'all don't waste any time, do you?"

James's gaze swiveled to her. The redhead in heat had slipped a hand between her thick thighs, although it hadn't moved up to her pussy.

Not yet.

He shot Corinne a wide grin as he let the cat girl push her big tits up in his face, her head thrown back as she surrendered herself to her dirty desire.

And as he feasted on Sara's big tits, Lucy wrapped her plump lips around his throbbing rod and took it as deeply as she could.

Lucy was like a professional; she worked his cock with a practiced ease that had him moaning in pleasure.

When she reached the base of James's cock and pulled her head back up to look at him, he could see that she was smiling, a runner of saliva and precum hanging from those lips that were perfect for sucking cock.

"That's it, baby," she purred. "Give it to me."

James had only a moment to gasp in delight before Sara claimed his mouth for another passionate kiss, her hand guiding his to the slick heat down the front of her slutty lace panties. Her lips were like fire; James was almost surprised she didn't burn him with her passion.

She pulled back to glance at him, her eyes full of lust and need, and when she parted his lips with her tongue, he moaned in pleasure, his fingers pushing against the silky lips of her delicious pussy as she kissed him.

Her sweet, creamy womanhood twitched as he massaged her lips, and a low purr rose from the base of her throat. James slipped a finger into that warm, wet, and welcoming opening. With a gasp of pleasure, she pulled back to look at him.

"Oh, sweetie," she moaned. "That's so good."

With a groan of delight, James slid a second finger into her, and she mewled again.

"Ohhh, yes!" she cried. "Yes! That's it! Fuck me with your fingers!"

James chuckled; she was his horny little kitten. With a smile on his face, he pushed one more finger into her pussy.

She let out a cry of pleasure as his three fingers pillaged her wet hole. And as James fingered Sara into submission, Lucy gagged and slobbered on his cock with worship and dedication, making his balls tighten in his sack, eager to spurt into her hot MILF mouth.

Sara was the one to break the kiss, pure lust in her

eyes as she moaned: "Ohhhh fuck! So good. I love it when you do me with your fingers."

With a grin, Lucy pulled away from James's cock and freed her big breasts from her halter top by pulling the straps aside.

James gave a deep, lustful moan when he saw her dirty little plan for him; she took his cock between those two big MILF tits of hers, pressed them together, and gave him the boob-job of a lifetime.

"Fuuuck," James moaned, leaning back.

Sara gave an impatient mewl at that, grinding her pussy on his fingers to make it clear he should not stop what he was doing.

With a hiss of delight, he continued as she desired, pounding her pussy with his fingers.

Sara looked up at the ceiling with a purr of pleasure. "Oh, yes!" she moaned, her eyes slipping shut as his fingers pleasured her pussy. "More! More!"

Lucy gave James a teasing wink before studying the way his cockhead popped up from between her big tits with every tug. Already, a bead of precum sat on the tip of James's engorged cock, and he was ready to explode.

With a purr of satisfaction, Sara grabbed James's cock between Lucy's big boobs and stroked him. The cat girl's eyes were closed in bliss as she added her efforts to the boob-job that Lucy was giving James.

"That's good," Lucy purred. "We need to work together to handle this big dick."

Then Lucy hitched up her own skirt, pulled down her panties, and began massaging her pussy.

"Ugh," James groaned. "You girls are driving me crazy."

They both giggled, exchanging naughty looks as they worshipped James's cock.

Then, a soft moan from the chair opposite the couch drew James's attention.

Corinne, unable to contain herself much longer, had hitched up her dress and pulled her cute, striped panties to the side.

Doing so had revealed a wet and ready slit with the cutest triangle of ginger pubic hair. She bit her lip as she began playing with her plump pussy lips, her free hand teasing her perky nipples through the fabric of her summer dress.

Corinne wasn't getting fully involved yet. There was some apprehension left as she teased herself — some vague notion of 'butting in' perhaps — but she was also clearly enjoying it. She would grow into it.

And for now, she was a delicious sight.

Beside James, Sara stirred on his fingers, and leaned

forward to lick the bead of precum from his tip. Her soft, warm tongue teased his cock, winning a little spurt of extra precum, which she lapped up with dirty lust.

"Hmm," she purred. "James... I'm... Ah... Don't stop."

"Oh, fuck," James groaned, feeling her tight pussy clench on his fingers as he pounded it.

"Is she coming?" Lucy purred. "Ahn... that's... that's so hot."

Heated, she began tugging on James with her boobs even faster, while Sara moaned and sucked on his tip.

Behind them, Corinne was now drawing circles around her little clit, her face flushed, and her eyes fixed on Lucy's jiggling backside and the way James's cock popped up from between her luscious tits.

With a groan, James gave in to the pleasure.

It was almost too much. His fingers pumped into Sara, his other hand kneaded her tits, and Lucy worshiped his cock while pleasing herself. It was every man's dream to have three abnormally hot women all to themselves like this, and James was actually living it.

As his fingers moved faster inside Sara's pussy, he could sense her tightening and clenching him; she was close.

"Come for me," he groaned at his hot little cat girl as he felt his own orgasm rise from his very toes.

"Yes... Ahn... Yes!" she purred, her left ear twitching and her tail curling as her orgasm came on.

She let out a high-pitched cry of pleasure, and James felt her tighten up, every muscle tense as she came trembling. Sensing her pleasure, James's own orgasm came suddenly, jumping on him.

"Fuck!" James groaned. "I'm gonna cum..."

"Yes!" Lucy moaned. "Cum for me. Please, baby, cum!"

"Ah," he groaned, even as Sara moaned and squirmed on his fingers. "I wanna cum in your mouth, Lucy."

"Yes!" she purred, then wrapped her plump lips around his cock without another word.

Their delicious warmth and softness caused James's body to tighten. "Fuck... Here it comes."

"Don't... ah! Don't swallow it yet," Sara purred. "I want some too!"

Across from him, Corinne was shaking as an orgasm lashed her too, and the sight of that delicious bounty of flesh jiggling as her pleasure lashed the redhead only made things worse for James.

With a deep grunt of need and command, he grabbed a handful of Lucy's blond locks and pulled her down harder on his cock, winning a squeal of delight at the rough handling.

And with that, he spurted a jet of hot seed into her warm and welcoming mouth.

She kept her big, blue eyes on him as emptied his balls in her mouth. Those blue lookers stood wide, some of the eyeliner running from the deepthroating, but she took it all like a pro and with obvious pleasure. James could see the joy in those big blue eyes as he spurted another rope of cum into her mouth.

But as Sara had asked, she didn't swallow, and her cheeks expanded with the thick, juicy load he blessed her with.

He spurted his last with a groan, and Lucy pulled back from his cock. The movement made him twitch, and a last gob of cum shot from his glistening tip over her big tits.

Then she opened her mouth and showed him his load.

Her tongue wasn't even visible in the thick, milky pool of cum. She gargled it, and bubbles came up.

"Fuck," James moaned. "You are crazy hot..."

With a purr of delight, Sara hopped down from the couch to her knees before Lucy, even as the blonde rose to one knee.

She took Sara's head in her hands while the cat girl

opened her mouth wide, cute canines flashing.

Then, in what was easily the hottest moment in James's life, Lucy shared his load with Sara, snowballing it down from her mouth and into Sara's.

Sara let out a long moan of pleasure as she took his cum like a goddess; she made him proud to be a man.

Then, with a smile on her lips and a look in her eyes that told James she was going to be a very naughty cat girl, she turned around and faced Corinne.

The redhead, still recovering from her orgasm, blushed as all eyes in the room turned to her.

"Yes," she said, soft but audible, and they all knew what she meant.

Lucy and Sara moved to her — Lucy with swaying hips; Sara crawling on all fours, tail a-swooshing.

Lucy sat down beside Corinne on one armrest; Sara on the other.

James's soul roiled with pure joy as Sara and Lucy cuddled up with Corinne, kissing and stroking the redhead before Sara hovered above her and opened her mouth.

A snowball of cum came from Sara's mouth.

It was messier this time — in tune with the cat girl's personality — and some of the sticky cum landed on Corinne's dress or down her cleavage, but the majority went into her mouth.

And she swallowed it all like a good girl.

"Fucking hell," James chuckled, shaking his head at this extremely hot display. "You girls are amazing."

With a grin of delight, Sara licked her lips.

Corinne's eyes were bright with wonder as she gazed at the cat girl.

"That was so hot," Corinne muttered.

"Hottest thing ever," Lucy agreed, running a hand through Corinne's coppery locks.

Then, Sara kissed her, and Corinne moaned into the kiss as she returned it with passion. The redhead's hands went to Lucy's tits, squeezing them while James's cat girl explored her with kisses and gentle bites of her neck.

When Sara pulled away, the redhead was panting, a little light-headed from the intensity of the kiss.

Then Sara broke out laughing and hopped to her feet to return to James.

She sat down on his lap, and the gentle light of the flickering flame highlighted her beautiful body. As she took her rightful place, the other girls and James joined in on her laughter, the tension having washed out of them.

For now.

Lucy and Corinne exchanged a glance, then joined James and Sara on the couch.

The couch wasn't big enough for four, but they made it work.

Chapter 49

Dawn came full of promise and found James in bed with three women. To say that any of them had slept well would be a lie, but James still rose at the first hint of light breaking into his small bedroom.

The heap of hot women in his bed just moaned lazily as if with one voice, and he chuckled as he made his way to the living room and kitchen to make some coffee.

The women could sleep in, but he had work to do.

He would have thought that after a night like that, he would have wanted to stay in bed.

But nope, not him.

Even more so than before, he sensed an urgency to get to work on his cabin and improve it. If he was going to host these women more often, then his cabin needed to be the best it could be.

With a sigh of happiness, he made some coffee and considered the work ahead of him.

First, he had to get this whole workshop taken care of. It would be the foundation of whatever followed. He expected he would need about two more days to flatten the land and make it ready.

Next, he would need to get building materials.

Those were not hard to find; he was in the middle of the woods, and everything came from the forest itself. And if the women wanted anything exotic, then they might try to order it — but that wasn't likely.

Finally, he would need to make some improvements. Furniture, more space... Electricity so they might switch to proper coffee.

But first things first: he needed to call the lawyer and tell him he'd made up his mind.

He was going to stay here.

Quit his job, terminate his lease. No more rat race in the city.

James smiled to himself as he finished boiling some water. Part of him was looking forward to making that announcement to the lawyer and to his brother.

They'd probably think he was weird for wanting to live way out here, but who cared what they thought?

And there was more to do. Not just stuff with the cabin. He wanted to learn new spells, increase his powers. He could help Lucy restore the farm to its former glory so that the pretty redhead could make a living.

And who knows? He might get a plot of his own...

His mind was already hard at work as he considered the potential of using magic to farm. What if you could strengthen crops, make them grow faster... or even out of season?

And then there was Astra... She'd been standoffish so far, but she had definite interest in him. Perhaps there was a crust for him to break there? And what would lie beneath? She seemed to have a lot of knowledge of the magical world.

And who might say what an *actual Dragonkin* could teach him?

He wanted to know more about Kesha, too; perhaps even meet the elusive fox girl. He had seen the regret in Lucy's eyes when she talked about her mysterious daughter.

Maybe he could help make things right?

Behind him, soft chatter and giggling announced that the girls were getting up.

Within a few minutes, they all sat at the small table in the living room, the girls wrapped in whatever oversized shirts and jerseys they could find.

They laughed and joked as they shared their morning coffee, and a sense of great happiness filled James.

Life was finally going his way.

THANK YOU FOR READING!

If you enjoyed this book, please check out my other work on Amazon.

Be sure to **leave me a review on Amazon** to let me know if you liked this book! Like most independent authors, I use the feedback from your review to improve my work and to decide what to focus on next, so your review can make a difference.

If you want to stay up-to-date on my releases, you can join my newsletter by entering the following link into any web browser: https://fierce-thinker-305.ck.page/45f709af30. You can also join my Discord, where the madness never ends... Join by entering the following invite manually in your browser or Discord app: https://discord.gg/ex5rEJdtwu.

<u>Jack Bryce's Books</u>
Below you'll find a list of my work, all available through Amazon.

<u>Aerda Online (completed series)</u>
Phylomancer
Demon Tamer
Clanfather

<u>Warped Earth (completed series)</u>
Apocalypse Cultivator 1
Apocalypse Cultivator 2
Apocalypse Cultivator 3
Apocalypse Cultivator 4
Apocalypse Cultivator 5

<u>Highway Hero (ongoing series)</u>
Highway Hero 1
Highway Hero 2

<u>Country Mage (ongoing series)</u>
Country Mage 1

A SPECIAL THANKS TO...

Stoham Baginbott and Maikeruu for beta reading. You guys are absolute kings.

If you're interested in beta reading for me, hit me up on discord (JauntyHavoc#8836) or send an e-mail to lordjackbryce@gmail.com.

Made in the USA
Monee, IL
18 March 2024